THE ART OF GETTING EVEN

J S Langley

The first two "Agaricus" novels.

Abuse of Privilege

Reasons to Deceive

For Janet, Robert, Iain, Michael

'If you can't get ahead then be sure to get even.'

Toni Malguzzi, Toronto, Canada

The sign on the door said "Interrogation Room 2". Inside the room the walls were lined with white sound muffling tiles that served no sonic purpose but were rather part of a psychological subterfuge designed to give suspects the illusion that here, in this room, it was safe to talk. The grey concreted floor was worked smooth and shiny by the volume and variety of footfall that the room had seen. The furnishings were sparse and bright fluorescent strip lights produced a severe light that bounced back off the white tiled walls.

In the centre of the room was a metal table and three chairs. Both the table and chairs were bolted to the floor.

The wall to the right hand side of the door as you enter held a large mirrored one-way observation window. A panic strip ran around all four walls at waist height.

On the table sat some completely unnecessary recording equipment. Carefully positioned cameras and microphones recorded everything that happened in the room and relayed their output live to the observation room that lay behind the mirrored wall.

Of the three chairs arranged around the table two were on one side and faced the third that stood alone, directly across the coffee cup ringed surface. All of the chairs were hard and bare and uncomfortable to sit in for any length of time.

The two interrogating officers sat alongside one another. One of them was male and the other female; one was black and the other white. The man had a notebook in front of him whose open pages were covered in his almost illegible scrawl.

It was the female who was black. She was about 5' 3" tall, slim, and had medium length braided black hair. The man was large, tending towards obese, his fair hair was greying and his demeanour was sour. Although hatless both were otherwise in the dark blue uniform of the Ontario Provincial Police.

The interrogation was in progress.

The light on the recording equipment indicated that it was switched on. The man slapped a thin manila file of papers onto the table alongside his notebook.

'Switch the recording off,' he said.

The female officer reached forward.

Click.

'You bastard,' he growled through clenched teeth.

The man on the far side of the table sat motionless. He was also a big man and although getting on in years was well dressed, broad shouldered and had a head of thick silver hair cut short and neat.

'I cannot count the times I've been forced to go through these motions with you over the years. You know you're a damned crook and a killer and this time, finally, you're not going to slither away back into the long grass.'

The man looked steadily into his interrogator's eyes, his calmness increasing the other's level of irritation.

'I'll miss these little chats with you, Officer Logan,' he said.

The interrogator started to rise but a hand on his arm gave him pause and he glanced at his colleague. She nodded upwards towards one of the cameras.

'Damn it,' he said and let out a deep, resigned sigh before resuming his seat.

'We're waiting for the results of the DNA analysis,' said the female officer, 'we're pretty sure we're going to get a match, Mr Malguzzi.'

'Ah please, you can call me Toni,' said the big man, 'I feel like we could be friends.'

'Friends!' yelled Officer Logan.

'Not with you,' said Toni Malguzzi, 'I think we got too much history, too many misunderstandings between us, but with your beautiful colleague, maybe, yes,' he smiled, two gold teeth glinting in the artificial light.

'Officer Jones does not want to be your friend. Why would she? We've got evidence from the body that is finally going to get you nailed.'

'I never said I never knew the guy. I admit I saw him the night he was killed, we shared a few drinks, had a few laughs. Ask the boys in the bar. There's plenty of witnesses. So of course there's going to be traces of my DNA all over him. It don't mean a thing.'

Logan didn't want to let it go, 'Where were you when Ray Chaucer was shot?'

'I dunno, you haven't told me the time of the shooting. Maybe I was on my way home, maybe I was already tucked up in bed. I feel for the guy, tough luck on him, a real shame, he wasn't so bad.'

'Why did you turn yourself in?' asked Officer Jones.

'He knew we'd be after him that's why,' blurted out Officer Logan unable to control his frustration, 'I guess he was just saving time.'

'Is that right?' asked Officer Jones.

'Nah, much as I enjoy my visits here I didn't feel the urge to make things easy for you,' said Toni Malguzzi.

'Then why?' she asked.

'Logan, it's time for you to leave,' said Malguzzi, 'I got an offer I want to make and I want to make it to Officer Jones here. Just the two of us and whoever's watching from in there,' he said, nodding towards the mirrored wall.

'You know we can't do that,' Logan spat, 'is this another one of your games?'

'No game,' said Toni Malguzzi, 'I could not be more serious.'

Officer Jones squeezed Logan's arm.

'Give us a few minutes,' she said.

'Don't worry I got nowhere to be. I'll wait right here.'

The two officers left the room. Toni Malguzzi sat quietly staring into space. Twenty minutes later the door opened and Officer Jones entered. Alone.

'What took you so long?'

'There was some convincing to do. Now I hope you're not going to waste my time Mr Malguzzi. So what is it you want to say?'

Toni Malguzzi straightened in his chair, his shoulders stretching the seams of his designer-label suit. He leaned forward and in a few words outlined his offer.

Officer Jones gulped.

'Are you serious about this?'

The question hung in the empty space between them. Officer Jones sat, her brown eyes shining out from ebony skin, her shirt sleeves rolled up. The big man opposite fell silent and stared up at the ceiling.

Officer Jones was experienced enough to know when not to push it too hard. She took out some gum, unwrapped it, put it into her mouth then held out the packet to Toni Malguzzi. He shook his head. She chewed slowly, methodically, mechanically, and waited.

Finally Toni Malguzzi took a deep breath, glanced up at one of the surveillance cameras mounted high in a corner of the room and then redirected his gaze to look piercingly into Officer Jone's expectant eyes,

'Yes,' he said.

'Say again,' she said.

The big man's dark eyes peered out at her from under his thick white eyebrows.

'I say OK,' he said more loudly, knowing that the repetition was in order to supply a clear recording of the interview. He had no problem with that. He'd made his decision. Now he had to follow through on it.

Officer Jones stopped chewing and raised her own voice ever so slightly. Now was not the time for indistinct language.

'So just to be clear Mr. Toni Malguzzi. You want to make a deal. You want to provide us with information and in return you want witness protection and all current and future charges against you to be dropped.'

'Don't make it sound like you do me a favour,' said the big man, 'you know I got stuff that can clear a whole lot of cold cases out of your pending tray.'

His voice had hardened, his hands clenched into fists. On the back of his left hand was the tattoo of a spider with its legs extending down his fingers and backwards up his arm to disappear beneath his shirt cuffs.

'You came in here with regard to a felony...' Officer Jones said, her voice calm, even. She was determined not to lose control of this interview. It was an interview that could lead on to bigger things, she thought, something that could bring her to people's attention, give her career a much needed boost. She was a black girl from Regent Park and she wanted to make good. She wanted to show all the disbelievers that she was a good cop, a real good cop, and could be an even better one.

Toni Malguzzi looked at her straight and unwaveringly. His face was like old leather, worn and wrinkled, blemished. Disconcerting though it was she held his gaze.

'I came in voluntarily because I wanted to make you this offer. Now do we deal or not?' he said.

In another room two men peered at a series of screens each giving a different angle on the interview room. One of these men was Officer Logan, long in the tooth in a game that had worn him down close to the point of burn out.

'Have we got the DNA results on Ray Chaucer's remains?' he asked.

The young man standing beside him shuffled a few sheets of paper before replying. He was just another rookie in Logan's opinion, someone who'd find out soon enough that he'd chosen the wrong profession.

'Not yet sir, should be later today,' he said.

Logan's face seemed to partially relax, to move from grimace to resignation. He turned to the young cop,

'I don't expect it'll matter in any case,' he said and then pointed to one of the flickering screens, 'So let me ask you, here we have Toni Malguzzi, better known on the street as Cazzuto, a badass, tough and mean-tempered, someone you wouldn't want to cross swords with, someone we've been trying to pin down for more than 20 years, and here he is sitting as meek as a lamb, opening up his arms and offering friendship, willing to turn in his old colleagues, wanting to throw away the loyalty he's built his whole life around. What do you think are the chances of this being as good as it looks?'

'When you put it like that, sir, it sounds like zero to nothing,' said the rookie, 'but what have we got to lose? You never know.'

Its either an old head on young shoulders or the naivety of youth, thought Logan.

'Look at him, a man like that would cheerfully stare down a charging bull but now he's gone all doughy eyed, acting like he's putty in our hands.'

'He says he wants to turn state witness, sir, do we take him at his word?' asked the rookie.

'I don't know,' said Logan stroking his chin with his hand. Turning to each of the screens in turn he took in all the angles and then lifted a microphone to his mouth and spoke into it softly.

His voice entered Officer Jone's head through the earpiece she was wearing, invisible beneath the covering blackness of her braided shoulder length hair. In front of her Toni Maliguzzi had started to talk, had started to offer random pieces of information, nothing yet of any great importance, but tantalizing, like a fisherman baiting his hook.

'Keep him happy. I'm going to inform Witness Protection and start the ball rolling. I may not understand what the hell is happening here but I'd be a goddamned fool to look this gift horse in the mouth,' said Logan.

Chapter 1

In my business you have to do what you're told even when it involves wading out into a swamp where survival is not the prerogative of the righteous. If I ever got in too deep I would just have to rely on being either smart enough or lucky enough to get through - my hopes were pinned on the latter.

My name is Mark Wilson and I get bored easily. I always get this way when I'm between assignments. My wife used to get frustrated with me when I was in this mood but that's all in the past now. When I'm working I'm not bored.

It was a gloriously sunny day. A cloudlessly clear azure sky domed above me and the silvery light seemed to intensify the colours of the world filling them with life and vitality. I hated it.

The devil makes work for idle minds, I thought, and my mind was drowning in its idleness.

My phone beeped.

I knew the sound. It was the activation of my call sign "Agaricus".

The message was a simple one, "The Store" wanted to see me and they wanted it to be now. It was time for me to break away from this humdrum morning of leisure, this wandering aimlessly from park to park, filling myself with over-priced caffeine and getting increasingly annoyed with a world full of busy, happy people enjoying the sunshine. It had felt to me that I was all alone in my boredom. Everybody else seemed to be having a really good time.

I was so upset to leave all this behind me that my face involuntarily cracked into a smile.

Soon I was sitting in an anteroom that smelt vaguely of furniture polish and disinfectant. I sat in a corner shrouded in as much shadow as there was. It seemed appropriate somehow, my natural condition.

The room was straight out of one of those 60's spy movies; oak paneling up to a dado, then deep red wallpaper stretching up to a stuccoed cream-coloured ceiling.

It had been too long since my last assignment and I had been going stir crazy. Just yesterday I'd caught myself jogging on autopilot; the same streets, the same London parks, the same avoidance of eye contact and I'd realised I was becoming predictable. That had hurt. Thankfully the summons from "The Store" had arrived before the rut I was digging got too deep.

I sat twiddling my thumbs in one of the 'shut-up-and-sit-there-and-wait' chairs. Samantha, the PA of the person who'd called me in, sat at her desk on the opposite side of the room. She looked both stern and alluring, something that she always managed to pull off though I could never understand how. The daily newspapers lay on a low oval table in front of me but I was in no mood to read somebody else's version of yesterday's news.

I looked across at Samantha who, as well as being a PA, was also my first point of contact when I was out in the field. Today she was wearing a dark blue jacket over a white blouse that was teasingly unbuttoned. Her faux blonde hair was tied back and away from her face, her gaze was focussed on the glowing blue screen in front of her. This was her lair and she was fully in control of it.

As she and I were old sparring partners I thought I'd pass the time by engaging in a little bit of harmless small talk,

'How are you Sam?' I said.

Her eyes swung round to meet mine.

'Don't call me Sam, my name's Samantha. And by the way you're late.'

'You're looking particularly fetching today,' I said.

'You are so full of sh…'

The blinking of a green light on a console to her right broke into our playful banter.

'He's ready,' she said.

I got up, made my way across to the dark oaken door that marked the entrance to "the Sanctuary" and reached out my hand for the shiny brass doorknob. My contorted reflection peered back at me.

'His mood's a little strange today,' said Samantha, her words stabbing sharply between my retreating shoulder blades. I was pleased she couldn't see that my hitherto engaging smile had frozen and melted away. I straightened my back and pushed open the weighty door.

Chapter 2

As soon as I entered Sir Anthony Baxter's office (I called him AB, but never to his face) I was conscious of an uncomfortable atmosphere made more clammy by the heated exhaust of overused computer equipment and an underlying odour of stale tobacco.

Natural light streamed into the room through three tall gothic windows. To their sides long red curtains were pulled back and secured by brass stays. In front of the windows was a large mahogany desk arrayed with screens. Behind this sat AB, his strong shoulders hunched and tense.

'Sit down and keep quiet!' he said without lifting his head, his glassily bald pate reflecting the sunlight that flooded in over his shoulders.

This was not an auspicious start.

AB was my link into the wider "Superstore". If, in a weak moment, I were to accept the overrated concept of hierarchy then I would have to accept that AB was my boss and, if pressed, I would grudgingly admit that he was damn good at his job. One of the things he was not well known for was extravagant displays of emotion. Something must have upset him.

I sat obediently in a red leather Chesterfield that faced his desk, the studded back reminding me to sit upright. Having nothing better to do I glanced over at a half-full decanter and tumblers that sat atop a polished regency half-moon table away to my left, far, too far, and out of reach. The contents of the decanter glimmered amber. It was early in the day but I knew how well AB chose his tipple.

As I was still being ignored I looked down at my Rolex watch. It was a GMT Master II with a black face and a bi-coloured black/blue cerachrom bezel and was attached to my wrist by a finely polished stainless steel strap. It was a kind of memento from a previous assignment and the only blemish on this amazing feat of Swiss engineering was a scratch on the glass running from above the 2 on the dial down to the 5. It was not a significant scratch but because I knew it was there I couldn't help seeing it. What made it worse was that it had been all my own fault. I had been using a Dremel drill with a diamond tip to do a bit of DIY and it had slipped. I had not been amused and was still not amused. For the record the rest of the DIY job went well but it had felt like a failure. So much for the old Scottish proverb "If you want something doing well then you should do it yourself (and save some money)". The outcome of this particular activity was more akin to the sentiments expressed by Scotland's greatest bard, Robert Burns, when he wrote, "The best laid schemes o' mice an' men gang aft a-gley." At least the scratch was in a nice straight line.

I sat and watched the seconds tick by. It gave me something to do.

After a few minutes of energetic keyboard tapping AB stopped, slapped his open hand on the surface of his desk, got up and turned to look out of the window. I had never seen him this agitated, his normal calm and collected demeanour had, for some reason, been badly ruffled.

I sat like a naughty schoolboy in the headmaster's office, not knowing what I'd done wrong.

As I looked around I was reminded that there was nothing light nor frivolous about this office. Heavy bookshelves lined the walls and seemed to groan under the weight of their own accumulated knowledge. The far corners hid themselves in shadow, brass poled floor lamps drooped their heads apologetically at being unable to provide a satisfactory luminance.

AB returned to his desk, sat down and started drumming his fingers on the mahogany surface. He was irritated. The drumming of his fingers did not ease the general mood.

He stopped and looked me squarely in the eye.

'There are many clandestine organisations like "The Store",' he said, 'that fill the gaps between what governments want done and there reticence to do it themselves. Where there's gaps there's need and where there's need there's always somebody willing to satisfy it, for a suitable price. For example if a government wants someone relocated without the risk of precipitating unwelcome attention from the interfering eye of the media and is struggling with the legal niceties whilst believing that their cause is just but having their hands tied in the Gordian knot of their own bureaucratic processes. In such a case if the person concerned were to go missing for a while and then serendipitously reappear within the desired legal jurisdiction then why would they not take advantage of such a piece of good fortune? Such things can happen and anyway does it not serve the cause of "justice"? After all it would be foolish to let such a person return from whence they came wouldn't it?. One could not look such a gift horse in the mouth. Much better to just accept that at least one tricky international problem has been solved. No need to notice that coincident to this happy event an amount of money has been quietly transferred into an offshore bank account.' He paused and then he continued.

'Over time you grow a reputation for getting things done quietly, effectively, but not cheaply, and the order book fills up. Even so it is always relationships that count, built and nurtured through constant networking, customer satisfaction and word of mouth. Then suddenly you're asked to do a "little favour" and most of the time you don't mind but sometimes you do and if you do, well, it doesn't matter. If you're instructed to do it then do it you must. This is one of those times.'

I just listened. He wasn't really talking to me, he was just venting his spleen. He paused. I got the feeling I was about to find out what it was that had upset him.

He shook his head slowly, took a deep breath and looked around as if seeing me for the first time.

'There are times,' he said, 'when I wonder what we are trying to do.'

AB wore a slim fitting black pinstripe suit over a pale blue shirt and a regimental tie secured by a neat windsor knot. His grey eyes were piercing. I tried to look away.

Relaxing slightly he leant forward and withdrew a mahogany cigar box from the top drawer of his desk. He took a few moments to make his selection and then rolled the cigar between his fingers, clipped the end and, using a Ronson lighter, drew it into life.

As far as I was concerned he could take all the time he wanted. Anything that might have a restorative effect on his composure was good with me.

He took a lungful of smoke and then slowly exhaled watching the stream of rich smelling tobacco spiral slowly upwards, past the chandelier and onwards to the ornately decorated ceiling.

'Well now,' he said, 'and how are you today?'

For some reason I was not entirely convinced of the sincerity of this enquiry.

'I'm just fine, sir,' I said, and bit my tongue to prevent myself from adding, 'and how are you?'. Call me perceptive but I thought that now was not the right time to ask.

AB nodded and took another deep draw on the cigar before regretfully placing it on the edge of a silver ashtray and leaving it there to smoulder.

Walking over to the drinks tray he poured two large whiskies into cut-glass tumblers and added a single ice cube to each. Without a word he handed one to me and then returned to his side, the proprietary side, of the desk.

I contemplated the depths of the straw yellow liquid and rolled it around in the glass picking up a hint of smokiness in its aroma. It showed all the signs of being a single malt of distinction.

'It's a little early…' I said, raising the glass to admire the contents.

'You'll need it,' he said and took a long pull from his own glass.

I thought it only polite to do the same. The liquid seared the back of my throat shocking my brain into an even higher degree of alertness.

'Before I go into this,' said AB, 'I want you to know I was against getting involved in this assignment.'

Oh thanks, I thought, that's a great start.

I gave a slight nod in acknowledgement.

'But,' he continued, 'the powers that be are adamant,' he paused before adding, as an irrefutable conclusion, 'so there we are.'

I found it difficult to imagine any "powers that be" that could overrule AB. But then again what did I know of the captain's cabin, my place was below decks, down in the engine room with an oily rag and a spanner.

At least the whisky tasted good.

AB steadied himself. After such an uncharacteristic show of emotion it was time to get down to business.

Chapter 3

AB leaned back in his chair,

'There is a Toronto ex-mobster called Toni Malguzzi who appears to have done our Canadian colleagues a number of favours,' he began, 'and has succeeded in convincing them that his revelations to date are but a taster of the golden seam of knowledge that it is in his power to reveal unto them. All he wants in return is a little favour.'

Super, I thought.

I had the distinct feeling that whatever AB's problem was it was soon to belong to me.

'Thanks to our friend's "cooperation" a number of cold cases are being warmed up,' he paused, 'so far so good and very routine but our man, bless his cotton socks, wants a trophy for his troubles.'

'A trophy?'

'Yes, as you know many criminals have things of value tucked away, assets that they believe can be liquidated should there come a rainy day.'

'OK,' I said, thinking that I should try to show that I had a grasp of the situation, 'and our prospective client would like to rub salt into the wounds he's inflicting by acquiring some of these?'

AB winced. He was not enjoying this.

'Not "prospective" and not "some",' he said, 'Just one particular item. A piece that will act as a last poke in the eye before he disappears into the re-born oblivion and the subterranean depths of the Canadian witness protection system.'

I'd seen this happen before, help rewarded by a brand new identity and a new life in some obscure part of the world. Somewhere you could while away the rest of your days in taxpayer funded luxury. An individually unfair outcome for the sake of the greater good. I hoped it was going to be worth it.

AB took another pull at the whisky glass. I followed suit. I was increasingly feeling the need.

'You'll get the normal thorough briefing of course but I want to pencil in some of the background myself, just to make sure that it's clear.'

'Yes sir,' I said, wondering why he seemed to be taking this assignment so personally. He always had a lot on his plate and was normally calm, collected and in control, distancing himself from specifics in order to retain his objectivity. For some reason he seemed emotionally attached to this assignment.

'As I've said, our client's name is Toni Malguzzi. This is not the new name he'll be given for his new-life, his rebirth, and I would strongly advise that you do not inquire into any of those arrangements.' His look emphasised the point, 'The main thing to remember is that he is well known, and probably disliked, by the people you'll be working with on his behalf to make the deal. They must not know that it is Mr Malguzzi that you are representing. If they were to find out then the consequences would, in all probability, be fatal,' he glanced in my direction, 'Fatal to you I mean… and that would be a shame.'

'Yes,' I said, meaning it and wallowing in the shallows of his concern. I'd got the message loud and clear that protecting our client's identity was an essential part of the deal.

AB shrugged, 'Until a few years ago Toni Malguzzi was a senior figure, a capo but born an outsider, in a family run Toronto mob that specialised in protection. It was during routine questioning about a recent killing that he took the authorities by surprise by offering his services as an informant. As he was, in all probability, the perpetrator of the killing they were investigating then perhaps he made the move out of self preservation although the evidence against him was, as usual, full of holes.' AB took the cigar from the ashtray, drew it back to life, took a few lungfuls of smoke and then returned the cigar to the ashtray, 'This mob of which he was a long term member has more or less disbanded so it was even more unusual for the Ontario authorities to receive an offer to help clear up what are, after all, cold cases. Cases whose files are already gathering dust down in a Toronto basement somewhere.' AB gazed up at the ceiling and sighed before he continued, 'It is rare to get this kind of offer voluntarily from this kind of man. It was a gift horse that couldn't be ignored. His offer was accepted and, in all probability, a number of police careers are currently on the up as a consequence.'

AB was such a cynic. But he knew how the world worked and there was a high chance he was right. In which case there would be more than one set of vested interests involved in this assignment.

'Nice guy,' I muttered.

'Quite,' said AB, 'with his help a number of his old friends have already been taken into custody for questioning. For his own protection the authorities have let it be known than Malguzzi himself has also been arrested on charges that are likely to put him away for at least 15 years. They hope, and I'm sure he does to, that this will serve to distance him from any suspicion of being a source. Rather than residing in prison he has in actual fact been whisked away and settled, at least temporarily, in a Toronto safe house. His location is a closely guarded secret but I'm sure that wherever he is his hosts are delighted to have him.'

'Yes, I bet,' I said quietly.

'What?

'Nothing sir, just muttering to myself.'

'Well don't, it's bad enough having to take you through all this without having to put up with your incoherent mumblings. If you've got something to say then say it, if not then keep quiet.'

'Yes sir, sorry sir.'

AB dislodged a cylindrical length of ash that had accumulated at the end of his cigar, dirtying the polished surface of the silver ashtray. After taking a further deep therapeutic lungful he rested the cigar back on the rim of the now soiled ashtray and sighed.

'Life must have become too easy for Toni

Malguzzi,' he said, 'or perhaps he just wants to flex his informant muscles while he still has the power of undisclosed information, information for which his captors and protectors continue to salivate. Either way he's demanded help in a little scheme he's cooked up and, god knows why, we have apparently agreed to be the ones to give it to him.' His unhappiness was evident, his grey eyes dull and brooding. He began drumming his fingers on the polished mahogany surface of his desk. I thought he might be wanting me to say something.

'Nothing illegal I hope,' I said, to break what was becoming an uncomfortable silence.

AB looked at me aghast.

'Of course it's illegal,' he said.

It just gets better and better, I thought.

'Toni Malguzzi has found out that a painting owned as an underground asset by his old chums has been put on the market through the dark web and he has decided he must have it.'

A painting? Buying a painting didn't sound too bad.

'A painting that doesn't exist,' added AB, as he saw me start to relax.

'A painting that doesn't exist?' I said, tensing up again.

AB was exasperated, 'I don't need an echo,' he said.

You don't need an echo? I thought.

'Yes, the painting is one of those hidden gems, stolen some years ago then seemingly vanishing from the face of the earth. The kind of piece that sometimes resurfaces decades later to be found in a deceased's private collection or reappearing mysteriously in a hedge. This particular work of art has the added attraction of reputably having been destroyed. Anyhow, it appears to be now up for sale and our client has seen it, recognised it, and wants it.'

This all seemed pretty unreal to me.

'So I guess this painting is to be sold extremely privately,' I said.

'Ah yes, you're excelling yourself today,' said AB. I made a mental note to be quiet and avoid the temptation of stating the blindingly obvious. I took a comforting swig from the whisky glass that was now almost empty.

'The painting is a Picasso and is available for sale to someone with deep pockets, a secure vault and a mouth that is able to remain closed.'

A Picasso! Even I had heard of him, although as a cultural philistine my appreciation of his work was somewhat limited.

'Obviously Malguzzi cannot make the deal directly himself so he needs an intermediary.'

Here we go…

'…and as I've already said we have been instructed to help…'

Riiiiiight…..

'…and we have no choice but to provide this intermediary…'

Yeeeeees……

'…and that means you. Just you.'

Great, marvelous, wonderful, although not totally unexpected. He hadn't brought me in just for the pleasure of my company. Without asking I got up and refilled my tumbler with whisky.

'Do I have a choice?' I asked.

'What do you think?' said AB, reaching out to re-gather the smouldering remnants of his cigar and rising to his feet. He turned towards the windows and stood quietly, seemingly distracted by other thoughts. The interview appeared to be over.

'Yes sir, thank you sir' I said, finishing my newly poured whisky in one and getting up to go.

'And make sure you keep in touch with me personally on this one, Mark. Once you get to Toronto I want you to check in regularly. I want to know what has happened, what is happening and what is going to happen every step of the way,' he paused, 'and just one last thing. Remember, you don't have to like someone in order to work for them, efficiently, professionally and quickly.' He put an emphasis on "quickly".

I knew that already but just said, 'Yes sir.'

'My operational days are over,' said AB, 'so you are my surrogate on this assignment too, Mark. Remember that. If you need help of any kind then ask. If you feel like you're getting in too deep then shout. Above all, don't fuck this one up. '

I nodded my head to signal my understanding and then vacated his presence with alacrity and a strange feeling of relief.

Chapter 4

Out in the ante-room Samantha pushed a slim manila coloured folder across her desk. It had my code name "Agaricus" written across it in a large, neat script. I'd always suspected Samantha of having an artistic temperament burning deep inside her and had often thought about stealing one of these folders and framing it as a memento. She was a woman who liked to be precise in everything that she did.

'Basement room 090 is available to you for the rest of the day. Your briefing agenda is the first paper in the folder. Everyone's lined up, they'll all be prepared and on-time. Good luck.'

She didn't normally say "Good Luck" and the way she said it struck a nerve and worried me more than anything AB had said.

I turned away.

Samantha was already focussed back on her screen, busily tapping away at the keyboard.

'I don't know what it is,' she said to nobody in particular, 'but I've not seen him this upset for a very long time.'

Thanks for that, I thought, that really helps! I already knew that these particular coloured files were reserved for assignments of high risk – high risk to the assignee that is.

'Now off you go, Mark,' she said, 'don't keep people waiting.'

I looked up from the folder.

'The name's, Michael,' I said, 'Michael Stewart. You know how important it is to adopt your new identity from the start.'

Samantha said nothing, she just pointed to the door.

I heard her mutter "smart ass" under her breath as I left.

The briefing room was bare and smelt of disinfectant. It was reminiscent of a cell in a private clinic. The walls were a stark white, both cold and humourless. The briefing was thorough.

As I'd seen in the file my identity for this assignment was to be Mr. Michael Stewart, a representative of a Scottish law firm. In terms of the associated cultural persona this was an easy one for me to adopt as it was a close but not too close fit to my own reality.

In my capacity as Michael Stewart I was the authorised legal representative for a client who had granted me the delegated authority to act on their behalf in the forthcoming negotiation and transfer of goods. I was to tell the seller that the buyer preferred to remain anonymous. I was sure this wouldn't be a big surprise under the circumstances. If pushed I would reveal that he was male, European and living in Switzerland. If pushed further then I could say that he was newly moneyed, a rising star in criminal circles and shy of making personal appearances. If really necessary I could further add that he wished to purchase the Picasso for his own emerging private, very private, collection. If you're going to start an illegal art collection of any standing then it's got to contain at least one Picasso hasn't it?

I was offered a pair of thick rimmed tortoiseshell glasses but decided I wouldn't use them, they were too obvious an artefact and as they were fitted with normal glass they could easily become more of a risk than an asset. I did however allow my medium length fair coloured hair to be cut shorter and dyed a deep auburn. My new wardrobe was a suitcase full of smart casual clothes and a promise that there would be more waiting for me on my arrival in Toronto.

A background of family, friends, career to date, favourite foods etc… was all drilled into me. I learnt the necessary details by rote and was then tested through interrogation until I achieved a "satisfactory pass".

I was also given a crash course in the history of art and in particular the Picasso painting that was up for sale or auction…

The Art Theft

It is 2006. Four young men move from an Eastern European town to the Netherlands intent on crime. They break into a series of homes but this brings only small reward and they decide they need to up their game.

The leader of this small pack of hyenas has heard that Art is worth a lot of money and there are plenty of galleries in Amsterdam and Rotterdam. They plump for Rotterdam.

They find a cheap apartment above a shop, move in and begin to look for opportunities. By a stroke of good fortune they find that a "remarkable exhibition of Avant-gardes paintings" loaned from a private collection is due to begin in a few days time and last for over a month.

Three of the gang buy tickets. Two walk around the gallery taking a close look at the artwork on display. The third ignores the artwork and concentrates on identifying the security systems.

The next day they go back again. This time their roles are reversed. Back in the apartment all four sit and compare notes.

Target artworks are chosen with care. Firstly on the basis of size. Nothing too large, nothing more than 70cm x 70cm which would fit into an average sized suitcase. Secondly the work is chosen by artist. It must be by a famous name, at least a name that they believe most people would have heard of. They're thinking practically, prioritising ease of transportation and commercial potential.

Their examination of the security systems also pays off. They use their burglary experience and find that the ground floor fire exit door is a weak link. It can be opened at any time with very little effort, even from the outside. Also, to their amazement, they find that the exhibition space is not covered by security cameras.

During the next few days they make several trips to reconnoitre the area around the museum. They drive to the gallery after dark to see how busy the roads are at various times of night. They note with further surprise and pleasure that there are no guards located physically within the building at night.

As far as they can see their activities thus far attract no particular attention.

They buy large bags from a local shop. They are made of black raffia and can be used to carry the canvases. They get new SIM cards for their phones and purchase black hoodies.

Six days before the break-in the leader pays a last visit to the gallery, this time alone. He spends two to three hours there, going over the plan in his head, step by step. Nobody approaches him or seems to notice anything unusual. He is taken to be simply an avid lover of the Arts – which, in a way, he is.

Now they are ready.

For two nights in a row the evenings are clear and dry and therefore the risk of being observed, of there being too many people about for comfort is judged to be too high.

So they wait.

The third night is cloudy and wet.

They borrow an unsuspecting friend's car and call in at an all-night kebab shop that is close to the gallery. They order pizzas that they share between them; one large margherita and one large pepperoni. They all drink Diet Coke..

Two of the four will carry out the burglary, one will wait in the car and the fourth will return to their apartment to await their return.

At 3 o'clock in the morning two black shapes, hunched against the rain, walk towards the gallery.

The gallery's fire exit door is equipped with a push-bar on the inside which, when pressed down for a few seconds, deactivates the electronic lock and then opens the mechanical door lock and the door opens. As it is designed for emergencies the electronic lock remains active 24 hours a day, 7 days a week. It is never de-activated.

The two robbers break in through this door from the outside. Later investigation will fail to account for how this was done but the police will come to the conclusion that the robbers knew how, by banging against the outside of the door they could activate a "panic system" response that would deactivate the electronic lock. As experienced burglars it would be assumed that they could then handle the mechanical lock from the outside by inserting something between the door and the doorjamb and pushing back the latch. The police would reject the alternative idea of an "inside job". Either way the two robbers had no difficulty in entering the gallery.

Once inside they knew there was a Matisse on their immediate right. It is fixed to the wall by a cable but this is easily cut. In the diagonally opposite corner there is a Meijer de Haan, a Gauguin and a Picasso hanging side by side.

The Picasso is a late work. It is a relatively small drawing entitled *Tête d'Arlequin* ("The Head of Harlequin") and was drawn by Picasso in 1971 when he was already ninety years old. What the picture demonstrates is that, despite his advanced years, Picasso was still a very proficient artist.

As a work of art the *Tête d'Arlequin* is both a comic and a desperate portrait of a wrinkled man, perhaps even a partial self-portrait of a man who feels that the end of his life is approaching. It measures only 38 cm x 29 cm, well within the limits of a suitcase, and is drawn in pen and brush in black ink, coloured pencil and pastel on thick brown woven paper. At the time of the robbery it had an Insurance value of $800,000.

In all they take 7 works of art and at some point set off the remote burglar alarms that sound an alert in a control room some distance away.

2 minutes and 48 seconds after entering the gallery they are back outside, standing on the wet grass. They have closed the door behind them.

They then load their black raffia bags into the boot of the waiting car, get into the back seats and are driven away by their accomplice.

Once back in the apartment the pictures are transferred to sturdier suitcases and the car is returned with thanks to the still unsuspecting friend.

The art collection from which the pictures have been stolen has been amassed by a single family over decades and generations. It is one of the top 200 in the world in terms of size and value. This is one of the few times that a selection of pieces has been loaned to a gallery in Europe.

The family are informed later that morning – they are not amused.

The gallery is closed.

The investigation begins.

The hunt is on.

The police, authorities and insurers all know that in this type of robbery speed is of the essence. Action must be taken before the trail goes cold, before the paintings disappear underground.

At a press conference that day a gallery representative refuses to give details about the break-in, the security systems, the on-going investigation or the combined value of the paintings. All she will say is,

'Each of the artworks that have been stolen are described and registered internationally: they are not sellable.'

The gallery is re-opened the following day.

Gaps on the wall show where the stolen pictures used to hang. Visitor numbers are significantly up.

The news of the audacious theft goes global.

The pictures are now in two suitcases in the hall cupboard of the robber's apartment.

The following day they take the paintings from the hall cupboard and part them from their frames. Now they are even smaller and lighter and easier to transport.

The investigation goes into overdrive.

It is not just the artworks that are at risk but reputations too. The police, the gallery, the experts and the insurers repeat over and over again that the pictures are "unsaleable" and appeal for their safe return. They imply that if this is done promptly and without damage to the works then no action will be taken against the perpetrators.

Due to the lack of any real facts the media fills its columns with speculation, valuing the missing artwork at "somewhere between $50-100 million". As the news spreads the valuation is inflated to $300 million.

The actual estimated value of the haul is significantly lower but the insurance companies are very concerned at the media coverage. They believe that such inflated estimates are likely to push up any potential ransom demands to unacceptable levels.

The public are asked to help and swamp the police with suspects, sightings, suspicions and speculation.

Meanwhile the stolen goods are driven quietly across Europe as the four robbers start looking for a buyer.

After failed speculative, arms length attempts to sell the pictures through their own criminal contacts they attempt to sell all 7 pieces to an art dealer in Eastern

Europe. He has only half-listened to the news, the theft was in another country, another world as far as he is concerned and he does not immediately recognise the artworks as the stolen property from the Rotterdam art gallery. He cannot however believe that the pictures are genuine, especially when they are in the hands of such a seller. He passes up on them.

It is two and a half months since the robbery was committed and the robbers are increasingly anxious to sell the pictures. They offer the Picasso and Matisse to a moneyed trader for $50,000. He thinks about it but believes that if anything seems too good to be true then it probably is and he refuses.

The police are closing in.

The failed sales to the art dealer and the trader spark tip offs to the police. Identities, names, faces are implicated, tracked down, and matched to video surveillance footage recovered from the art gallery CCTV cameras.

The robbers are arrested but without the paintings.

Before the ensuing court case the mother of one of the three accused (the fourth is still on the run) at first says that she has been so anxious for her son's predicament that although she has had the pictures in her possession for safe keeping she felt, after her son had been arrested and charged, that the best thing to do to help him was to destroy the evidence. She says she is sorry but she has burnt all the paintings, later clearing out the ashes and throwing them on a local dump. She had thought that if the paintings could not be found then her son could not be charged. She admits that she acted in haste and now wishes that she hadn't.

She then withdraws her statement saying that she had been forced to make it under duress.

Following up on her first story detectives manage to recover some ashes from a stove and a rubbish dump.

After four months of expert scientific analysis it is reported that paint residue, canvas remains and tacks recovered for analysis contain certain chemical residues that are unique to the kind of paints and materials known to have been used in some of the stolen artworks. It seems therefore that at least 3 or 4 of the 7 stolen canvasses have indeed been burned.

The scientists cannot prove that all the artworks have been destroyed.

3 of the works, the one by Picasso and two by Monet were produced on board or paper which, the scientists explain, would not leave any identifiable traces if they had indeed been incinerated.

So in truth it is unlikely that it will ever be known with one hundred percent certainty whether the 7 stolen artworks were burned in the stove or not. Paintings stolen and lost for decades have been known to reappear. For example a Matisse painting worth £600,000 was returned to a museum in Sweden 25 years after it had gone missing.

International news agencies and journalists attend the court case. In their live reports from the steps of the court building the reporters still talk about the stolen paintings being worth hundreds of millions of dollars even though it had been long known that the insurance value of all 7 totalled a mere $18.1 million.

Soon after the court case is over and the three robbers (the fourth is never caught) are found guilty and sentenced, an insurance syndicate at Lloyd's in London pays out the $18.1 million to the family that owned the stolen artworks.

*****

'So the Picasso was burnt to ashes,' I said to the person in my briefing team who was responsible for bringing me up to speed on the *Tête d'Arlequin*.

'Probably but not conclusively,' she answered.

'So I'm being sent on a wild goose chase. If the Picasso I'm supposed to buy is anything then it's a fake isn't it?'

'Not necessarily. It depends on whether you think these crooks were completely incompetent people who simply got far too far out of their depth, or if you think that maybe they were smarter than that. They'd found out through repeated failures that if they were ever going to sell the pictures then they had to find some way to take the heat off, stop people searching for them, maybe see it as a long term investment, a pension plan and not a short-term windfall as they had originally intended.'

'So to take the heat off they put them in a stove?'

'Very funny I don't think. Remember they were smart enough to complete the robbery in less than three minutes. There is even an unsubstantiated story that they offered to return some of the artworks after they were supposedly burnt in return for leniency in sentencing.'

'Maybe they didn't know they'd been burned when they made the offer,' I said, 'or maybe they were trying it on. Maybe the robbery was "to order" but only for some of the pictures. Maybe once inside the gallery they got carried away. Maybe they got inside help to get in. Maybe…'

She interrupted me in mid rant.

'Exactly. It's in the "maybes" that you're going to be operating. The grey spaces, the areas of uncertainty,' she paused, 'Maybe this harlequin is living up to his reputation as a trickster. He's a character that represents many uncomfortable aspects of human nature, you know, from his origins in Italian street theatre of over 500 years ago to the still extant but pale reflections we see in the pantomimes of today. If you want my advice don't think too much about it. Just do your job, do it quickly, get out unscathed and come home.'

She was sounding increasingly like a combination of AB, my daughter, my girlfriend and my mother. I realised that there was nothing to gain from pushing the speculation any further.

Chapter 5

The most technical part of the briefing was to do with the *Tête d'Arlequin* itself; the context of its production, the pigments, style, technique, distinguishing features and its place in the world of modernist art.

I was also given a lot of "homework" to do.

Fortunately one of my few talents is information assimilation and retention so that although it wasn't easy to compute so much information so quickly it wasn't impossible either.

Finally I was informed of what was known of the sellers; why they might be selling, how much they were probably looking for and most importantly, how dangerous they were.

The patriarch of the family was a man called Lejon Vandla who had risen through the ranks of prostitution, gambling and drug pushing to run a very successful protection racket for almost two decades although for some reason he had recently "retired".

His daughter, Sky Vandla, had been sent away for private schooling in Vancouver, just about as far away from Toronto as it's possible to get whilst still being in Canada and not getting your feet wet. Her father was determined she should get the education that he never had. He believed it would give her new and different chances in life. There was no intention for her to ever enter the family business. She had two brothers and the family succession plan was all about them.

Unfortunately the protection business is not free from risk and the brothers found themselves on the wrong end of a turf war confrontation. Unluckily for the Vandla family both brothers were in the same wrong place at the same wrong time; a car with a remotely activated bomb strapped underneath.

Lejon Vandla did not grieve. Instead he went on the rampage. More than 20 people were killed. Torture and interrogation were used to find out the names of the bombers. The culprits, there were three of them, were skinned. It was never clear at what point their pain stopped and their lives ended. Pictures of their bodies were circulated. The turf war stopped.

Sky was kept clear of as much of this trauma as possible being kept on the sidelines by an increasingly protective father who was determined his daughter would not suffer the same fate as her brothers. After all she was all the close family he had left.

With the succession plan in tatters Lejon Vandla remained at the helm until deciding to simply wrap up the organisation and walk away. This wasn't an easy thing to do. Normally any sign of weakness is fatal in a world such as his. But he managed it and is still breathing.

Although geographically distanced for a lot of her formative years Sky has always had a strong bond with her father, a relationship that has only been strengthened in recent times with her return to Toronto.

Whilst at college Sky was a vigilant and intelligent student who showed a natural aptitude for art. Her father was content to finance the development of his daughter's talent and she impressed some critics with her first exhibition. After graduating she tried to develop her own style further and started to build her reputation. Most recently she had contributed 4 canvases to "Toronto's up and coming young artists" exhibition held at the AGO, the Art Gallery of Ontario, situated in downtown Toronto. Although critically commended she had yet to actually sell any of her pictures.

It's amazing what you can accomplish in 72 hours if you put your mind to it and I was getting increasingly impatient to get out of the basement and into the fresh air. Not only that but I was impatient to go and meet the prospective buyer of a non-existent Picasso. The man who was to be my client, Mr Toni Malguzzi.

The first leg of my journey was a trip to a laboratory in Manchester. I travelled by train and was greeted at door by Professor Kieran Lansbury a very down to earth scientist. We knew each other from our active service days.

'Hey Mark,' he said slapping me on the back, 'long time no see. How's things.'

'I'm getting there,' I said. We knew each other too well for me to insult him with the normal 'I'm fine' response.

'You're always welcome at our house,' he said.

'Thanks, you never know I might take you up on that one day soon.'

'Please do, now to what do I owe the pleasure of this visit?'

'You know already,' I said.

He smiled.

'Aye, I do, you want to know what scientific tests can be done to authenticate a painting. You're in luck Mark, we've got just about everything in this laboratory from a magnifying glass to a $1500^{0}C$ furnace we can use for melting metals, including gold.'

'I don't think I'll be needing the furnace,' I said, remembering the picture's already chequered history.

He laughed, 'I guess not but you never know. At least you know where to come if you ever do.'

'What I hope you've come up with,' I said, 'are tests that you can do with portable equipment and that won't take too long.'

'Indeed,' said Kieran, 'I've had a bit of time to think about that and on the basis of gaining maximum knowledge in the minimum amount of time using only portable equipment I would suggest infrared reflectography, multispectral scanning, X-ray fluorescence and a microscopic substrate analysis.'

'Seems thorough enough to me,' I said, the truth being that he'd lost me at "reflectography", 'Is all the equipment you need stuff you can ship out to Canada?'

'I won't have to,' said Kieran, 'it's all pretty standard. I'm sure it'll be readily available over there. We can specify the model types to ensure they pull out the right portable versions.'

'Would you come over? I need somebody I can trust,' I asked.

Kieran didn't hesitate.

'Just give me 24 hours notice and a First Class return ticket and I'm yours,' he said.

'It's a deal,' I said, 'even if I have to pay for the ticket myself.'

'With your Scottish blood,' he said, 'I'd be more likely to have to swim across.'

I laughed. My reputation went before me.

'Just remember,' I said, 'next time we meet I'm Michael Stewart not Mark Wilson.'

'Of course, Michael,' he said, 'who the hell is this Mark Wilson guy anyway?'

Before I left I asked if he had any contacts in Toronto. Kieran said that he had and we managed to make a Zoom call and some brief introductions that I could follow up on when I got over there.

Chapter 6

My flight to Toronto was due to leave from Manchester Airport, Terminal 2.

Once I arrived I took the lift to the Departures area on the 3rd floor. I'd checked in on-line which meant I only had to join the "Bag drop" queue and was pleased with the comparative smoothness of the process.

I took my hand luggage through security and with time on my hands I sought out a "traditional English breakfast". The place I found offered fried egg, bacon, sausage, baked beans, tomato, mushrooms, a slice of toast and butter and a pot of tea for a little less than £20. Extortionate but what can you do?

I ignored my Scottish conscience telling me that I should have haggled the price down and passed on optional extras like the offer of a three inch diameter half inch thick circular fried concoction of shredded potato and onion that they called a rosti on principle - when did that become part of a traditional English breakfast?

Next I thought about my girlfriend, Teresa, who was living in the States. It was tough keeping a cross-Atlantic relationship alive and although we did our best using Zoom calls with a dodgy internet connection (mine not hers) there was no substitute for the personal touch.

There was definitely a chemistry between us. We'd

known each other long enough for any "honeymoon period" of forced best behaviour to be well gone. If she didn't have any feelings for me then it would have been very easy for her to dump me by now, and she hadn't done that. Since my wife died of cancer this relationship with Teresa had been my first proper foray back into the risky world of dating. I didn't find it easy. Perhaps the fact that we saw each other so seldom was helping. I hoped not. Whatever the case I was looking forward to seeing her face-to-face again. I gave her a call,

'Hello'

'Hi Teresa.'

'You're not calling to tell me the trip's off are you?'

Oh, she of little faith.

'No quite the opposite. I'm calling to tell you I'm in the Departure Lounge at Manchester Airport waiting to be called to the flight.'

Her voice softened, 'That's good, Mark. I'm looking forward to seeing you. We have a lot to talk about.'

I read the warning signs.

'Do we?'

'Oh yes,' she said, 'we sure do.'

The rest of the call was spent confirming the when, where and how of our meet up. I'd had to organise the time as best as I could around the needs of my assignment. I knew it wasn't ideal. Teresa was also clear on that point.

'It's not ideal,' she said, 'but I guess beggars can't be choosers.'

I wasn't clear whether she meant me or her… or both.

She ended the call with a, 'Have a good flight, stay safe.'

Even though I've travelled a lot I have a healthy respect for flying. I always hope the laws of physics do not decide to take a holiday when I'm in what amounts to a tin can with wings 30,000ft up in the air. The "stay safe" therefore wasn't as comforting as I'm sure it was meant to be, instead it made me wonder whether she knew more about this flight than I did and was giving me warning.

As I was finishing up my meal I thought about my daughter, her live-in boyfriend, Brett, and their new baby, my granddaughter, who also live in the States. It's been quite a revelation becoming a grandfather in my forties and I recalled the time I visited my daughter while she was still in the hospital.

I'd turned up the day after the birth, my daughter was in bed looking lovingly into what looked like a heap of towelling. Brett was alongside beaming. My daughter looked up as I entered. She looked tired.

'Hello dad,' she said, 'come and look.'

'Yea hi pops,' said Brett.

I didn't look at him. I wasn't sure whether I'd forgiven him yet for what he'd put my daughter through. If I understand it aright childbirth can be a bit uncomfortable.

'How are you?' I asked my daughter.

'I'm fine, don't worry, everything went just fine.'

'19 hours...'

'Oh dad, it's OK.'

'You look a bit tired...'

'You'd look a wee bit tired too...' she stopped, I knew she wanted to add 'if you'd had your insides ripped out, convulsions the strength of a tsunami and only gas and air for company!' I saw the fire flare in her eyes. Yep, this was my daughter. She was exhausted, but alright.

I smiled.

She smiled back.

'Do you want to hold her?'

I moved to her side. Brett moved away to make room. Maybe he wasn't such a bad choice after all. She held out a nest of towelling. I looked inside. Bedded down, eyes closed, lips puckered, was a new life. I took her very carefully and held her a little way away from my body. The air conditioning in the room must have been a bit faulty because I felt moisture welling up in my eyes.

'Your Mum would have been over the moon,' I said.

'I know,' she said, not making eye contact.

Brett said nothing.

It looked like I'd managed to put a dampener on proceedings. I really am an idiot.

My daughter raised her head, there were tears in her eyes,

'Although she would have already been telling me the best way to breast feed and I'd be swamped in baby clothing ranging from 0 to 6 months.'

Dammit, I thought, I can't help with the first but I should have remembered to buy some woollens.

'You're absolutely right,' I said, 'I'm going to have to up my game.'

She smiled.

'You're quite alright as you are. I wouldn't have you any other way.'

I swallowed hard, but recovered quickly.

'Not even if I could advise authoritatively on breast feeding made easy?'

'Particularly not,' she said, 'but if you come across a foolproof method for dealing with sleep deprivation don't keep it to yourself.'

'Yea, pops, we'd sure appreciate it,' said Brett.

I'd forgotten Brett was still there.

I met my daughter's eye. She was so like her mother.

'She's...' I said. I've always been good at finding the right words at important moments, it's a talent.

'Seven pounds two ounces,' said my daughter.

I looked at her.

'A good weight,' she said, 'although the midwife tells me she'll lose a little in the first few days and then hopefully start to build.'

'Ah,' I said. I'd run out of questions. There was nothing to say. I was just in the moment.

'We're thinking of naming her Amelia,' said Brett, breaking the spell.

'Oh,' I said.

From the look on their faces this wasn't quite the enthusiastic reaction they'd been hoping for. I handed Amelia back to her mother.

'Nice name,' I said, trying to recover.

'And what do you want to be called?' asked Brett.

'Me?'

'Yep, are you gramps, grandpa, grandfather...'

I had to think on my feet. I hadn't realised that this birth meant that I got re-christened as well.

'Grandad will do just fine,' I said, straightening my shoulders, trying not to look old.

'We hope you'll be around for this little gal,' said Brett.

What did he mean, did I look like I was at death's door or something?

'Spend quality time with her when she's growing up. My grandpa had some land in Texas, taught me to shoot, taught me to ride,' Brett added.

A light went on. Here was a chance to pass on some SAS hand-to-hand combat moves, maybe go out for a few nights camping under the stars, maybe...

My daughter read my mind and broke into my thoughts.

'She's less than 1 day old,' she said.

'Absolutely, shouldn't be jumping too far ahead.' I said, wondering what the price of modern camping equipment was like these days.

She laughed. It was good to see her laugh. It was good to see her happy. I looked at Brett.

'You'd better look after them' I glared at him using only my eyes, without saying it out loud. He took a step back. I think he got the message.

I looked down at my granddaughter. Time marches on, I thought, things happen, some good, some bad, some you can't do anything about, some you can. But some things change your perspective, like a bolt of lightning would if you got too close. Seeing my granddaughter for the first time was something like that.

As I was making my way to the departure gate I thought about calling my daughter but decided not to. I didn't know how long I was going to stay in North America and whether or when I would have the time to visit them. So to avoid awkward questions I put it off until later. Anyway they needed their sleep and it might be the wrong time to call.

Chapter 7

My flight was an Air Canada Boeing 767-300 flight to Toronto. Take off was at 12.00hrs with a flight time of 7 hours 20 mins. With a time difference of minus 5 hrs compared to the UK the local landing time would be about 14.20 hrs. It all seemed very precise on paper. In practice we took off 35 minutes late.

Once on the plane I tried to settle in. I'd been forced to travel Economy. Even though it was an aisle seat the narrowness of the spaces ensured physical contact with my neighbour and we carried out the obligatory silent ballet that is the competition for elbow room on our shared armrest.

I was seated fairly close to the emergency over-wing exits and could overhear the additional safety briefing being given to those lucky passengers who were seated by there, able to revel in the luxury of the additional leg room at no extra cost.

'Do all of you understand English?' asked the rather attractive young stewardess in the deep red tee-shirt, light grey slacks and deep red neckerchief decorated with splashes of pale blue, yellow and white that is the Air Canada livery. Her long fair hair was carefully tied back from her face, her make-up expertly applied to enhance her already naturally attractive features.

The passengers in the emergency exit row seats

nodded. She took this to mean 'Yes'.

'That's good,' she said, although it wouldn't have reassured me. 'Now, as you know you are sitting next to one of the over-wing emergency exit doors and I need to give you an additional briefing on what to do in the ...' She paused for effect, '...in the very unlikely event of an emergency. Is that OK?'

No response.

'Great. Firstly then, do any of you have any medical condition that could prevent you from opening the emergency exit door?' she asked and then added quickly, 'but only, and I mean only, if instructed by one of the cabin crew to do so.'

Vacant looks. The silence was taken as reassurance that the passengers so addressed were indeed fit enough to take on the task ... if, and only if, they were instructed so to do by a member of the cabin crew.

'Moving on then,' her smile had slipped just a fraction but she was determined to finish this, something she'd done hundreds of times before, no matter what. 'If and only if you are instructed by a member of the cabin crew to open the emergency doors you do it like this. Firstly look out of the window and if you see fire or smoke billowing around, or for example there is water lapping up at the windows or any other indication that opening the door would not be a good idea, then immediately tell a member of the cabin crew and do not open the door even if you've been instructed to do so.'

Seemed sensible enough to me, there must be times

when opening up pretty big holes in the fuselage would not be a big help.

A grunt from one of her tutor group served as permission to proceed and she leaned over and touched a part of the door marked "Pull".

'If it's safe to open the door, and when you've been instructed by one of the cabin crew so to do …'

Even I had got that message and I was 3 rows away.

'… pull on this cover, see, where it's marked "Pull" …'

There's a clue there somewhere I thought.

'…and the cover will come away revealing the lever that actually opens the door. Pull this down and this will release the door, see there's an arrow showing you how to do it. Lift the door into the plane, turn it at an angle and fling it out of the plane through the hole you have just created.'

I looked at my potential saviours. I wanted to demand a recount on the physical and mental prowess required to do this task, which, in the event, would need to be carried out under duress.

'Is that clear? Any questions?'

One of the passengers reached up and started to move his fingers under the cover marked "Pull".

'You mean this one?' he said, his grip tightening, 'how hard do you have to pull.'

The stewardess' expression froze, a sign of thorough training on passenger management I thought, and she calmly reached across and moved his hand down and away.

'Please don't touch this unless instructed by a member of the cabin crew,' she said with practiced politeness.

I think you mentioned something of the sort, I thought, projecting my mental support in her direction.

'You will not have to pull that hard,' she said, 'you'll know when you've pulled hard enough because it will come off.'

Seemed logical.

'Any more questions?'

There were none. One of the passengers had slipped earphones into his ears early in the proceedings. The stewardess moved away. Her job was done.

I wasn't sure that I felt reassured, my main hope was that the need to rely upon the newfound knowledge and skills of these few frail fellow travellers would never arise.

I looked at the Safety card. If we were to land on water, which most of the Atlantic route between Manchester and Toronto is made up of, then there was a life raft that would need to be deployed through the over-wing exits. The deployment routine was shown graphically on the card. I looked above the emergency exit seating where I could see there was a large luggage compartment made unusable by the sign "Contains Life Raft". The complexity of deployment was obviously a step too far for the Stewardess to include in her briefing, keeping my fingers crossed seemed a better bet.

The meal was a very passable piece of roast chicken with gravy, a herb infused mash and mixed vegetables. I overcame the temptation to pay for an alcoholic drink on principle, the Scotsman in me whispering in my ear that it should have been included, and settled for an orange juice.

The in-flight entertainment was delivered through an app you could download on a phone or tablet, or you could rent an iPad for $10.

I should have got one.

The guy beside me, medium build, height, medium everything, was a motor mouth. He was one of those people it was impossible to be anything other than polite to, even if he did have a Yorkshire accent. I was only half listening,

'What are you going to Canada for?'

'Just a business trip.'

'It's my first time in Canada how about you?'

'No, I've been there a few times.'

'I won this trip as a prize. Still, as soon as I'm off the plane I'll be over to the hotel, checking out the gym, pushing some weights. I'm in training to be a physical trainer you see, so I can help people regain their fitness. I want to give something back.'

I'd been concentrating on other things. We'd hit some "bumpy air" and the plane was rising and falling like we were white water rafting. As I wasn't re-assured by the exit seat experts I needed a distraction and was therefore more interested in carrying on this conversation than I would normally have been.

He pulled out his phone, scrolled through his photos and then held one up so I could see it.

'This was me 18 months ago.'

The phone waved about in front of me. It was in danger of making me feel seasick. I held onto his wrist to steady it. The picture showed what I could only describe as a fat face sitting on top of a fat body. He looked very different now. I sat up in my seat and gave him my attention.

'Couldn't walk properly, never ran, borderline diabetic I reckon. Did it to myself, fried breakfasts, take-aways for lunch, dinner and supper. Some days I just couldn't get out of bed. It was when I saw my mum crying that I knew I had to do something. It was hard, it was very hard,' he paused as if inwardly remembering just how hard it had been, 'I lost 8 stones in a year. It was almost too much, too fast. There were lots of times I wanted to give up but I kept seeing that picture of my mum in my mind's eye.'

'I'm impressed,' I said.

'Don't be. I didn't want to die. That's what drove me. Now I have to watch myself. I'm like an eataholic in remission. I don't want to slip back.'

I wasn't sure I wanted all this information from a complete stranger. I moved my arm to give him more room on the armrest. The air turbulence was still evident and we had to raise our voices to hear each other speak.

'I've got so much more energy now, I feel like I've

got a future. I'm mid-way through my training and I'm determined to finish it, then I can get a job or be a freelancer. Lots of people need help. I know what it's like. I can earn a living and help people like me at the same time.'

If the ability to talk non-stop without taking a breath is a sign of fitness then you're almost there, I thought, holding onto my seat. But I had to give him respect. I thought about the photo he'd shown me and then looked at the man sitting beside me, in the flesh. Well done, I thought, bloody well done. Selfishly, I was also a bit relieved because sitting next to his old self in cramped seats for over seven hours wouldn't have been much fun. I looked down at my own midriff, promising myself a better diet and more exercise starting from right now.

'What do you do?' he asked.

I thought about my answer. Next to the effort he was putting into life I didn't seem to be doing very much.

'I'm between jobs,' I said, feeling this was at least half-true. All the things I did seemed to be betwixt and between other people's desires.

'Oh, I'm so sorry,' he said.

As the air turbulence subsided so did our conversation and he soon reclined his seat, put his head back and fell fast asleep. He snored loudly, enjoying his beauty sleep.

I didn't want to sleep so I attracted the stewardess' attention and invested in an iPad. As I settled back to watch a movie I couldn't help wondering to myself, 'Buying a painting, even if it's a fake, how tough can that be?'

Chapter 8

I went to the WC an hour before landing having first opened the overhead locker and taken my toiletries out from the zipped compartments of my hand luggage. Ablutions, a quick wash, shave and cleaning of teeth was all the freshening up I could achieve in such a cramped space. It did make me feel better though and took my mind off the 5 hour time difference.

Just before the landing procedure commenced I returned the rented iPad, wishing I'd chosen better movies, and woke up my snoring companion. Refinding your way in life is no easy matter. Realising you need to is difficult enough in itself. No matter where he'd come from or where he was going to he deserved credit for his courage in trying. His efforts had clearly been successful so far. I didn't even know his name, I'd forgotten to ask. But that didn't matter,. I wished him well on his way.

We landed a little late at Toronto's Pearson airport, gate E75, Terminal 1. The local time was 15.00hrs (20.00hrs UK time). Thankfully we had not had the need to use the emergency exits or deploy the life rafts.

I joined the flow of passengers making their way to Passport Control and made a point of avoiding any sign that said "Visitors on Business" as I knew from past experience that this led to tighter scrutiny and more questions.

As I was dressed casually I had no problem blending in with the milling crowd of mainly tourists and was happy to show my passport, which identified me as Michael Stewart and explain that I was here for two weeks, had an hotel address and could show them that I had a return ticket. Although I felt I'd been somehow singled out for closer scrutiny I kept any semblance of a scowl off my face. I got through unscathed and the whole process felt less threatening than the same procedure feels when you're entering the USA.

After collecting my luggage from the carousel, which was just a single medium sized suitcase with wheels and a pull out handle, I slung my small black back-pack, that I'd used as hand luggage, over my shoulder and made my way out through Customs.

I went through the green channel and was not stopped.

As I had plenty of time I dawdled in the Arrivals Hall, visited the shops and picked up a few local purchases, some of them quite expensive. I slipped these into my backpack.

Pearson International Airport is located 22.5 km (14 miles) northwest of downtown Toronto. Rather than take a taxi I took the Union Pearson Express train and was standing outside Toronto's Union Station looking up at the imposing site that is the Fairmont Royal York Hotel less than 30 minutes later.

The Hotel, more commonly known as the Royal York, is situated at the southern end of Toronto's Financial District. It was originally built by the Canadian Pacific Railway company and was opened on 11 June 1929. It has changed hands a few times since then and undergone many different refurbishments. At 124 metres tall it was briefly the tallest building in Toronto and indeed the tallest building in what was then the British Empire.

Now it stood opposite me gleaming in the afternoon sun like some kind of gigantic chateau, its 28 floors housing 1,363 guest rooms, 4 restaurants and bars, a gym and a spa amongst other things.

Front Street West stood between me and luxury and a few easy steps would take me up the ladder from economy to first class. I hurriedly dragged myself and my luggage across the road, passed under the giant flags of Canada, the United Kingdom and the USA, walked through the automatic revolving doors and emerged into the marbled, richly carpeted and air conditioned interior. I paused for a moment to take it all in.

Although a porter offered to help I carried my own case up the few steps that took me towards the reception desks. Before I could get there a young lady dressed neatly in a dark green trouser suit rose from her seat in a side lounge and walked over to intercept me.

'Mr Stewart?'

She'd clearly done her homework. I must actually look like my photograph.

'Yes,' I said.

'Officer Jones' she said, holding out a hand. I took it. She had a surprisingly strong grip, 'We have your room all ready for you if you would like me to take you up.'

I glanced at the table she had left. A half-full glass still sat there.

'Tell you what,' I said, 'Why don't I join you for a drink first, I can see you haven't finished yours. We've got plenty of time and I need a coffee.'

As we settled at the table she said,

'We could have met you at the airport you know.'

'I know, but I wanted to do a bit of shopping and I enjoyed making my own way here. The train service was good and the views gave me a renewed feel for the place.'

'You've been here before?'

'Yes, over the years, and each time is different, the waterfront reclamations, the new high-risers…'

'Well I'd like to welcome you back but I'm afraid the business you're here to help us with is liable to be messy.'

'Ok,' I said, 'but before we get into any of that I could murder a black coffee.' Under the circumstances my choice of words could have been better. Hopefully the fate of the black coffee would be all I had to worry about. From the anxious look Officer Jones had on her face I thought not.

Raising a hand she signaled to a waiter and ordered my coffee but nothing else for herself, 'I'll just finish this,' she said.

'What is it?' I asked.

'Just a Diet Coke, I'm trying to watch my sugar intake.'

'The coffee is to help with the time difference. If I can stay awake till say about 10 o'clock tonight, 3 in the morning UK time, then I hope I'll get a good night's sleep and be on the ball tomorrow.'

'If I may say, sir,' she said, 'go careful on the caffeine. Too much of that and you won't be doing much sleeping at all.'

What is it about me and women? We'd only just met and already she was starting to mother me.

'You don't have to call me "sir",' I said, 'you can call me, Michael.'

'If you don't mind I'll stick to "sir", sir, I'd be more comfortable with that.'

'How about Mr Stewart then?'

Her black nose crinkled attractively as she thought about it. In her dark green trouser suit, white blouse and neatly braided hair she was clearly a good looking woman. I'd have put her height at about 5ft 3in and from the little I'd seen so far all her curves were in the right places. She sat in her seat so straight-backed I got the impression that she was probably more comfortable in uniform than out and about in civvies.

'I could throw in a few Mr Stewart's I guess,' she said. When she smiled her whole face lit up.

'And what should I call you?'

The smile disappeared.

'Officer Jones will do just fine, Mr Stewart,' she said. We clearly were never going to get onto first name terms.

'Ok Officer Jones, tell me how you fit into all this.'

She took a sip of her drink before answering.

'I'm an officer with the OPP, the Ontario Provincial Police, and proud to be.'

She didn't need to say it, I could tell by the look in her brown eyes.

'We're one of the largest police forces in North America with more than 6,000 officers. I'm in the IOC, the Investigations and Organised Crime command, that's how I came to be interrogating Toni Malguzzi.'

She paused as the waiter brought my coffee. It smelt of freshly ground beans and from the aroma I guessed it was a Kenyan variety, medium roast. Not a Peaberry but a good one nonetheless.

'You were one of the original interrogating officers?'

'Yes sir, me and Officer Logan.'

'Officer Logan?'

'Yes, you'll be meeting him soon.'

'What's he like?'

She paused, then shook her head.

'You'll meet him,' she said.

I took a sip of the coffee, it was hot but drinkable. The taste was full, round and rich with a complexity of berry flavours and a sharp edge that did its work. I could feel myself perking up.

'So tell me about Toni Malguzzi, bring me up to speed.'

She clicked into professional police officer mode and began to give me her report. I'd obviously hit the right button.

'Not for the first time we suspected him of murder,' she said, 'this time it was a man called Ray Chaucer a well-known fence. But before we could bring him in he turned up voluntarily. We were surprised as we knew our evidence was weak and we were unlikely to have enough for any charge to stick. Malguzzi knows how the system works, he would have known that he was likely to be in the clear. However as we had him we began to go through the motions...'

'Back up a bit,' I said, 'tell me about his history. I want to know more about where he comes from than I do.'

It's always good to know your... well what was he? I couldn't quite get my head around it but I guess the closest I could get was... client.

'How far back do you want me to go?' said Officer Jones.

'As far as you like. I've got the time. I've got the coffee.'

'Well, as you can tell from the name he's from Italian extraction, but who his father was or how far back his roots go nobody knows. His mother died when he was a child, drug overdose I think, and he was shuffled between homes, institutions, fostering but didn't stick anywhere, kept getting into trouble and being moved on. Not a surprise then, as he got bigger and older, that his crimes evolved with him. From shoplifting to burglary, from car theft to ram-raiding, he was in an out of custody. And prison didn't provide any road to rehabilitation. Instead it became a kind of college of crime and each time he emerged more educated, more dangerous and more plugged in to a wider network of fellow criminals.'

She paused to take breath and ask if I wanted a refill. I replied in the affirmative although I could detect her disapproval at my level of caffeine consumption. If I wasn't careful I was probably going to get a lecture on the dangers of caffeine as a drug, the long term effect it can have on the body etc. After the coffee arrived I tried to head that off with flattery,

'You've certainly done your homework,' I said, 'it sounds like a pretty sad story.'

'Don't feel any sympathy for Toni Malguzzi,' she said pointedly, 'he's had lots of chances along the way to take different roads,' she paused, 'he took advantage of some of the prison classes for example and became quite an art lover,' I raised an eyebrow, it seemed out of character for the rough, tough man-of-the-streets that had been shaping in my mind, 'oh yes, whilst incarcerated he took the opportunity to take a lot of the courses on offer, a promising student apparently, a sponge for knowledge. He's become quite the art snob and believes he has taste. At one point he had amassed quite a good but small collection of mainly Canadian artists I understand. But it didn't make any difference, once he was out of prison he was soon back to his old ways,' she shook her head, 'there's just no helping some people.'

She took a drink. I sipped my second coffee.

'Go on,' I said.

'Well it got worse,' she said, 'he was accused of his first murder over 20 years ago, a young female, British I believe, a mugging gone wrong. The evidence should have been strong, he has a tattoo of a spider on the back of his left hand and that's quite a distinguishing mark. But in this case the assailant wore gloves, we didn't have all the forensic tests we have now and the rookie cop who was first on the scene basically trashed any possibility of extracting reliable evidence. Malguzzi used his right to remain silent, something he's become a real expert at over the years, and we couldn't make anything stick. A few years later he hooked up with the Vandla family, a criminal gang involved first in drugs and prostitution before moving on to specialise in protection. As a department we've rubbed shoulders with him many times over the years but when witnesses are too scared to come forward it's tough to build a case that can stand up in court.'

Her summary confirmed my own briefing in the UK, except for his apparent interest in the arts. Maybe that explained his interest in the Picasso. I could tell from her body language that she was reaching the end.

'The family disbanded the gang recently. We know that because of the turf war that ensued as others tussled to fill the lucrative gap left behind. Toni Malguzzi slipped off our radar, his file was moved to the basement, we didn't expect to hear from him again. We in the office felt a mixture of frustration and relief.'

She stopped, relaxed, took a drink of her Diet Coke. I thought about telling her it contained caffeine but I resisted.

'That was a great summary, thanks,' I said.

She smiled, 'No problem.'

'So it must have been a big surprise when he reappeared?'

'It was, it was another gangland killing. It was pretty obvious who had done it, it was probably over some kind of deal gone wrong. It was equally obvious we wouldn't be able to take Toni Malguzzi down for it, unless he'd been careless that is. We were looking into that possibility. But the game changed when he decided to use the murder as a convenient cover, a reason for coming to talk to us, to make us his offer.'

'Why does it matter?' I asked, 'why does he matter? His time has gone hasn't it? All the cases he's left behind, other than the one you were questioning him about, are cold aren't they? What difference does it make if you re-open them now?' I was being provocative. I wanted to see her response. I didn't have to wait long. It was immediate. Her face hardened. She glared at me.

'Victims deserve justice, Mr Stewart, however long it takes. Our motto in the OPP is to serve with pride, professionalism and honour. What pride, what professionalism, what honour is there in giving up, sweeping things down into the basement, switching the lights off, trying to pretend they never happened or worse, that they no longer matter?'

I'd got the response and it was a strong one.

She sighed.

'Also,' she said, 'there's the politics. Think about it. How much would you give to be known as the person who cleared up 30 or 40 old cases and put 10's of old villains behind bars, villains that none of your predecessors managed to touch.'

'But they'll all be old people, it'll be like putting them in a care home ... at the taxpayer's expense.'

'So you're not an expert in PR,' she said pointedly.

She was right, I wasn't. But I was also testing the waters, trying to be clear why Toni Malguzzi, a lifelong criminal, was getting such special treatment.

'And how has it been working out?' I asked.

'It's going well, we've already run a number of cold cases past him, he's selected a few and from his info we've made arrests, got court cases in progress and pending.'

'So?'

'So?'

'So why this charade, why this pandering when you're already getting what you want out of him?'

She dropped her eyes, she wasn't proud of this next bit.

'He's reeled us in,' she said, 'he's given us minor victories but he's pointed to other, larger, more serious cases, cold cases that still resonate in the public domain, and he's promised us he can unlock them for us. Easy as pie. Just help him do this little thing.'

'Buying a stolen painting off the dark web, dealing with criminals... you call that a little thing?'

I wasn't being fair. It wouldn't have been Officer Jones' decision. It was above her pay grade.

She didn't answer.

'Why does he want the painting anyway?'

She looked up, re-made eye contact, her brown eyes shining.

'I have no idea, and you know something, Mr Stewart, I really don't care.'

I finished my coffee. She left the remainder of her Diet Coke. It had been there a long time and was probably flat by now.

'The only thing that matters, Mr Stewart, is that we have a job to do. I'm here to help you but you're the one on point. It's important this goes well.'

Thanks for that, I thought, nice to know where I stand.

'Now, if you've finished your coffee let me show you your room.'

Chapter 9

The suite they'd booked for me was on the 16th floor, at the front, high enough up to get a view over the station and on over Toronto's Harbourfront and out into Lake Ontario. Although it was luxury accommodation I was under no illusions as to why I'd been put here.

'There are cameras and microphones in every room,' said Officer Jones, 'no one can move an inch in here without being seen and recorded.'

'Even the bathrooms?'

'Almost everywhere,' she said, 'we'll be constantly monitoring from the next room down the corridor.'

Now I am not a prude, years in the army rid you of any semblance of that, but at the same time I wasn't looking forward to being treated like I was in a modern version of the "Truman Show".

'Is that really necessary? Even when I'm in here on my own.'

'I don't think so but the powers that be do. Remember you'll be dealing with people proficient in the art of witness intimidation. We don't want you bothered by any unwelcome visitors. Visitors that may arrive at any time of the day or night.'

Far from making me feel secure this outlook served only to make me feel a wee bit nervous.

The door to the suite opened onto a short hallway. To the right was a locked door that I assumed was the adjoining door to the next suite, the "surveillance centre". At least they were close at hand in an emergency, I thought.

Opposite the adjoining door there was a small toilet/shower/bathroom and straight ahead was the access to the main lounge with plenty of seating, coffee table, bureau, TV, and desk. It was a large room with large windows giving plenty of natural light. A good room for difficult meetings and conversations.

Off the lounge a further door led to the bedroom with its king-size bed, wardrobes, further TV and en-suite bathroom. It was definitely a well-appointed suite and I was pleased I wasn't paying for it myself.

'What do you think?' asked Officer Jones.

'Fine,' I said, already watching my words, aware I was now a fish swimming in somebody else's goldfish bowl.

'We've got you some extra clothes suitable, we think, for this time of year and for what you're likely to be doing.'

It'll all be tagged, I thought, so you can monitor my movements.

'Thanks,' I said, not really meaning it.

I strode through to the bedroom dragging my suitcase behind me and opened a wardrobe. It was full of black, navy blue and dark grey jackets and trousers, and white and pale blue shirts. I'm not a big fan of ties and I normally wear my shirts open at the neck. It was a reasonable selection and would do for normal everyday use. I took my back-pack from my shoulder and dropped in on the bed leaving my suitcase to stand alongside.

It took another 30-40 minutes for Officer Jones to show me the locations of the carefully concealed cameras and microphones, and she asked me to go into each room, every corner, and say something so that she could check reception with the surveillance team next door. We did it twice, three times until everybody was satisfied.

'Sometimes your voice sounds very soft,' she said, 'try and keep it up, make our job easy.'

'Sure,' I said, although I wasn't going to artificially raise my voice all the time. I wasn't a stage actor. I wasn't here to play to the audience, projecting my voice to make sure that those in the cheap seats at the back could all hear me. It was their responsibility to make sure their equipment was good enough. I would just be me and they would have to live with that.

I wanted to be left alone now, all this attention was stifling. In an attempt to get her to leave I said,

'I think we're about done for now, aren't we? Just remind me of the next few steps in the timetable you've got lined up for me.'

'Well, I think you're right. I think we're just about there,' she said.

Good, I thought, at least we are in agreement on that.

'I'll leave you to unpack and my partner, Officer Logan, will come along and meet you for dinner.

You've asked and we've given you the day tomorrow to settle in and then the following day you'll meet with Toni Malguzzi and we'll move on from there.'

'Great,' I said, 'taking it easy tomorrow will help me get to grips with the 5 hour time difference. I never sleep well on the first night.'

'All that caffeine won't be helping,' she said, switching back into mother hen mode.

Chapter 10

I took my time unpacking. It was important to me to be clear on what clothes I had that were not tagged versus those that probably were. It was also important for me to arrange them so that if they were tampered with whilst I was out of the room then I would know about it.

I left my airport purchases in my backpack.

Once I was satisfied with the unpacking I took a shower. If they were going to get the benefit of seeing me naked then they may as well start early. After that, and feeling cooler, cleaner and fresher, I dressed in some of my new clothes; a blue shirt with button-down collar, boxer shorts, black slacks, red socks and black polished shoes. Everything was a perfect fit, they'd done a good job.

I then went back into the bathroom on the pretence of cleaning my teeth, as if it were something I'd forgotten to do. The toothbrush shaft contained an electronic sweeping device which confirmed my fears that my new clothes were indeed tagged.

Returning to the bedroom I took a jacket from the wardrobe, which again was a perfect fit, and picked out a pen from my backpack which I slipped into an inside pocket. Taking the card key to the door of the suite with me I headed out to the elevators, determined to find one of the hotel bars.

It was easy. I found a bar on the 3rd floor and a corner to sit in. I ordered a Molson Canadian lager beer. It would have somehow felt disloyal to order a Budweiser even though I think Molson Canadian is now part of a larger American group, so it was probably misplaced loyalty. At least I was trying.

The beer arrived together with a bowl of salted peanuts which were very welcome. As I settled back to drink I reached inside my jacket and clicked the top of my pen. I could just imagine the consternation in the surveillance suite when all of a sudden their tracking screens turned into white noise.

Sod 'em, I thought, I had some personal calls to make and I may as well test their responsiveness at the same time.

I took out my phone and dialed. A new face entered the bar looking around anxiously. Once he spotted me he settled on a bar stool and ordered a beer. I was impressed at their speed of reaction. I was clearly important to them right now.

'Hello.'

'Hi Teresa, just checking in. I'm here in Toronto and looking forward to tomorrow.'

'I'll be arriving later tonight,' she said, 'we could meet up straight away.'

Ah, this was going to be trickier than I thought.

'I can't tonight, they've organised a meeting over dinner, and anyway by then I'll be feeling groggy from the time difference.'

'So you don't want to see me.'

Told you it was going to be tricky.

'Of course I want to see you. I'm desperate to see you.'

'Well then?'

'Well then I've still got this job to do and I don't want you coming over to this hotel.'

Shit, as soon as I said it I knew it was wrong.

'So you're ashamed of me!?'

What I should have said was, 'No, it's just that I don't want you getting caught up in all this, who knows it might get dangerous. My every move is being monitored right now and I don't want you to get caught in the net. I think too much about you to allow that.' What I actually said was,

'No, no, of course not,' the guy at the bar was getting up, I was in fear of him coming over to join me, 'Listen I'll explain everything when I see you. Just trust me OK, just trust me.'

Silence.

'Hello...'

Silence, and then,

'OK, I'm not happy,' I'd already got that impression, 'but OK,' pause, '...your reasons had better be good.'

'See you tomorrow.'

I reached into my jacket again and clicked the top of the pen. I could picture the surprised and relieved faces in the surveillance room. I'd leave them to their investigation of what went wrong. I certainly wasn't going to help them out.

The man who had been sitting at the bar did not come towards me but instead headed out of the bar. Maybe I'd got it all wrong. Maybe he wasn't watching me.

I was confirmed in my former suspicions however because as he left another man entered and I saw them nod to each other. It was like watching a relay, the smooth passing of the baton. The new man was large, made to look larger by the tightness of his suit which seemed to be at least two sizes too small. He didn't dally, he came directly to my nook in the corner and sat down opposite me whilst holding out his hand in greeting,

'Good evening, Mr Stewart, I'm Officer Logan.'

I took his hand, it was clammy and the grip was lukewarm, like shaking hands with a large sausage.

'Hello,' I said, 'Officer Jones told me you'd be along.'

He grinned.

'Yea, she's very efficient is Officer Jones. I sometimes think she's almost too efficient for her own good.'

Call me perceptive, but I could see immediately why Officer Jones had declined to give me a description of Logan, if you can't say anything good about a person...

The two officers were like chalk and cheese. I was amazed that they could work together without the cracks beginning to show although I knew from the army that working towards a common good could overcome many a personality clash.

'Do you mind if we go for an early dinner?' I said, 'early for you that is.' It was already after midnight for me.

'Sure,' he said, 'OK if we just eat in the hotel? They do great food but on my salary I can't normally afford to eat here.'

At least he was honest.

'That's good for me,' I said, 'but I really just want a good steak.'

He seemed disappointed, maybe he was hoping that I would be into gourmet food and would be an excuse for a large expense claim. Anyway, he came around pretty quickly,

'Sounds good,' he said, 'I know just the place. Bring what's left of your beer and follow me.'

In the hotel restaurant chandeliers hung from the ceiling and provided subdued lighting. The décor harked back to a golden age. More importantly the food was spot on.

I didn't want a starter and quaffed a glass of Canadian Pinot Noir as I watched Logan make mincemeat of a duck pate with melba toast smeared thickly with butter. Here was a man who liked to eat.

'What more can you tell me about Toni Malguzzi,' I asked. It was only fair I made him sing for his supper.

'Toni rose through the ranks,' he said, talking mainly with his mouth full, 'he was a key enforcer for the Vandla family firm. He was someone to be feared and wore the spider tattoo on his left hand like a badge. When the family firm broke up my guess is that he got a pretty healthy nest egg to take away with him.'

The main course arrived. I'd taken a chance and gone for a flat iron steak, a shoulder cut that can be tough if not handled well. I'd asked for medium rare to try and be on the safe side. When it arrived I realised immediately that it had been in safe hands, the fascia membrane had been removed and the meat was full of flavour. To go with the steak I'd gone for french fries, garlic mayonnaise and chimichurri, an Argentinian mix of chopped parsley, oregano, garlic, olive oil, vinegar, and red pepper flakes. The Pinot Noir was a successful accompaniment with lots of smooth berry flavours and a satisfactory level of acidity.

After his apparent gourmet aspirations Logan had chosen the "Royal Cheeseburger" a beef burger layered with smoked bacon, white cheese, sour pickle, tomato and the house special and secret "royal" sauce. It also came with french fries and a side salad that he turned his nose up at. His drink of choice was Budweiser and he wasn't shy to drink it in quantity.

'So why has Toni Malguzzi turned against his old friends?' I asked.

'Who knows,' said Logan, 'and who cares? Maybe he feels like he's been slighted for some damn stupid reason. But while he's doing us favours I'm happy to take advantage of it.'

It seemed like Logan was happy to take advantage of anything that might fall his way, this dinner included.

After polishing off his two courses he still had room for dessert and chose something called Whoopie pie; two red velvet cake pieces, made with cocoa powder, vinegar and buttermilk, the chemical reaction between the ingredients giving the cake a dark maroon colour, with a filling of cream cheese marshmallow. It wasn't the low calorie option.

I didn't want to just sit and watch him eat again so I asked for the cheese and biscuits. The selection was of Canadian cheeses; a smooth cheddar from British Columbia and a Belle Creme, Mamirolle and Camembert from Quebec. I knew I wasn't going to finish it but I could at least try a little of each.

'Why do you think he's so obsessed with getting this painting?' I asked Logan, who had transferred all his attention to his dessert.

'Obsessed?'

'Seems that way to me. Why doesn't he just finish off welshing on his mates and disappear into the big unknown of your witness protection system.'

Logan stopped eating for a moment, but only for a moment.

'Toni Malguzzi is a dangerous guy, Michael, I wouldn't go throwing around words like obsessed within his hearing, he might not like it,' I didn't have any intention of doing that but I took the warning on the chin, "tread carefully, Michael, dangerous people are sensitive people.". Having delivered his warning and satisfied he'd drilled it home sufficiently, he carried on,

'In my opinion,' he said, 'it's a final power play, a look what I can do moment before stepping off the stage. Or maybe, you know about his artistic pretensions don't you, yea, well maybe he's seen this picture before and has always wanted it, you know, envy, jealousy, that kind of stuff.'

He took mouthfuls while he was talking, his plate was emptying fast. I nibbled at a couple of pieces of cheese.

'But don't you think they'll know that it's him? Don't you think it's too obvious a move?'

Logan finished the final crumbs, they'd hardly need to bother washing the plate, then he smacked his lips together appreciatively and looked me straight in the eye.

'Well, Michael, I can call you Michael can't I?' I nodded, he didn't seem a "sir" kind of guy, 'well, Michael, that's where you come in, that's why you're here, that's your job, to do the deal so as they don't know Toni Malguzzi's behind it,' he paused to take breath and to grin at me, I didn't find his attitude reassuring, 'that's why you're in this 5 star accommodation, that's why you're getting treated like a pop star. We trust you'll get the job done, make the deal, get the goods, go home, that's it, that's all you have to do,' he paused again, the grin had gone, 'just don't mess it up, Mr Stewart, you'd be very unpopular if you did that, very unpopular indeed.'

Hmm, so that was clear then, everything that was going right was in their court, everything that might go wrong was in mine. I noted the change from "Michael" to "Mr Stewart". Logan was happy to smile and be friendly but he was making it clear he was never going to be a "pal". Fine, great, thanks for the clarity, I thought, and my thanks to AB for another problem-free assignment!

'So Michael, would you like a coffee, maybe a brandy to go with it?' his bonhomie was back.

'No, I'm done. I don't want to take on too much caffeine when I'll probably struggle to sleep anyway.' Officer Jones would have been proud of me.

Logan looked visibly upset. He called over a waiter.

'Can you bring the check. I'll give it the once over and my friend here will put in on his room.'

His use of the word "friend" was definitely a misnomer.

Back in my room I checked my clothes, suitcase, and backpack. As far as I could see they had not been disturbed.

I got showered and ready for bed and before settling down with a nightlight, a good book and a couple of whisky miniatures I made my final call of the day.

Buzz, buzz,

'Hello?' the voice sounded full of sleep.

'I'm here,' I said.

'Oh good.'

I left a pause...

'Do you want me to guess the rest?' she said.

Samantha sounded suitably irritated. I decided not to tease her any further and gave her a rundown of the events so far using a code word to let her know that there were people listening in to our conversation.

'OK,' she said, 'got it, call me again after your first meeting with Malguzzi,' pause, 'or sooner if anything important happens.'

'OK, will do,' I said, 'I'm hoping this'll all be over in 4 or 5 days.'

'Don't rush it, we're after a good result not speed.' I wasn't sure whether the surveillance microphones were good enough to pick that up. If they were I was sure they'd be pleased with the sentiment. In contrast I couldn't help remembering AB's emphasis on "quickly".

'Oh, and just one more thing,' she said.

'Yes?'

'Try and call at a more sociable hour than 3 in the morning!'

'Will do, sleep tight now, and don't let the bedbugs bite.'

Her groan was audible.

Click.

Chapter 11

The next morning I took an early and light room service breakfast at 05:00 hrs (although still a late one in UK terms). Just croissants, Canadian raspberry jam (not as good as Scotland's), fruit and coffee. I'd actually slept well under the influence of last night's alcohol and felt fit and ready to go.

I dressed in my travelling, untagged, clothes. They might be a bit smelly but the advantage of being untrackable was more than compensation for that. I slung my backpack over my shoulder and got up to leave, leaving my phone behind on the bedside table.

The suite had two entrances and I exited by the second which was directly off the bedroom. I took the elevator down two floors, retrieved a hoodie from my backpack and put it on. I got out of the elevator as others were getting in and took the stairs down five floors. Then I walked across to the alternative set of elevators and exited, with hood up, as close to the access to the underground walkway as I could.

Toronto nestles on the western side of Lake Ontario, one of the Great Lakes, and is the most populous city in Canada with around 3 million people. It's people are a diverse mix reflecting its current and historical role as a destination for Canadian immigrants. As an international centre of business, finance, arts, and culture, it is recognized as one of the most multicultural and cosmopolitan cities in the world.

In reality Toronto is made up of two cities, one above ground and one below. The one below ground is known as the PATH and is a network of more than 30 kilometres of underground pedestrian tunnels and elevated walkways connecting major buildings and containing the largest underground shopping complex in the world with an area of 4,000,000 sq ft. Over 200,000 residents and workers use the PATH daily and it's constantly being developed and expanded. If you're not a local you'll need a map, it's easy to get lost in there. I know.

I decanted at Union Station and made use of the public washrooms to change into the "I ♥ Toronto" t-shirt and baseball cap I'd bought at the airport. I'd also bought and activated, with the help of a young and knowledgeable shop assistant, a pay-as-you-go phone and I now took this out of the backpack and put it in my pocket. I then rejoined the PATH and made my way to one of Toronto's most iconic landmarks, the CN Tower.

At over 550 metres high this concrete communications and observation tower rises like a giant pointer into the Canadian sky. For obvious reasons it acts as a tourist magnet and city navigational aid and attracts more than two million international visitors every year. The main pod contains a 360 degree restaurant and viewing platform, that protrudes like a skewered donut at a height of 350 metres above the ground and for those of an adventurous disposition there is an EdgeWalk where for a tourist-sized sum of money you can be tethered to an overhead rail system and walk around the edge of the roof of the main pod on a metal walkway just 1.5 metres wide. I'm sure, like me, you'll be glad to know that this walkway is closed to the public during high winds or electrical storms.

I shielded my eyes and gazed up at the tower, it was bereft of the red be-helmeted, harnessed hangers-on of the EdgeWalk. Such adventurous souls clearly needed a lie-in prior to their adrenaline rush. Maybe another time, I thought, but then again maybe not.

I carried on walking between the CN Tower and the Toronto Blue Jays Baseball stadium and picked up a taxi to take me the rest of the way. No point in overdoing the exercise.

Once I got to Hotel X, which overlooks the Harbourfront and has views out across Lake Ontario, I went first to the shops on the ground floor. They were only just opening their doors. I purchased a new set of clothes from a young assistant with sleep still in her eyes. I changed in the public washroom and felt less like a "look at me I'm a tourist" than I had in my t-shirt and baseball cap.

Then I gave Teresa a call,

'Hello?'

'It's me.'

'I don't recognise this number.'

'It's a disposable one. I bought it yesterday.'

'Why?'

'I'll explain when I come up. Are you awake? Are you decent?'

'Yes I'm awake or I wouldn't be talking to you, and no I'm not decent.'

Perfect.

'Give me your room number and I'll be straight up.'

She did and I was.

Chapter 12

Teresa's room was on the 10th floor with large windows making the most of the view. I didn't take much notice of this though as my eyes were only for Teresa and as she opened the door I fell into her arms. Luckily she caught me.

We spent the next hour or so getting reacquainted and after we'd both showered we ordered a substantial room service breakfast. Although this was my second of the day I felt I had earned this one and was in need of more sustenance.

We sat gazing alternately at each other and then at the view as we tucked into fried eggs (over easy), crispy bacon, beans, tomato and mushrooms with breakfast tea as the perfect accompaniment. I'm not sure what happiness is but if it's counted in moments then you could chalk this one down for me.

Unfortunately such moments do not last forever.

'So why did you not come and see me last night and why the new phone?'

Teresa pretty much knew the world I inhabited and my irregular lifestyle. She'd got used to my different assumed personas and although she had been surprised by my new auburn look she didn't seem to mind it. So I saw no reason to lie. I trusted her. I told her the truth. I told her what I was doing and that I was under close watch.

She looked around uncomfortably, she was only wearing a bathrobe, 'Are we being watched now?'

'I hope not, I don't think so,' I said, 'I've taken what precautions I can,' I described them to her, 'but they won't be happy, they will be looking for me.'

'Can we go out?' she asked.

'I think so, I've got a new change of clothes, I've got you with me, they won't be expecting that.'

'I'm going to buy you a hat,' she said.

'I've got this baseball cap,' I said, reaching for it and holding it up.

'I'm going to buy you a hat,' she said.

We spent the rest of the morning wandering the streets of Toronto. Teresa bought me a black stetson. Who in their right minds would be trying to hide from view by wearing a black stetson on the streets of Toronto. It was a double bluff that worked for me.

I bought her some clothes. I'm not great at shopping. No patience. And I'm particularly bad at choosing clothes for women. When Teresa was trying things on I tried not to yawn and when she asked my opinion I tried to read the right answer in her eyes and body language. I hit lucky about 50% of the time, well above my average.

After organizing for all Teresa's purchases to be sent on to the hotel we lunched in the CN Tower restaurant. It was a relatively light lunch because I'd booked us some jet skis for the afternoon. We bought swimming costumes down by the Harbourfront and the tight fitting safety gear was included in the rental. I'd done this before so the briefing was a bit of a waste of time for me, but Teresa hadn't and she hung on every word.

Once out on the water she soon got the hang of it and we had a great couple of hours racing out ovals and figures of eight on the rippling surface of the lake.

Afterwards we wandered around the streets for an hour or so just enjoying each other's and then we found a patisserie where we sat and shared a big slice of Saskatoon pie with vanilla ice cream followed by freshly ground coffee, Brazilian Arabica beans, ethically sourced, hand-roasted with a mild nutty body. It was good.

'How's business,' I asked. Teresa ran an importation business between the States and Costa Rica, her home country.

'Very well,' she said, 'I've had to employ two more people to handle the increase in sales. I've started a subscription service and that's gone down well.'

'And you're still doing it all online?'

'Sure, I don't want the hassle of retail premises. Where would I locate them? The United States is a big place. I'm happy to rent out some storage spaces and distribute out from them.'

'And Canada?'

'Why not, I've never thought about it, but why not.'

We chatted on and then, out of the blue, she got serious.

'So where are we going?'

'Well, I thought we could just go back to the hotel. I'll get changed because unfortunately...'

I'd stopped because she'd held up her hand.

'I didn't mean today, although I've had a really good time,' that was nice of her to say, I'd had a good time too, 'I mean us.'

'Us?'

'Yes us.'

'I'm not sure I know what you mean. I'm just having a great time. Why don't we just go back to the hotel. I've got a present for you.'

'What kind of present?'

'A girl's best friend,' I said tantalisingly.

'Hmm,' she said.

We got back to the hotel as it was beginning to get dark and went up to Teresa's room.

I reached into my backpack and took out a gift box. Who doesn't like diamonds, I thought. What a great way to finish a great day.

I handed the box over to Teresa.

She took it eagerly and ripped off the gift wrapping.

'Strange shaped box,' she said.

She opened the box and took out the contents.

Her face contorted.

'What is this?' she said. I could see that she was fighting to keep control. Something was wrong.

'Erm, it's a real Canadian diamond,' I said, 'I bought it for you at the airport, it's a friendship bracelet, a diamond on a gold band.'

Teresa is Costa Rican by birth and when she gets particularly emotional she speaks in Spanish, her face becomes very expressive and her whole body joins in the conversation. She was like that now.

'Have I upset you?' I asked both puzzled and completely unnecessarily.

With great effort she fought to regain her self-control. She balled her hands into fists, clamped her arms by her sides and took a few deep breaths.

There was a horrible silence. Then she exploded.

'A fucking friendship bracelet! I don't want to be your fucking friend!'

I think I might have mentioned that the honeymoon period of our relationship, when each of us had been keen to be only on our best behaviour, was well and truly over. However I was still taken aback by the vehemence of her reaction. I had thought that she'd like it. I was way wrong, way, way, wrong.

I wasn't sure where to go from here.

'Well?' she said, then paused for a second, her body tense, her brown eyes piercing, 'Well!?'

She threw the friendship bracelet at me. I picked it up and put it in my pocket and in less than 5 minutes I found myself outside the hotel staring up at the sky, wondering what had just hit me. Didn't she like diamonds?

Chapter 13

I decided to walk back to the hotel in order to clear my head. It was a calm, clear evening with a healthy nip in the night air. I didn't have a map but was happy to rely on my unerring sense of direction to find my way back; or the satnav on my phone if that didn't work.

It was growing darker and I walked along the waterfront with my head down, not paying any attention to my surroundings. This is not a sensible idea in any big city at night, it's always best to keep your wits about you. Anyway, in this instance I didn't and wandered blindly on into one of the lesser lit areas.

I was just thinking about whether there was anything more I could or should have done or said this evening when I realised that a shape had unfurled itself from the shadows and now stood blocking my path.

My first thought was, 'Shit,' after all it was hardly professional of me to get caught out so easily. My unerring personal spider-sense had let me down.

A man's voice gravelled at me, 'Money, just give me your money.'

He held something in his hand. It glinted at me. His hand shook.

'I don't have any money,' I said.

Brown discoloured teeth formed a smile in the shadowed face.

'Well now, that would make two of us,' it said, 'but I think one of us is lying and it t'aint me.'

His hand twitched. I was lucky it was only a knife, a relatively long knife with a cerrated edge, but still only a knife. He lifted the point towards my face but struggled to hold it still.

'I been trained to use this,' he said, 'now no more shitting with me. Just give me your money. I don't want to use this.'

I didn't want him to use it either.

I lifted my left hand to reach inside my jacket. The sleeve fell back.

The man leered at me allowing me to get a whiff of his foul-smelling breath.

'Nice watch,' he said waving the knife around, 'take it off, I'll take that too, hand it over.'

Now money is one thing but my watch is quite another. I've become quite attached to it and I was certainly not going to hand it over.

'Come on,' he drooled, 'I don't have all night. You don't want me to cut you up do you?'

It had been a bad night and it just kept getting worse.

I moved my left hand towards my right intimating that I was going to unhook the watch strap.

'That's better,' said the shape, 'nice and slow.'

'Wait,' I said, 'let me get the money first.'

I could feel his eyes following my left hand as it reached inside my jacket. I readied my right.

With my left hand I started to withdraw my wallet. His teeth parted and the tip of a wet tongue showed itself. He was tense. I looked straight at him.

Then I made my move.

Time seemed to slow.

My right hand darted forward and grabbed the wrist of the hand holding the knife and swung it forcibly way.

He did not release the knife.

With his other hand he made a lunge for my eyes. I was only just quick enough to turn and take the blow on the side of my head and at the same time strike out into his groin with my foot. It might not have been Queensberry rules but it was effective.

He exhaled in a painful whine and doubled up.

As his head fell forward I met it with my knee. I think he lost another tooth. As he jerked back I used his own momentum to push him backwards into a wall, the back of his head cracking on the brickwork. As he slipped to the ground I smashed the hand I was still holding into the concrete.

The knife clattered free.

It was clear that at some point he had had training but he was a pale shadow of whoever he had been then.

He lay on his back, unconscious. I took C$50 from my wallet and scrunched it into a pocket of his dirty, torn trousers. I then took a handkerchief from my pocket and picked up the knife. I didn't want him to hurt himself with it.

I straightened and patted down my clothing before carrying on into the reds, yellows, and whites of a better lit thoroughfare. Finding a waste bin I dropped the knife into it.

There was bar just up the street. I popped in for a beer, relaxing in the white noise of multitudinous conversation. While I was there I took a trip to the washroom just to make sure nothing was too out of place and splashed my face with cold water. Outside the bar I took a taxi back to the Royal Oak compensating for the short journey with a C$20 tip.

Once inside the main entrance I took the lift up to my room. When I opened the door I could see Officer Jones in the lounge, sitting on the settee, looking at her phone. She stood up immediately.

'Where have you been!' she said, her voice a mixture of anxiety and relief.

I felt like telling her to piss off, but instead I said, 'Have you missed me?'

Chapter 14

In reply to a stream of questions I told Officer Jones I'd had a good day, thanks. No point telling her the truth.

They'd kept it a secret that there were trackers in the clothes they'd provided me so it was difficult for her to ask me difficult questions like why I'd gone out in my soiled travelling gear or why I'd left my phone behind. We just danced around the subject until she got tired of the game. Although it was quite late I hadn't had dinner yet. I had hoped to eat with Teresa but that idea had obviously been scuppered.

'I'll eat in the room tonight,' I said, 'get my mind ready for the meeting tomorrow.'

'Logan will be disappointed,' she said.

I'll get them to send him a doggy bag, I thought.

She paused and looked at me quizzically.

'There's nothing wrong is there, sir?'

Women knock all men into a cocked hat as far as emotional intelligence is concerned. I softened a little.

'No, I'm fine thanks,' which was not true, 'I'll be ready for tomorrow,' which I hoped was true.

'Well if there's anything we can do to help, anything we're not doing to your satisfaction then please let me know. We're here to support you in the best way we can.'

By keeping me in a surveillance goldfish bowl, I thought, yea that really helps a person relax.

'I'm fine,' I said.

'OK, then I'll leave you alone,' she said shrugging and turning for the door.

"Alone", yea that would be nice, but it definitely wasn't the case. I felt like there were eyes and ears on me whichever way I turned in this suite of rooms.

I watched her leave, listened to the clunk of the door closing, and then went into the bedroom and retrieved my normal phone from the bedside table. As anticipated there were a series of missed calls, voicemails and increasingly irritated texts. They were all from the same source. I didn't bother reading or listening to any of them, I just made the call I knew I needed to make.

'What the hell do you think you're doing,' said Samantha through clenched teeth, her icy calm worse than any shout, 'do you know that I've had to sit here trying to explain to people why you decided to just fall off the grid for over 10 hours.'

Had it really been that long? It had flown by.

'I didn't realise I was being kept on a lead,' I said, although I absolutely did realise it, 'this was my settling in day, I went out to explore the city.'

She made an exasperated noise that is hard to describe. I'd put her in a tight spot. To drive home her point she would have to admit there were things she knew but hadn't told me, like that my new clothes were tagged.

'Look,' she said, 'this is a sensitive assignment. I've had to keep AB at bay until I could tell him that although you'd got lost you were now found again. He'd have gone through the roof otherwise. I was running out of time, I don't like withholding information, and especially not from him.'

But you don't mind withholding it from me, I thought. Her loyalties were at least transparent.

'You might not think it's important,' she continued, there was a lot she wanted to get off her chest, 'but this is an important assignment for us and for our friends in the Canadian police. Don't fuck them about!'

What was it with women and bad language today?

'OK, OK, I'm sorry, it was a mistake, I've got that,' I said in what I hoped was both an apologetic and a conciliatory tone.

'I don't want to have to pull you off this case,' she said, 'but you're walking a fine line. I look forward to your report back tomorrow.'

I now knew she was getting "report backs" from at least two different directions and would be cross-correlating them, believing that were they intersected was most probably the truth. Once she'd made her assessments she would pass on progress reports to AB.

'Do you understand.' she said.

'Yes,' I replied.

Click.

I had a shower and then put the same, untrackable, clothes back on. Despite everything I had said I needed some air and was going to venture out again. However, on a conciliatory note, I kept both phones with me this time so they could keep track of me if they wanted, Then I went back out onto the streets of Toronto in search of dinner. I didn't care what I ate I just wanted to find a restaurant with dark recesses where I could put in a call for help. I knew I needed it and I knew there was only one place I could go to get it.

I found an Italian restaurant just down the street where the food looked authentic and freshly cooked and, more important for my purposes, where the lighting was low and there were tables in alcoves that gave a semblance of privacy in an otherwise busy city.

I ordered a bottle of chianti and a bowl of pasta and then took out my pay-as-you-go phone and called my daughter. She and her partner Brett lived in California with their new daughter, my granddaughter, Amelia (who as well as having a nice name was beautiful, although I may be biased).

Ring, ring

Ring, ring

'Hello?' it was a tired voice that answered.

'It's me,' I said.

'New phone?'

'Sort of,' I said.

'Where are you?'

I told her.

'Are you going to pay us a visit before you leave the continent? It'll give you a chance to play with your granddaughter, she only knows you as a face on Zoom.'

'I hope to,' I said, meaning it.

'So what's wrong this time?'

She's always been perceptive.

'I've got to warn you I'm heavily sleep deprived,' she said, 'so you'd better spell it out clearly and in words of one syllable.'

I knew I was being unfair sharing my problems with her, she had enough on her plate to worry about but I didn't have anybody else I could talk to about this.

I explained what had happened.

She groaned.

'Oh god, Dad, not again!'

'What do you mean?'

'You never learn do you, were you this way with Mum?'

The mention of my wife hit me like 20,000 volts shooting up my spine. My wife, who I had loved and who had battled her cancer. My wife who had thought of others all the way through her illness,

'Be happy,' she'd said to me, 'live, Mark, love and look after our daughter.'

I shook myself back into the present.

'I loved her right from the start,' I said, 'she made me chase her, drove me mad, and then reeled me in. I was caught on her hook. I never wanted to get away.'

'I know, Dad, I know.'

Her voice sounded serious and sad both at the same time.

'So although I might like someone, they could never replace your Mum, it would be disloyal to her memory...'

I trailed off.

'Don't be so selfish,' she said.

That was harsh, I had been expecting sympathy.

'What do you mean?'

'Firstly,' she said, here was the schoolteacher showing through, 'firstly, Mum would always want you to carry on, you can never find the same thing again but you can find different, and different can be good, can be very good.'

Teresa was very different to my wife.

'Secondly, you are looking at this only from your own point of view, what you'd be happy with, the easy way out. You've done this before with Teresa and then you decided to build the relationship. But to be honest you didn't decide, the two of you did. Teresa took you to the edge, showed you the way, and you both decided to jump.'

That was true and I had admitted to myself and to Teresa that I loved her. That wasn't an easy thing for me to do and the subsequent trans-atlantic nature of our relationship certainly hadn't made things any easier.

'She's got her own life to lead, dad. Things change, they move forward or back, they never stand still.'

'So what does she want?'

'Commitment you idiot, a life together or not at all. She's 10 years younger than you, she has to move on, one way or the other. And when you did all that teasing, that your present was "a girl's best friend" what do you think she was thinking?'

'Well a diamond of course, and that's what I'd bought her.'

'A diamond what?' she said pointedly.

The penny finally dropped.

'You think she thought I meant a ring?'

'And when she found out it was a "friendship" bracelet...'

'I was lucky not to get killed.'

'Right you are, dad, right you are.'

Silence.

'Listen, dad, I've got feeds to give, nappies to change and you've got some thinking to do.'

'Right you are,' I said.

I finished the pasta. I'm sure it was delicious but I didn't really taste it. I drank the chianti and finished off the meal with some Italian ice cream. I walked back to the hotel. The evening had closed in, the city lights burned in reds, blues, and yellows. I needed to compartmentalise. I needed to think about Teresa. I needed a good night's sleep in preparation for meeting Toni Malguzzi. I needed to do my job.

When I got back to my room there was a message. The meeting was set for 10 o'clock the following morning.

Chapter 15

I had had a restless night and was pleased when the unnecessary bedside alarm went off. I was showered and dressed by 08:00 hrs and a knock at the door signalled the arrival of Logan who chaperoned me to breakfast. I wondered how long he'd been waiting and watching from the surveillance room next door. He almost led me by the hand. He wasn't going to let me out of his sight.

The buffet breakfast was fine although my mind kept drifting and Logan ate much more that I did. I wondered if it was his first or second breakfast of the day.

'Do you know,' he said, just to pass the time, 'that this hotel has its own roof-top herb garden.' It clearly impressed him. I didn't really care one way or the other, 'and it has beehives, imagine that, hundreds of thousands of bees searching the gardens and parks of Toronto for pollen and nectar,' he picked up the miniature jar of honey that he'd collected from the buffet and read the label, 'see, here, this is honey from this very hotel,' he stuck his dirty knife into the jar and lifted a dollop of honey to his lips, 'tastes good too,' he said, 'wanna try?'

I declined his generous offer on the basis of hygiene. I'd had a run-in with stinging insects and as a consequence was not a big fan. I didn't mind good honey though, but not today, and definitely not from a jar Logan had already stuck his knife into.

He did his best to keep a conversation going while I drank my coffee. Then he switched to more important stuff,

'Malguzzi will be here on time at 10:00 hrs. He'll be escorted to your room. You'll sit in the lounge with him, in the corner by the main window. There will be others who stay in the room but they will keep their distance and will not interfere,' he paused, 'unless they absolutely have to.'

I nodded that I understood.

'We pretty much know what he's going to say but he is unpredictable so be careful,' I watched as a bead of sweat formed and started to trickle down one of his temples, he really needed to take care of his health. I could see he was mentally checking off a list of things that he was supposed to tell me. 'There is no time limit,' he said, 'take as long as you want, but if I were you I wouldn't take any more time than is absolutely necessary. We need Malguzzi to accept you as his intermediary and for you both to agree whatever the next steps need to be.'

'That's it?' I said.

'That's more than enough,' said Logan, licking his knife clean and preparing to stand up.

At precisely 10:00hrs the door opened and Toni Malguzzi entered. He was just like his photographs although maybe a bit older looking in the flesh. His hair was thick, silver and cut short, his face was tanned and craggy. His shoulders were broad but whereas Logan's girth showed obesity Toni Malguzzi's showed muscle. Once in the room he seemed to command it and he strode straight across to me and stuck out his hand.

The two agents who had escorted him in took up station at the door and tried to look relaxed. Toni Malguzzi wore a light grey suit that contrasted with his tanned complexion, a dark red waistcoat and a white shirt, open at the neck. The spider tattoo was visible on the back of his left hand, legs spreading down onto his fingers and upwards to disappear beneath the cuffs of his shirt. It was obvious that this guy was not shy and had a sense of style that was all his own.

'Toni Malguzzi,' he said, 'you can call me Toni.'

'Michael Stewart,' I said, 'you can call me Michael.'

Toni Malguzzi's grip was firm and the handshake took the form of a kind of unarmed combat. He was clearly keen to establish his position. We sat on opposite sides of a low table and Malguzzi called across to his companions.

'Hey you guys get me a Jack Daniels Old No.7 willya, on the rocks.'

One of the guys nodded and got on his phone.

'Hey, and not a small one, you got me?'

The guy nodded again.

Malguzzi turned to me, 'You want?'

I didn't see why not. After all I was trying to build a

relationship here and it would show that I was trying to be friendly.

'Sure,' I said.

The guy with the phone doubled the order.

Malguzzi peered at me.

'You're a Brit, right?' he said.

'Yep, though I like to think I'm more of a Scot than a Brit,' I said.

'Well, see, Michael, I'm Canadian, but I feel more Italian,' he half-smiled, gold teeth showing alongside white and shining against his dark skin, he obviously had a good dentist, but the smile lacked warmth, 'you get me, capisci?'

'I guess so,' I said, meaning that I'd no idea what he was talking about. I thought he was probably trying to wrong foot me. If that was his intention he was making quite a good job of it.

'Well, listen Brit,' he said, emphasising the last word. If this was an another attempt to prickle me then it didn't work as I was used to it and had grown a thick Scottish skin over the years, 'you know anything about me?'

I thought it better to play along.

'A little, not much,' I said.

At this point the whiskeys arrived. The glasses were large and generously filled, the ice clinked as the drinks were put down on the table in front of us.

'Thanks,' I said.

Malguzzi said nothing.

When the waiter had gone Malguzzi leant forward,

keeping his voice low. I also had to lean forward to hear him properly.

'I got brought up hard, Michael, but I got to know the streets, got to know how to look after myself,' he took a swig of his whiskey, 'you could say the Vandla family took me in, adopted me. That family and their business became my family and my business. And I grafted. If you wanna have respect you gotta earn it. You gotta be willing to go that extra step, do things that ain't normal. And I got respect all right, the kinda respect that counts.'

He was almost making it sound as though he was the good guy, fighting against the odds that were unfairly stacked against him but still able to rise high although the arrogance with which he held himself gave an entirely different impression. Here was a man who would take easily to the role of bully. I don't like bullies, yet here I was working for one. What was it AB had said 'you don't have to like someone to work for them, efficiently, professionally and quickly'. He must have guessed what my first impression was going to be. I bit my tongue and listened. This was going to be a challenge.

'If somebody raises a fist, you hit them with a baseball bat. If they have a baseball bat you use a knife,' Malguzzi shrugged, 'you got to keep one step ahead.'

Nice guy. I got the message. He'd go as far as he had to to retain the upper hand. He was not a man to be crossed. He was not a man that you could easily associate with an appreciation of art.

'I was their right-hand man, their capo,' he said, 'We built the business together. Without me it would have gone nowhere.'

By "business" I assumed he was referring to their journey through prostitution and drug dealing and on to the elevated plains of protection racketeering.

'And then, what do you think? Do you think I got a fair share of the success?'

I shrugged. These were rhetorical questions.

'No. Do you think they ask me before they decided to retire? No. And do you think they care that I had some bad luck and needed a hand? No. And after all I done for them… all I done…'

His hands were clenched into fists, the spider tattooed on the back of his left hand coiled, ready to pounce. The guys by the door tensed.

'Nobody likes to be humiliated,' he said, 'I'm owed, so now I give it back a little, the guys in uniforms gotta lot to thank me for.'

I was struggling to see him as a hero.

'Well,' I said, forcing a smile, 'I'm here to help you.'

'You're here to do as I say,' he said.

It probably meant the same thing but it sounded a lot less palatable the way he said it. I wondered what would happen if I just turned around and took the next flight back to the UK. As much as I wanted to I knew it wasn't an option. I tried to smile.

'The gal done me bad,' said Malguzzi.

'The girl?' I said.

'The daughter, Sky,' he said, 'I'm sure it was her that got in the way. All I wanted was a little extra help after all those years and she wouldn't give it. Whispered poison into her father's ear. For years she's gotten in between Lejon and me. It wasn't my fault her brothers got killed and yet I always thought she blamed me, standing in the background giving me those accusing looks. If it wasn't for her things would be a lot different for me, a lot better. Well let's see where it all gets her in the end shall we.'

If I ever thought this was just about buying a painting, which I didn't, then I had just been disabused. This was about settling a score and the painting was somehow a pawn in the game.

Toni Malguzzi's glass was refilled. I was still less than halfway through my first one.

'How does the painting figure in all this, Mr Malguzzi?' I asked. I wasn't comfortable calling him Toni.

What I should have asked was, 'Isn't it enough to welsh on your old mates, get them denuded of their proceeds of crime, probably get them incarcerated?' But I didn't ask him that. I was trying to be friendly.

Toni Malguzzi took his time, he wanted me to know.

'I know about art,' he said, 'in the past I have invested in some good Canadian art, those artists whose paintings capture the Canadian landscape, it's wildness and it's beauty in a way that shows what it means to be Canadian.'

Really, I thought, as far as I knew Toni Malguzzi had never been out of the city of Toronto for more than a week.

'The pride of my collection,' he continued, 'was a Tom Thomson piece. You know Tom Thomson? He is very famous, very good, an artist strongly associated with our Canadian "Group of Seven",' he saw my blank look and decided to educate me, 'the Canadian "Group of Seven" is really a misnomer, Michael, as there are actually eleven artists closely associated with it, it was a Canadian national art movement of the early 20th century. They captured a mood, produced art that made you feel as well as look,' he paused, 'works by these artists now sell for millions of dollars, sketches sell for hundreds of thousands. My collection would have been a wise investment if I had not had bad luck and lost them.'

I didn't want to know how. I guessed gambling or poor business. Whichever it was it wasn't my concern. It had helped fuel his grudge and that's all that mattered to me.

'If Lejon had just helped me a little when I asked him to they would still be mine,' he said, 'I am sure it was Sky who turned him against me.'

'So why a Picasso?' I asked, 'why is it so important?'

'It's always good to spread your risk,' he said, 'and keep some assets safe that you can liquidate if needs must, you know what I mean?' From what he'd just said it seemed either he'd not always followed this sage advice himself or he'd recently had an urgent need to liquidate his own assets.

'I understand,' I said, wondering how many people keep a stolen Picasso up their sleeve.

'As I told you I know about art,' he continued, 'Lejon and Sky do not have the taste, the love of art, they are not like me, they only got this artwork by mistake, by chance, in part payment of a debt. But I saw it, I saw Lejon hoard it away. I appreciated it for what it was, a masterpiece.'

But it is supposed not to exist, I thought, it is supposed to have been destroyed. Dare I ask. In for a penny in for a pound, I thought.

'The history of this painting,' I said, 'it's somewhat chequered isn't it. I mean it's...' I shrugged, hoping he got what I was trying to say.

'This deal I've made with the cops,' he said, 'you think they would let me keep a stolen Picasso?'

I was getting confused.

'The only way I get to keep the Picasso is because it doesn't exist.'

OK, I saw it now. The authorities couldn't possibly help a felon to acquire stolen goods. But if it's politically expedient, if there's pressure to squeeze the most out of a gift horse, if positive headlines, promotions and chances of re-election hang in the balance, and if no-one finds out because the whole thing is nothing, then to help Toni Malguzzi acquire a nothing, just to make him feel good, and in return to get lots of somethings, lots of somethings that are of value to the wider community then that was something they might do. It was a stretch but I could just about swallow it.

'Do you know where it's kept?'

'He moves things around,' said Malguzzi, 'Lejon is a clever guy.'

'And how did you find out this painting was up for sale?'

'I saw it on the dark web, when I came across it I recognised it, a stroke of good fortune at last,' he said, 'I have access,' he paused, 'I don't want to say more.'

'Why would they be selling it now?'

'Things are moving, Michael, sands are shifting beneath their feet, I'm shifting the sands,' he smiled, 'and there's lots more sand to shift.'

It felt like I was interrogating him. He seemed used to it. I just had to be careful not to push it too far.

'Sorry, but I need to ask you more questions,' I said, 'how far have you got with the deal? Where do I pick it up from?'

He didn't seem to mind.

'It's important to know your enemy,' said Malguzzi, 'or your friend, their likes, dislikes, their virtues, their vices, their obsessions, particularly their obsessions.'

He signalled for a Jack Daniels refill. They'd brought in a bottle. His glass was replenished.

'I've made an anonymous virtual connection. I've offered a trade not a sale. I've got a bite. There's a meeting fixed for tomorrow. You go. Sort it out. Bring me the picture.'

He made it sound so easy. But the apparent simplicity begged some complicated questions.

'What's the trade? Why would they accept a trade? I thought this was all about cashing in.'

'You got to understand obsession,' he said, 'if you offer a collector the very thing their collection is missing, the very thing they've always wanted, don't you think they'd trade to get it?'

'I guess so.'

'Well, Lejon Vandla is a compulsive numismatist, a collector of rare coins, and I've offered him the holy grail. Of course he wants to trade.'

'The holy grail...?'

Eagles and Double Eagles

The twenties in the United States roared on through. The economy was constantly expanding and investing in a burgeoning stock market was like making a bet that always came off. Everybody wanted a piece of it. Who in their right mind wouldn't?

But nothing good lasts forever.

On October 29th 1929 investors got nervous and started selling stocks they knew were overpriced. A trickle turned into a stream, a stream turned into a torrent as mass panic kicked in and investors tried to off-load millions of shares at fast declining prices. Lifelong savings, built up over years, became worthless in less than a week.

As consumer confidence vanished spending

declined, factories slowed down their production or closed altogether, and more and more workers were laid off.

By 1930 unemployment was at four million, rising to six million in 1931, fifteen million in 1932. The number of bread lines and soup kitchens increased to try and cope with the increasing number of homeless in a society that had no unemployment welfare safety net. Crops rotted in the fields as farmers couldn't afford to harvest them.

In 1930 severe droughts blew dust on high winds that killed people, livestock and ruined crops all the way from Texas to Nebraska.

The result of these combined catastrophes was a mass migration of people from the land and into the cities looking for work.

Increasingly large numbers of people began to fear that their money was no longer safe in the hands of the banks and rushed to withdraw their funds as cash. As their cash reserves vanished the banks liquidated loans as fast as they could but under this kind of pressure the number of defaulters increased. By early 1933 thousands of banks had simply given up and closed their doors.

When Franklin D. Roosevelt became the new President in 1933 he took immediate action. Amongst many other things the circulation and private possession of United States gold coins was outlawed, with an important exemption for "collector coins". This meant that gold coins were no longer legal tender and people had to hand them in and exchange them for other forms of currency.

Some 445,500 1933 gold $20 Double Eagle coins were struck **after** this order had passed into law and none were officially released into circulation. On government instruction all of these coins except 2 were ordered to be melted down. The 2 intentionally spared coins were to be held as the sole surviving examples, on behalf of the country, by the National Numismatic Collection.

However, somewhere along the line between instruction and destruction a small number of coins were stolen. Even to this day the actual number is disputed but is likely to be between 20 and 30.

Over a decade later, in 1944, examples began appearing at auctions. It is important to note that these coins are both a collector's dream and illegal to own. Secret Service operations were launched to investigate the source of these renegade coins and recover the "missing" Double Eagles on behalf of the state.

Over the coming years 20 coins were located and 9 of these were destroyed.

What most people overlook is that there was another gold coin minted in 1933, the $10 Single Eagle. In contrast to the Double Eagle the 1933 Eagle was issued **before** Roosevelt's withdrawal order. Therefore it is legal for private citizens to own this coin. However, although 312,000 were minted, the vast majority were melted down either prior to circulation or after return for conversion to other forms of currency.

Although the absolute number of extant 1933 Eagles is unknown it is estimated to be in the order of 40-50 pieces. The rarity of this coin means that it is a prime target for any serious, moneyed, collector of American coinage.

These two relics of a desperate and destructive time, the $10 Eagle and the $20 Double Eagle, have taken prime positions in the mythology and competitive nature of American coin collecting.

It is also worth noting that, although there were further significant bumps along the road, the worst of the US depression was over by 1934/5 but it's ripple effects traveled across the globe and the upheaval it caused in Europe fueled increasing support for Nationalist parties. A circumstance that lead on to the outbreak of WW2.

Chapter 16

Toni Malguzzi reached into an inside pocket of his jacket and withdrew a package of about 8 cm x 10 cm with his fingertips. He placed it on the table and slid it towards me. It was a plastic grip seal bag inside which I could see a plain brown envelope. I left it where it was.

'The envelope is sealed,' said Malguzzi, 'don't open it. Inside the envelope are photographs of the item I'm offering to trade. I've prepared this package very carefully. The plastic outer bag is to ensure my DNA is not on the envelope. When I've left the room I want you to take the envelope out of the bag and throw the bag away.'

He seemed to be going to a lot of trouble. Hopefully it would make my job easier.

'Photographs of Lejon Vandla's holy grail?' I asked.

'Yes,' said Malguzzi.

I shook my head.

There was a question I needed to ask. I wasn't sure what reaction I'd get but I had to take the risk. It was important. Better to ask it sooner rather than later, I thought. Even if the answer I got was a lie I still had to ask.

'Is it real?' I asked.

Malguzzi laughed, 'You're a brave man, Michael. You're asking me, Toni Malguzzi, if I'm dealing in fake goods! I like you, you got balls.'

His response could have been a lot worse. He was a violent man. I could have needed help from the guys by the door.

I wasn't sure the risk had been worth it as he hadn't actually answered the question. I decided not to push it.

'And why not let me have the real thing?' I asked.

'Are you crazy? Do you think I'd let you take the real thing into the first face to face meeting? You'd just leave without it.'

So I couldn't rely on that old "honour amongst thieves" adage then. To be fair I'd always found it overrated.

'One last thing,' I said, 'I understand I'm meeting with Sky tomorrow. Why not Lejon? He's the father, he's the collector, it's his holy grail.'

Toni Malguzzi waved his hand towards the two be-suited guys standing at the door.

'Because these geniuses, or people just like them, got Lejon detained in prison on suspicion. They jumped the gun, Michael, and now they can't let him go. He might flit and they can't get charges to stick without my help. It don't pay to be impetuous, Michael, it just don't pay.'

I saw the awkward position the authorities had managed to get themselves into. No wonder they were willing to support Malguzzi on this crazy quest.

'Anything else?' I asked.

Malguzzi drained the remaining whiskey from his glass.

'Nope. Go do it, Michael,' he said, 'and don't fuck it up.'

I was pleased I hadn't tried to match Toni Malguzzi's drinking because if I had I would have been just about out of it for the rest of the day. Once he'd left Officers Jones and Logan came and joined me. They'd obviously been following proceedings from the surveillance room next door.

'We heard most of it,' said Logan, 'just when he dropped his voice we couldn't really make it out.'

Worth remembering, I thought.

Logan shrugged, 'We don't want to know what's in the envelope, OK,' he said, 'When you find out you just keep it to yourself. What we don't know can't hurt us.'

'All we want,' continued Officer Jones, 'is to get the deal done, the goods transferred and Toni Malguzzi talking to us.'

'If you need anything that helps that happen,' said Logan, 'then you just ask, you understand? We're here to help. In fact we gotta help, you just gotta ask.'

It sounded like a double-act they'd rehearsed. I could almost taste the relief that they'd got over what they had to say without interruption. They were playing by the rules. Keeping themselves clean, making sure that if there were any blame to share around none of it would stick to them.

'Thanks,' I said, 'Anything else?'

'Here are the details of your first meeting with Sky,' said Logan, passing over a single sheet of paper. I had been given the details before leaving London but there was no harm in checking that nothing had changed. I looked at the times and locations. Nothing had changed.

'OK.'

'You will not have a tail when you leave the hotel,' said Officer Jones, although she failed to add that they would be aiming to track my movements through my phone and the tags in my new clothing, 'and we do not want to know the detailed content of your discussions with Sky. We just want to know what we need to know to help you get the deal done as quickly as possible. If necessary we have funds at our disposal to oil the wheels.'

"...funds at our disposal..." that sounded interesting.

'Malguzzi is being held in a safe house,' said Officer Jones, 'if you need to speak to him between meetings you can call, give me your phone.'

She took it, touch-typed a number, saved it to memory as "Jason", and then returned it to me.

'OK?'

'Why that name?' I asked.

'It'll do,' she said. 'reminds me of the story "Jason and the Golden Fleece", my grandpa was always telling me stories, this was one of them, just seemed appropriate.'

'OK,' I said, hoping this quest was a little less eventful than that one.

'So you call, then you get a call back when we've made the connection to Mr Malguzzi.'

'Got it,' I said, they were clearly taking this witness protection thing very seriously.

'We don't want anything to get in the way of a successful outcome,' added Logan, 'we, at this end, already feel pretty nervy about having to rely on somebody from outside to get this done. Please don't increase our anxiety, you know what I mean?'

I could imagine how little they were enjoying having a Brit foisted on them at such a delicate moment. I was fairly sure that some poor police officer had already been sent out to police the polar bears at the far end of Hudson Bay for being too impetuous in bringing Lejon Vandla in on suspicion. To be fair my disappearing act of the day before probably didn't help build their confidence. Ah well, I'd do my best from here on in.

'Just one more thing,' I said, 'don't send me out in wired clothing.'

The look on their faces was priceless. They looked at me, they looked at each other.

'We were going to tell you,' said Logan.

Yea right, I thought.

'It was for your own protection,' said Officer Jones.

It was more likely to get me into deep trouble, I thought.

I gave them a reassuring smile. It's not fun when you've been unexpectedly caught out.

'If Sky is worth her salt at all she'll check to see if I'm wired. It wouldn't be a good way to start building trust if I immediately set off an alarm, she's sure to be suspicious anyway.'

I could see they got my argument. If I could suss it out so easily then a seasoned criminal would have no problem.

'I bought some fresh clothes when I was out yesterday,' I said, 'I'll wear those.'

I nearly said "we bought", now that really would be giving the game away.

'You can track me though my phone,' I said, 'everybody carries a phone so she won't be as suspicious of that.'

'Sorry,' said Officer Jones.

'No need to be,' I said, 'I understand the rules you're working to, I just don't want them to get me killed.'

Chapter 17

I asked to be left alone for lunch and walked down to the Harbourfront to find a cafe and get my mind into gear for the early evening meeting with Sky. I wasn't sure what my starting position was going to be. I'd never met nor communicated with Sky or anybody else from the Vandla side about this deal. I was coming in briefed but cold. Toni Malguzzi, using an assumed virtual identity, had made the contact through the dark web. He'd got the deal to this point, set up the meeting and said that his representative, Michael Stewart, would attend on his behalf and with his full authority. And that was it. Here I was. It was up to me to pick it up from there.

I ran through various scenarios in my mind and eventually decided I was as prepared as I was ever going to be. I had Malguzzi's DNA-free envelope in my pocket. I had the briefings from London. But what did I know about Sky?

I'd seen her photograph and knew she was blonde, tall and slim with olive skin and clear blue eyes. I knew she had been born into the "family business", that she had known it all her life, that her mother was unknown, that she was the only surviving child of Lejon Vandla and as such his natural successor. I knew of her education far away in Vancouver. I knew that instead of handing the reigns over to Sky the family business had been liquidated producing at least one unhappy camper. That was about all I knew, I hoped it was enough.

I still had time on my hands and whilst I'd been in Manchester, UK, Kieran Lansbury had helped me make contact with an art expert who worked at the Art Gallery of Ontario (AGO) here in Toronto. I rang ahead to make sure he had time to see me and then walked up John Street, right on to Queen Street, left on to University Avenue and finally left on to Dundas Street West. It probably wasn't the best route and it was definitely longer than I thought it was going to be but I needed the exercise. The weather was fine though a little brisk so it was quite a pleasant walk.

Founded in 1900, the AGO's collections contain and eclectic mix of almost 95,000 items ranging in time from 100 A.D. right up to the present-day. It is a dynamic institution and engages in all forms of creativity, from music to film, from graphic art to experiential media. The building is on five levels and as well as the exhibitions there are places to eat and an ongoing range of events, workshops, conservation work and research.

The artworks on display include 20th century European works, including Picasso, and a significant collection of Canadian art both by the so-called "Group of Seven" and by emerging indigenous artists.

Overall it is a gallery for the people with all the ostentatious corners knocked off.

On entering the building I headed straight for visitor reception and asked for Dr Peter Meredith-Taylor. The blonde receptionist made a call, asked me to wait and in a few minutes a spritely though rotund middle aged man with greying brown hair, glasses, and a big smile on his face came bounding over to me, his hand outstretched in greeting.

'Nice to meet you in the flesh, Michael,' he said, 'getting to know people over Zoom is vastly overrated I find.'

I heartily agreed, the vagaries of unreliable internet connection, the protocols of who speaks when, the location of the "Mute" button all serve to get in the way of building up proper human to human relationships and understandings. I was pleased to meet him face to face.

'Come up to my office,' he said, 'we can talk there.'

We took the elevator and made small talk. How was my trip over? How was the hotel? Did I like Toronto?... that kind of stuff. I gave the normal polite replies; fine, fine, yes.

His office was on the 4th floor, looking out over the city and back towards the CN Tower. It was probably quite a large office but as it was stacked with papers and books it was hard to see. Thankfully there was still enough vacant space for me to make my way to the seat in front of his desk and I sat there while he went and grabbed us a coffee from a machine down the hall. He brought it back in paper cups that were almost too hot to handle and when I tasted it, it was raw, bitter, and dreadful.

'Thanks,' I said.

'No problem, Michael, no problem at all. I was pleased and surprised to hear from Kieran and it was good to be introduced to you. Now, how exactly can I help?'

He spoke fast and at a volume that was meant to be heard at the back of lecture halls. He took a bottle of what looked like brandy from a desk drawer and poured a sizeable measure into his coffee. That was one way to make it palatable, I thought. He offered the bottle to me.

'Thanks but no thanks,' I said, 'I have an important meeting later and I want to keep a clear head.'

'I completely understand,' said Meredith-Taylor taking the opportunity to put a little more into his own cup.

'What I would like you to help me understand,' I said, 'is the business of art theft, particularly if it is not done "to order" but is done by perpetrators with substantial personal gain in mind.'

This was no surprise to Meredith-Taylor, we'd introduced the subject on our Zoom call. He settled his expansive frame comfortably in the leather confines of his large padded desk chair, took off his glasses and polished the lenses with a monogrammed handkerchief he'd withdrawn from the inner reaches of his jacket. Once satisfied with the arrangement of his attire and the proximity of his brandied coffee, he turned his attention back to me,

'Let me start by telling you why art is important,' he said, 'what music is to the ears then art is to the eyes. As human beings we operate to a rhythm, the rhythm of night and day, light and dark, the rhythm of the seasons. It's built into our psyche, and music is the same, intrinsically part of our being, a basic need. Give us a pen or a pencil and we will soon start tapping it on the nearest hard surface, play us music while we work and we'll be soothed or energised, our bodies will start to naturally respond to the beat. It is the same with art. Show us a picture, flat on a surface and we can immerse ourselves in it, enter the landscape or, if it is abstract, see the colour as meaning, challenging our perceptions, playing with our vision. This is why art is important, it is fundamental, it is intrinsic to the human condition.'

Having stated to a cultural philistine like myself what was blindingly obvious to him he felt able to move on. He was clearly going to make the most of having an attentive audience of one.

'Unfortunately it is an enduring principle of mankind that if something is important then it's worth having and if it's worth having it's worth stealing. The art world is riddled with thefts and the scarcity of a piece or the fame of the artist only stands to enhance its apparent value.'

He paused to take a gulp from his cup, then he reached for the brandy bottle and poured some more in.

'But the art world has its own rules, Michael, and thieves tend to make the same mistake over and over again,' he said, 'they think that by stealing a famous painting they'll make a lot of money. But nothing could be further from the truth. Take the Mona Lisa for example. No one in their right mind would steal that. It is the most recognised painting in the world, painted by Leonardo da Vinci sometime in the first two decades of the 16th century, acquired by the king of France and hung in the Louvre until Napoleon took it to hang on his bedroom wall,' the look of disdain on Meredith-Taylor's face was clear to read, 'and after this unsavoury sojourn returned to the Louvre where it rested happily until the 21st August 1911 when it was stolen.'

He paused and took a gulp of brandy-coffee.

'Pablo Picasso was actually one of the early suspects but in reality it was stolen by a petty criminal who had worked at the Louvre and hid there overnight, taking the Mona Lisa out of its frame and walking out the following morning with it hidden under his smock, a common garment that employees wore at that time. The robbery itself was an audacious success. But who could he sell it to? Who would buy it? Where could he hide it? It remained missing until late 1913 when finally it was offered to an art dealer in Florence for a reward. An arrest and return immediately followed and the Mona Lisa was once again back in the Louvre.'

Another pause, another drink.

'So now, Michael, the Mona Lisa is surrounded by screens, security and 24/7 surveillance. Why? It is a waste of money except that I suppose it stops some lunatic from trying to deface the painting and all that security must be reassuring to the general public.'

He leaned forward, eyes sparkling,

'From my point of view I think what it does is to increase the Mona Lisa's notoriety, it's fame, which in turn gets more people through the gallery's doors, sells more posters, more reproductions, more coffee mugs, more fridge magnets. It's an advertising ploy and… it works.'

He paused to take a breath. He obviously revelled in his subject area and I tried to remain studiously attentive. He smiled.

'No, Michael, what smart thieves steal are works that will not justify a long, protracted, international police hunt. Art works that might hit a headline for a day, maybe two, but in a week the story has disappeared from public view, interest has been lost. Paintings that, when police discuss resource allocation and budget restrictions, when priorities are set, when risk versus reward calculations are made, fall beneath the cut off line. Thefts whose files are closed and moved to some dark, damp basement to gather dust and grow increasingly cold.'

I didn't interrupt I could see he had more to say.

'Savvy collectors, willing to build their collections for their eyes only, or those who wish to have the thrill of secret possession whilst keeping their items locked away in a vault somewhere, even they know this. "Theft to order" is overrated but where it does exist a savvy collector is the one who does not order a piece that will be forever too hot to handle. What would he or she do with it? What is it worth if it can't be sold or shown off? It is worse than worthless. It is a liability, an albatross around the owner's neck. There is the relentless hunt by the authorities, the constant threat of discovery. Who needs that?'

These were all good points but I needed him to come down from the clouds and get more specific.

'Where does the Picasso we discussed fit into all of that?' I asked.

Meredith-Taylor poured more brandy into the now empty paper cup. I had no idea how he had appeared to talk non-stop and yet the brandy laced coffee had still disappeared. I was still nursing my brandy free version.

'Let us look at the real problem,' he said, 'the real problem is not the picture, it is a late work, a minor work drawn in 1971 with pen and brush using black ink, colored pencil and pastel on thick brown woven paper. It has some interesting points yes, it shows that, despite his advanced age of 90, Picasso was still proficient, but so does every Picasso. Perhaps it has a deeper meaning, who knows? Picasso was prolific and produced more than 50,000 pieces of art. This picture can be worth no more than C$1-2 million. Here in this gallery we have Picasso's, better than this one, and more important pieces. The real problem is who would buy it?'

I could have given him one suggestion, I thought.

Chapter 18

'The so-called legitimate art market on the other hand is a fairly modern creation, Michael,' said Meredith-Taylor continuing my education, 'It is a strange beast with its own peculiar rules. I don't think you would like it, it's too full of people seeking to classify the unclassifiable. It seems that it is impossible to appreciate art if we haven't given it a name.'

He shook his head and took a drink.

'What do you mean?' I said.

'"isms",' he said, 'I live in a world full of "isms". I'll give you an example. Impressionism. Now that's quite a useful one referring to the trend, starting at the end of the 19th century, for artists to move away from the then traditional objective depictions and instead focus on their subjective reaction to their subject, freely experimenting with rough brushstrokes and use of colour, allowing some pieces to retain what was seen at the time as an unfinished look. It of course was scandalous, an attack on the accepted norm, the established conventions of art. The pieces were almost too hot to handle in their audacity, the artists were renegades and rebels,' he paused, 'although now, calmed by the passage of time, we see impressionists like Manet, Monet, and Pissarro as traditionalists, their techniques studied, copied and admired. We can now look at a painting and immediately classify it if it is in the Impressionist style.'

'Yes,' I said, 'even I take that for granted. It seems to me it's a useful shorthand in talking about a work of art, puts it in brackets, whilst still allowing it to be unique in itself.'

He ignored me.

'Then there is Cubism, art that portrays a large range of viewpoints within the same image, another example of a useful term but what about Synthetism, Fauvism, Futurism, Rayonism, Vorticism, and my personal favourite, Kitchen Sink Realism, to mention but a few?'

'Are they all real or have you made some of them up?' I asked.

'I'm afraid they are all very much real and not at all amongst the more obscure "isms". Some, of course, are better known than others. Pick one as an example,' he said.

He repeated the list.

'How about Futurism,' I said.

'Ah,' he said, 'an Italian movement from the early 1900's meant to capture and celebrate the dynamism of modern urban life, depicting movement, concentrating on new technologies which then included the motor car.'

'So we would call it Pastism now,' I said smiling.

Meredith-Taylor glared at me.

'Don't joke, this is not a laughing matter, and for god's sake don't invent another "ism"!'

I looked away, suitably chastised.

Meredith-Taylor burst out laughing.

'There you see the absurdity of it all in a nutshell,' he said wiping his eyes, 'we art experts do not just invent new words, we then force our own definitions upon them and shoehorn works of art into them to justify their existence whilst feeling free to disagree amongst ourselves which "ism" most perfectly suits a particular piece of art. I sometimes wish there were no "isms" and that we just looked at the art, closely, intuitively and allowed ourselves to have our own unique reaction to it untainted by the judgement of others.'

He took another drink.

'But then again, Michael, where would people like me be without our "isms"? They are a cloak of authenticity to our expertise. Every profession needs to invent its own language doesn't it?'

I looked at Meredith-Taylor's rosy cheeks. He was right, I couldn't survive for a minute in his world without being exposed as a fraud but he was perfectly at home there. I watched as he finished his brandy. I liked him and hoped he had a strong liver.

'Come, let me show you a small part of our collection so you can see the range and complexity of what museums call art.'

'Such artwork as this Picasso we are discussing is not rare,' said Meredith-Taylor as we descended in the elevator down into the bowels of the AGO on our way to the gallery's vaults, 'every national gallery has loads of the stuff.'

My eyes widened, 'Really? I thought value meant rarity.'

We emerged directly into a reception area where Meredith-Taylor showed his security pass and signed us in. We then walked on to a second security checkpoint and Meredith-Taylor signed us through again. By the time we'd got past the third security checkpoint, which was a keypad password and security card recognition, I'd got the distinct impression that whatever was down here needed to be well protected.

After all this ceremony Meredith-Taylor pushed open a pair of plain steel doors and I followed him through and into a grey concrete corridor lit by industrial strip lighting activated by motion-sensors. On both sides of the corridor were more metal doors, spaced approximately 15m apart.

'Pick a door, Michael,' said Meredith-Taylor waving his arm in the manner of a conjurer warming up his audience for an astonishing trick.

'I'll take the third one on the right,' I said.

We walked past large diameter aluminium ducts of what appeared to be the innards of a huge ventilation system. I asked about them.

'Down here,' he said, 'the climate is carefully controlled to protect the artwork. The temperature is maintained at 19°C and the humidity is also controlled. The lighting is only in operation whilst people are in the area and as you can see everything that arrives or leaves is carefully monitored. Let me show you into the room that you chose.'

He approached the door I had selected and again had to put a code into a keypad in order to gain entry.

As we entered the room the lights flickered on and I saw that there was a wide corridor-type space running down the centre with trackways overhead and row upon row of racks on either side.

'Pick a rack,' said Meredith-Taylor, still in conjurer mode.

'Number seven on the left,' I said, feeling like I'd become embroiled in some strange game of lucky dip.

Meredith-Taylor counted out the rows and pulled on the seventh which slid smoothly out on teflon runners. It made a soft whooshing sound.

Hung on both sides of the exposed rack were paintings of various shapes and sizes. Someone had cleverly arranged them so as to make best use of the available space. The rack was full.

'We have far too much artwork to display,' said Meredith-Taylor, 'every gallery of note in the world has this same problem. Each season committees of trustees and art connoisseurs meet to decide which of the works will be put on public display and which held here in the vaults. I would estimate that not more than 5% of our artwork is on public display at any one time. That is why galleries communicate with one another and regularly swap artwork to build interesting exhibitions and juxtapositions of artists. As you can imagine the packaging and transport of these artworks is subject to much secrecy and security. It's one of the things that makes the job interesting.'

He pointed in a general fashion down the left-hand row of screens, 'All the artworks without exception are carefully catalogued by screen number, barcode, room number, position, artist, title, etcetera, etcetera.'

At the end of the room by the far wall there was a table and past this I could see various pipes, valves and pressure cylinders. Meredith-Taylor followed my gaze.

'More climate control and fire protection,' he said, 'if you look around you will notice multiple alarms, CCTV cameras and the like. It is much easier to steal artworks from public display than it is to steal them from vaults like this.'

I looked around, 'I'm sure it is,' I said, 'I'm sure it is.'

He pointed to the exposed paintings on screen number seven.

'They are arranged on the racks by using an algorithm that manages the jigsaw of art pieces to make best use of the space rather than storing them more logically by genre, artist, or era. This throws up some interesting and serendipitous juxtapositions, look here for example...'

I moved closer to the near side of the screen.

'Here is a Degas and next to it a Hockney. Below them is a 17th century Italian landscape and further along a Warhol.'

He pushed the screen back into place and went to the table to consult a loose-leaf catalogue in a ring-bound folder. After studying it for a moment he moved to the left-hand bank of screens and pulled out screen number nine.

'Here,' he said, 'this is what I was trying to tell you. We have entered at random one of the storage rooms within the vault. I had no influence on the one that you chose and yet here is a Picasso.' He pointed to one of the paintings. 'This is a more important painting than the one that you are concerned with. In terms of value it is worth, in today's market, at least 20 times as much as your picture would fetch. As I mentioned Picasso was a prolific artist and every gallery of note will hold several or maybe tens of examples of his work.'

So the painting that was causing me so much trouble was 'just another Picasso'. It held no special interest other than it had been stolen and either did not or should not exist.

'Thank you,' I said, 'very enlightening. Why do you think Picasso's paintings bring such enormous sums when there are so many to choose from.'

He laughed, 'As well as being a genius, Picasso was a very successful self publicist and so now, of course, every collector worth his or her salt must have a Picasso amongst their collection. It has become a rite of passage.'

Yes, I thought, I think I can see that. There is so much hype around some artists; Picasso, Van Gogh,

Matisse, Renoir… that whenever one of their works comes up for auction it must start the glitterati salivating. The auction must resemble a feeding frenzy in shark infested waters.

'Just one more question,' I said, 'how much is your accumulated collection of artwork worth?'

He sighed, 'Always the dollar, Michael, must it always come down to money?' he shook his head. 'Today everything is predicated on the $ sum. It has gotten so bad that we no longer appreciate art for the art itself, the beauty of the image, the provocation of the colouring. Instead we hunt for the name, seek the provenance and find out the insurance value. It has become a rich person's game, just a game.'

I didn't want to let it go quite that easily, 'But can you give me an idea of worth?' I asked, 'just as an example.'

He grimaced but took the question and looked at the screen in front of him perusing its content from floor-to-ceiling. He then walked around to the other side and did the same thing.

'This screen for example,' he said, coming back to stand in front of me, 'could not be replaced for less than C$50 million a side. And we have many screens in tens of rooms. I'll leave you to do the math, Michael.'

Chapter 19

We returned to his office, resumed our seats and Meredith-Taylor dribbled a little more brandy into his paper cup. I again declined the offer to join him.

'Now where was I?' he said, it was a rhetorical question, 'Oh yes, your painting. The problem is not that it is a Picasso. The problem is that it was on loan from an exclusive family collection when it was stolen. In other words it was the responsibility of the gallery to keep it safe. To lose such a piece in such a shoddy way reflects badly not just on the gallery but also on the whole country. It sends out a message that this country cannot be trusted,' he paused, 'and then of course there are the insurers.'

He was right. From what I'd learned about the robbery it had all seemed too easy. 7 artworks removed in less than three minutes. And if the thieves really were amateurs at this game then that just made it worse.

'The insurers?' I asked.

'Insurers as you must know, Michael, are risk managers. They ask a little to protect a lot. They survive and dare I say thrive because the worst does not generally happen. The ship does not sink, the house does not burn down, the jewels are not stolen. The insured goes along with wasting their money because of the peace of mind it procures. And if the worst does happen then the insurers are the first to want to know how and why before they consider paying out any money. The more public the case the more they want to know what went wrong, the more they want culpability independently investigated and, most importantly following a theft, the more intensive the efforts they want to see have been exerted to retrieve the stolen goods, if necessary co-ordinated across international borders.'

He took a drink. Although his cheeks were starting to get flushed I was impressed at his capacity to consume so much brandy so quickly and still remain lucid.

'They do not want the dogs called off before the fox is hunted to its lair.' he said, 'and when it is run to ground they want the recovered goods returned in a blaze of public and journalistic glory. They want fanfares and cheering. "Look," they want to say, "Look, even when the worst happens you can trust us to get it sorted out." They won't mention that this retrieval has saved them paying out on the policy and they won't mention that they helped fund, behind the scenes, some of the investigation. No, they let the media do their work for them. The gallery and the country can recover their reputation. The world can return to normal and there can be more artwork swapped and loaned along, of course. with the associated need for insurance cover, at ever increasing premiums.'

That's very cynical, I thought.

'So here is the problem the people who stole this

Picasso had. It was too high profile a theft. The dogs were never going to be called off. No one was ever going to buy these pictures at sensible prices, their loss was too widely publicised. They'd made a big mistake stealing them.'

I tried to stop him refilling his cup but failed. I didn't know what else he had planned for the day but even with his capacity I feared for his ability to do it.

'So the only way to retrieve the situation was to return the pictures or...'

He opened his eyes wide, inviting me to continue.

'...or do something that took them permanently off the radar,' I said.

'Bravo, Michael, precisely,' he said, clapping his hands, 'and what could be better than having them destroyed and their destruction validated.'

'Even if they weren't.'

'Exactly.'

'So this picture may be genuine?'

'Who knows,' he said, shrugging his shoulders, 'that's what makes the art world so interesting, the intangibles, the unknowns.'

I didn't really care whether the picture was real or not but for my purposes it was important to believe that it might be. Why waste time trying to procure it if it was certain to be a fake. But if there were doubt then there, in that chance, in that uncertainty, hung the interest for a voracious collector. That was my story. That was what I had to believe as I prepared myself to meet Sky Vandla.

Chapter 20

The meeting with Sky Vandla was to be held in Casa Loma, a gothic revival castle complete with secret passages, towers and tunnels, that is situated within Toronto city and up on a hill 140 metres above sea level. It has great views over the city. One of the 98 rooms had been booked by Sky to accommodate us. It was a private room on the third floor.

I'd left Meredith-Taylor to the remainder of his brandy and taken a taxi from the AGO. I wanted to make sure I didn't get lost.

I arrived in good time and walked the paved way past the fountain and towards what to me looked like a fairytale castle. At the front entrance I turned to take in the view; the CN Tower stood like a pointer in the midst of the distant skyline. It was somehow reassuring.

Once inside I checked in at reception and took the elevator up to the third floor.

The room was elegant but sparsely furnished. Large windows in one wall gave the impression of space even though at this time of day there were enough shadows to require the assistance of the internal electric lighting.

In the centre of the room was a double leaf mahogany table. Around the table were six dining chairs, two on each side and one at either end. I left them as they were.

I had been there for about 10 minutes when the door opened and Sky Vandla entered. With her was a painfully thin man, tall with short cut red hair.

Sky approached me.

'Mr Stewart?'

'Yes,' I said.

'Good to meet you. Before we start my friend Spike here would just like to carry out a few preliminaries.'

Spike smiled, he had perfect white teeth, and took out of his pocket a small electronic handheld device about the size of a mobile phone. He put a finger to a wireless earpiece he had in his left ear and moved around the room waving the device about in his right hand and listening to the electronic buzz. After a few minutes he switched it off and shook his head,

'You can never be too careful,' said Sky, 'I've spent my whole life looking over my shoulder. The hunter and the hunted both need to keep their eyes and ears open, their wits about them at all times, especially when you're not sure which one of them you are. After all, Mr Stewart, there is only a thin line between them, the hunter is the hunted to a higher predator and there are many predators each one wishing to demonstrate their supremacy. And to add to this complexity there is the constant change, nothing ever stands still, there is no such thing as stability. You could be a willing worker one day, an amicable peer the next, a deadly enemy a week after that. It keeps you on your toes, Mr Stewart, but the stress can eventually wear you down eventually, after all we're not robots.'

She'd spoken calmly, slowly, in complete control of herself and of the situation.

Spike approached me and asked me to hand over anything metallic or electronic. I handed over my phone, my pen, and I even took off my Rolex GMT Master II watch covering the scratch on the glass with my thumb as I was sensitive about it.

'Nice watch,' said Spike.

I noted with satisfaction that Sky also followed the same instruction. She also wore a Rolex although hers had a pink dial with a diamond-studded surround. At least we shared the same taste in watch manufacturer.

I was then checked over with Spike's electronic gadget and manually frisked. This was a process that would have immediately caught me out if I had worn the wired clothing I had been supplied by Officers Logan and Jones. I thanked my lucky stars that I'd not fallen at the first fence.

Spike then withdrew to the corner of the room and sat down.

Sky was wearing a black jumpsuit, body hugging but zipped down at the front, the zip pulled far enough to confirm that she was definitely female. The legs of the suit ended above the ankle and on her feet she wore white high heel shoes. Around her neck she wore a silver chain from which hung a blue stone surrounded by what appeared to be diamonds. Although metallic this was obviously something she was not willing to be parted from.

'Would you like to frisk me,' she said, 'it seems only fair.'

I moved towards her. I could feel Spike tense behind me.

'I think I can see what I need to see,' I said, 'can you turn around.'

She obligingly turned through 180 degrees. The jumpsuit was a tight fit, if she was hiding anything in there it would take a braver man than me to find it.

'That's fine,' I said, 'thank you.'

Spike relaxed.

'I don't want this meeting recorded,' said Sky, 'I'm sensitive about that kind of thing.'

'I'm offering you a trade for a stolen Picasso,' I said, 'I definitely have no interest in this meeting being recorded.'

She smiled. The common ground rules had been set and agreed. If either of us failed to comply then whatever fragile trust we could build between us would be broken and the deal would be off.

'There is one question I need to ask up front,' I said.

'Please,' said Sky.

'Why am I not meeting with your father?' I asked, knowing the reason was that he was currently incarcerated, 'I thought he was the collector in the family.'

'He has decided to stand back from the messy business of negotiation,' she said without a flicker, 'but I have his full authority. If you agree anything with me then you will have agreed it with him too,' she paused, 'do you have a problem with that?'

She made it sound like a challenge.

'Not at all,' I said, 'how could I, I'm almost in the same boat, my client wishes to remain anonymous.'

'Ah yes,' said Sky, 'I'm not as comfortable with that. I like to know who I'm dealing with. It's difficult to negotiate with an unknown party.'

I spread my hands.

'I'm sorry,' I said, 'I do understand but I have my instructions.'

'Tell me something about him or her,' she said, 'I need to know more than nothing.'

'I can tell you that my client, the prospective purchaser of your Picasso, is based in Europe, that he is a he and that he makes his money in the same way that I believe your family did in the early years.'

'You have looked into our business?'

This was dangerous ground. How would a European criminal know what had being going on and who was responsible for it in a Canadian city ten to twenty years ago?

'My client is prepared to consider the purchase of a Picasso that is not just stolen goods but reputedly destroyed,' I said, 'You can't blame him for researching into who he's dealing with. He's no fool and he doesn't want to be taken for one.'

I left it there.

The silence hung in the air as she digested what I'd said, thought about it, considering how to respond.

I just let the silence do its work.

'You make it sound borderline too risky,' said Sky, 'why would your client bother?'

Good question. And one that I'd prepared for.

'My client is accumulating funds and simultaneously diversifying his holdings. His second passion, beyond making money, is art. My client, I'm not sure he would like me to say this,' I was turning up the "I'm willing to confide in you" dial, 'has an obsessive streak. His current obsession is art and more specifically the art of Picasso. He is hoovering up Picasso pieces from around the world, making anonymous or facilitated purchases. His aim is to amass a large private and hidden collection. Nothing else matters to him. Offer him a Van Gogh, a Matisse, or a Dali at well below market value and he wouldn't be interested. His obsession has tunnel vision,' I paused to let the personality of my fictitious client sink in, then I continued, 'The Picasso that you have on offer has an additional piquancy, it has an interesting history, it is not supposed to exist and it is a harlequin. My client shares Picasso's interest in the harlequin character with his gaudy chequered costume, his split personality between acrobat, trickster, servant and lover. Under those circumstances how could he do anything other than make you an offer?'

'There has been other interest,' said Sky.

I raised an eyebrow. I didn't know whether this was real or just a standard negotiating ploy.

'The reason we have put you in prime position,' she continued, 'is because we are intrigued by the trade you are offering.'

I noticed her use of "we". I took that to mean Sky and her father, and that this was a good sign.

'My client obtained an item in lieu of payment of an outstanding debt, a large debt. As I said his obsession has a narrow focus. He is no coin collector. He is aware that the trade he is offering is over-generous from his side and believes your father would appreciate the item much more than he does.'

Sky smiled, it lit up her face.

'I think I can understand obsession,' she said.

I had cast the hook. I could feel a pull on the line.

'I don't have the item with me,' I said, taking the envelope from my inside pocket, making sure I did it slowly and carefully as I was conscious of Spike sitting behind me, 'but I do have this.'

The envelope was still sealed and I hoped to god that Toni Malguzzi wasn't about to make a giant fool out of me.

Sky took it and carefully tore it open. She removed a series of photographs, laid them out side by side on the table in front of her. I saw them for the first time at the same time that she did. The photographs were high resolution images of a single coin taken from multiple angles, a combination of close detail and full face.

'Thank you,' said Sky, 'I'll take these away and if we're interested in proceeding we'll be in touch. Do you need anything more from me at this point?'

'My client has already seen images of the picture,' I said, 'but if we do proceed we will need to carry out detailed authentication although I'm happy to leave that for future discussion, so no, I need nothing more from you at this time.'

Our meeting was over. I retrieved my belongings from Spike and left the building.

It hadn't been a disaster.

Now I just had to wait.

Chapter 21

I walked down into the subterranean meanderings of the PATH. I took my time to ensure I wasn't being tailed. When I was satisfied I resurfaced, found a coffee shop, a dark corner and made a call to Samantha,

'Hello,' she said, 'it's after midnight. Again.'

I couldn't help that, I thought, she wanted immediate feedback didn't she? I couldn't stop the world revolving with the speed and direction it did could I.

I gave her a summary of my meeting with Sky, missing out a description of the item Malguzzi had put up for trade.

'I don't need the details of Toni Malguzzi's offer,' she said.

That's why I didn't tell you, I thought.

'OK, I'll keep AB up to speed. So now we just wait?'

'We just wait,' I said.

She yawned.

'Good night,' she said.

Click.

As I finished the call I was aware of a new presence in the coffee shop, it wore a dark hoodie and he or she was doing everything possible to avoid looking in my direction. It was disconcerting.

When I left the coffee shop the hoodie followed. It was dark now and I started to walk back to the hotel. As I passed the dark mouth of an alleyway the hoodie called to me.

'Excuse me.'

I stopped and turned and as I did an arm reached out from the blackness of the alley, grabbed me around the neck and pulled me backwards. It was a well executed manoeuvre and it took me by surprise.

Before I could react I felt a jab in my arm and as I began to lose consciousness a voice whispered in my ear,

'This is just a friendly warning, Mr Stewart, the Vandlas are history. There are new kids on the block now. Don't do anything to try and change that.'

The only other thing I remember is the smell of peppermint before blackness overcame me.

I came round sometime later, curled up in the foetal position, my head resting in my own vomit. It wasn't attractive. My head pounded like I'd gone twelve rounds in the ring and lost. I struggled to my feet and braced myself against the wall for support. I concentrated on controlling by breathing as I slowly regained my senses; in, out, in, out aware that the effects of delayed shock following an attack like this could be as devastating as the attack itself.

I gave myself time. I checked myself over. I seemed to be intact and as I searched unsteadily through my pockets nothing seemed to have been stolen except...

I felt the lightness on my wrist before I registered the loss. I pulled my shirt sleeve up to confirm my suspicion. The only thing that had been taken was my watch!

I gritted my teeth. That wasn't funny.

As soon as I felt able I straightened up and stood, shakily at first, without the support of the wall. My head pounded but not so loud as to stop me beginning to think, to hear my own thoughts. I whispered them aloud to myself to make sure they were real,

'Who the hell and why?'

In my muddled state I got nowhere with either of those questions. I knew I'd somehow been located and followed.

'How?'

This seemed an easier question. Either they miraculously saw my face in the shadows of one of a thousand different coffee bars and hit lucky or they traced me... and there was only one way they could have done that.

I took out my phone and gazed at it.

Assuming Logan or Officer Jones or one of the other police officers had not fallen out with me there was only one other person who had had my phone in their possession.

Spike.

I staggered out of the alley. My attackers had not taken anything from me except my watch so I got a taxi to the harbour front, found a bar and used their washroom facilities to smarten myself up.

The pain in my head had now subsided to a dull ache. Comparatively I was feeling better. I washed away any remaining traces of vomit as best I could and wetted my auburn hair, the cold water bringing further relief. I then returned to the bar and ordered a pot of tea, avoiding the disapproving looks of the mainly beer-drinking clientele. I drank it hot and sweet while I concentrated on what to do next.

My phone needed to be destroyed and disposed of and I needed to get back to the hotel with some kind of explanation for Logan and Jones.

I needed to think what to do about Spike.

I don't like bullies and I'd just been bullied by proxy. I needed to think why and what, if anything, I was going to do about it. I would like to get my watch back.

First things first. I saw a bunch of papers behind the bar and asked for the loan of the paperclip. A C$20 tip overcame the surprise and I straightened the metal and used it to prize the SIM card out of my phone and then curled the paperclip back into shape and returned it to the incredulous bartender.

After that I left the bar and walked down to the nearest water's edge. There I hunted for and found a large stone that I used as a hammer to smash the phone. Such an act was probably ineffective but it made me feel better. I then collected up the pieces and threw them as far out into the waters of Lake

Ontario as my aching bones could manage, which wasn't very far.

The night air had turned brisker and a light breeze had stirred. As I walked back to the hotel I appreciated the feel of the cold air as it brushed against my skin.

'Where the fuck have you been?' It was Logan at his most direct.

'Do you know your fucking phone went dead about 20 minutes ago!'

Officer Jones sat alongside him with her mouth clamped in a tight line. I felt her silent rebuke more deeply than his voluble one.

'I'll be needing a new phone,' I said, 'I was mugged in this great city of yours.'

'Fucking mugged! And you wanted to go out without backup. You could have fucked up this entire operation,' said Logan.

I should have warmed to the fact that he cared about my welfare so much, but I didn't.

'I didn't ask to be mugged,' I said, 'I must just be unlucky.'

Yea, I thought, and this is the second time I've been attacked. I was starting to feel unpopular. My head was clearing but I still felt unwell. I wasn't in the mood for this kind of friendly banter.

'The phone is disabled,' I said, 'and I've lost my watch.'

I uncovered my wrist and held it out as evidence.

'Hard fucking cheese,' said Logan, obviously lacking empathy.

Officer Jones reached across and squeezed his arm. Getting the message he breathed in deeply and battled to regain his composure.

'Would you like me to tell you how my meeting with Sky Vandla went?' I asked.

'Go ahead,' said Logan.

I summarised the meeting as best I could.

After I'd finished Officer Jones said, 'So now we wait.'

'That's right,' I said.

Logan sighed deeply.

'So now we wait,' he said.

I felt like I was hearing an echo.

'Yes,' I said, 'now we just wait.'

'We've replaced your wardrobe by the way,' said Logan, 'there's been a change in the weather, we didn't think the first set of clothing we got for you was still appropriate.'

You almost sent me into the lioness' den smelling of raw meat, I thought, remembering the electronic frisking that would have instantly caught me out.

'Thanks,' I said, 'very considerate of you.'

'That's OK,' he said.

As she was leaving Officer Jones turned and said, 'I'll get you another phone.'

'Thanks,' I said.

After they'd gone I went into the bathroom, filled the basin full of cold water and stuck my head into it. After that I took a long shower and changed my clothes.

By the time I came out of the bathroom a new phone was lying waiting for me on the bedside table.

I took it, activated it, but did not synch to the Cloud.

I sat on the edge of the bed feeling much better and used the hotel phone to order a room service dinner and a couple of beers. I then used my pay-as-you-go phone to call Teresa.

There was no answer.

It was just as well because I hadn't worked out what I was going to say to her.

Chapter 22

Waiting is a pain in the ass. And I'm no good at it.

After as leisurely a breakfast as possible I decided to at least start planning ahead on the basis of success. As Logan and Officer Jones did not seem to be around I decided to try contacting Toni Malguzzi via the safe house. I had something I needed to ask him.

So I put in a call to "Jason".

'I need to talk to Toni,' I said, when somebody had answered and the trick questions providing proof of identity were over, 'I assume someone will be listening in.'

'Someone is always listening in,' said the voice, 'we'll call you back.'

The call came 5 minutes later.

'How'd it go?' asked Toni Malguzzi without preamble.

'They're suspicious but interested,' I said.

'Tell me how it went,' he said.

I gave him a rundown of the meeting. He'd probably already got this via Logan or Officer Jones but a little repetition wouldn't hurt, besides it would allow him to compare the stories and hopefully confirm we were all on the same page.

'So we wait,' he said when I'd finished.

There you go, I thought, see, we're all on the same page.

'I hope we don't have to wait long,' I said.

Malguzzi laughed. 'You forget, Michael, I know these people, like I know my own family I know these people.'

As far as I knew Toni Malguzzi didn't have any family, but I let it pass.

'They will not take long,' he said, paused, and then added, 'or if they do or if they say no then you have made a mistake. A big mistake. If I don't get this deal then I clam up, I clam up good, comprendi?'

I comprendi'd alright, just like Logan and Jones he'd found a fall guy – and that was me.

'What I wanted to ask you,' I said, trying to ignore the not so veiled threat, 'was how do I get hold of the coin? After all the logical next step, if there is a next step, is that they will want to physically see the coin.' I felt like adding 'comprendi?' but I didn't.

Malguzzi laughed again. It was getting to be an annoying habit.

'Of course they will,' he said.

'Have you got it?' I asked.

'Hey, let me just check my pockets,' he answered sarcastically, 'you think I just carry it around, take it out every night, sleep with it under my pillow?'

My question may have sounded naive but wasn't sure that I deserved this kind of put down.

'Well can you get it?'

'What do you think.'

'I think that unless this is your idea of a big joke then you can get hold of it and now's the time,' I said.

'Not so stupid then, are you,' I guessed I was supposed to feel pleased to have gone up so far in his estimation but I wasn't, 'as a matter of fact you'll have to go and collect it. I don't want to risk being seen in the wrong places for a while, capeesh?'

'OK, I understand, so where is it?'

He laughed again. I was getting to really dislike his sense of humour.

'There's people listening,' he said, 'you think I just blurt it out? No, we do this face to face, you and me, mano a mano.'

'Tonight?'

'Whenever you like, my calendar seems to be open,' he said.

I said I'd talk to Logan or Officer Jones to see what they could fix and the call ended.

Two minutes later Officer Jones called.

'8 pm,' she said, in proof that our conversation had been overheard. She made it sound like a date but it definitely wasn't that, he wasn't my type.

'I need Toni Malguzzi to help me out here,' I said, 'or else this deal will be dead in the water no matter whether we hear back from Sky or not.'

Officer Jones picked up on the worry in my voice.

'OK, Mr Stewart, just you stay cool, we'll help you all we can.'

"Stay cool"! "We'll help you all we can"! I was the fall guy here stuck between the devil, the devil and the devil. I just wished there was a deep blue sea somewhere that I could go and jump into.

Chapter 23

From the first time I'd introduced Teresa to my daughter in Honolulu I had suspected that they had stayed in contact, that somehow they'd managed to exchange numbers when I wasn't looking. Not that I thought they were in regular contact but that, when needed, they had and would contact each other without my knowledge, knowing that the other would always be there and willing to talk. So it wasn't that much of a surprise when I received a call later that morning from my daughter that started with,

'Dad, what's going on?'

'What do you mean?'

'Teresa was in tears.'

'Oh.'

'It was very clear that you've hurt her.'

I sighed.

'Yes,' I said, 'I told you what happened and since then she hasn't answered any of my calls. It was a friendship bracelet, I thought she'd like it,' I said.

'Oh dad, really...'

There was an awkward silence.

'I have been trying to call her I really have,' I said lamely.

'Oh yes?'

'Yes, honestly, but I don't think she wants to talk to me.'

'Then keep calling until she does.'

'Hmm.'

'Dad, you can't leave it like it is.'

Couldn't I, wouldn't it be best to just let things slide, to move on and try not to regret?

'Dad.'

I hesitated.

'I suppose you're right,' I said, 'but I don't think it will end well.'

'Promise you'll keep trying.'

I kept quiet.

'Promise?'

If Teresa was going to vent her spleen at me again, if it would make her feel any better then maybe…

'OK,' I said.

'OK what?'

My daughter had turned into my mother.

'OK, I promise.'

'I've already told her that you're an idiot, that it was a mistake, that I think you care about her but that you're not that good at showing it.'

Thanks, I thought, it was like receiving a school report somewhere short of "Satisfactory".

'What was her reaction?' I said.

'She stopped crying... eventually.'

Teresa was a woman with a strong will. I knew she wouldn't cry easily and definitely not in front of somebody else. She must have called my daughter in despair and got carried away.

'Good luck, dad.'

I knew I needed to get my act together. Hearing

how upset Teresa had been by my thoughtless act, even though from my side it was well-meant, made it even more important that I made some kind of decision about where I wanted this relationship to go. Teresa had always set the pace and now I needed to catch up. It wasn't easy. I needed more time.

But at the same time I still had a job to do, a job that was currently on a knife-edge. I needed to make progress, I needed a distraction from going around in circles thinking about Teresa.

I called Meredith-Taylor and he gave me a name to go visit.

Before I followed up on the intro I decided the best way to clear my head was to write down what I thought about Teresa. I picked up a pen, took a piece of virgin white paper and started to write,

Teresa and I come from completely different places and cultures.

She was brought up in a warm climate. I wasn't.

We've lived completely separate and different lives thus far.

Our life experiences and the scars we carry are very different.

We currently live about a quarter of the world apart, I mean, how is that going to work?

Putting our past relationship track record to one side (although in my case I acknowledge that this is an almost impossible thing to do as I will always miss and love my wife) Teresa and I still don't seem to have much going for us.

I mean what did we have in common?

Teresa has a latin temperament, although that's one of the things I like most about her, she is passionate, enthusiastic, energetic. She is all the things I would like to be if it were not for my inbred Scottish dourness, the inherent belief that however bad things are today they can always be worse tomorrow.

I paused for a moment or two and stared at the almost unintelligible scribble. Was this writing your thoughts down really such a good idea?

I soldiered on,

Teresa is intelligent both logically (sometimes) and emotionally (always), has naturally bronzed skin, long brown hair and the most adorable brown eyes, her figure is curvaceous in all the right places (and I mean all!) and her demeanour is both determined and endearing, but most of all she is kind of spirit, and a loyal friend…

I put down the pen. I was on the verge of making her sound more like a devoted pet than a woman with a mind of her own. I battled on,

She is obstinate, stubborn, strong-minded and pushy…

Whoops, I was now in danger of pushing the pendulum too far the other way. I had to remind myself that I liked obstinate, stubborn, strong-minded and pushy women, that they're the best sort and more fun.

Now I was putting her in a category! She was an

individual for god's sake. Get a grip! I read back what I'd written. I wasn't sure this was helping. I sat gazing out of the window. Life was out there rushing about in all directions, falling down, getting up, carrying on. I picked up the pen again.

...and she seems to care about me, I don't know why but she does, and I care about her, I don't know why but I do.

I put the pen down. That was it then. Decision made.

Chapter 24

I was feeling naked without a watch on my wrist so on the way to meet Meredith-Taylor's colleague I stopped off and bought a new one, a Citizen eco drive. It was elegant in its simplicity with a deep blue dial and matching bezel, a date window and a stainless steel case and bracelet. I didn't need to worry about keeping it wound up as the eco-drive technology would generate enough energy to drive the watch by harnessing both natural and artificial light. It was a nice watch, very different from my Rolex. It was a temporary fix. I wanted my Rolex back.

Arriving at the designated apartment block I pressed the buzzer for Apartment 12B and was invited in.

I could see immediately on entering that Professor Amanda Harker's apartment was super-neat, everything seemed to have a place and be in it, quite a contrast to Meredith-Taylor's office at the AGO. Another big difference was that Professor Harker drank tea with nothing added except milk. We settled ourselves in comfortable lounge seats.

'Now, Mr Stewart, how can I help you?' she asked.

'I know nothing about coin collecting and more particularly about coin collectors but I need to be able to talk to one without making a fool out of myself,' I said, and then I told her what I thought I knew about Lejon Vandla's interest in North American coinage.

'I see,' she said, 'or at least I think I do. Coin collecting is a vast subject, you know, although to some it may seem like a boring and pointless hobby.'

She looked across at me. It seemed to be a test. I tried to look interested. Satisfied she continued,

'Some people collect coins because of a desire to own small pieces of history. If you hold a 1794 United States Large Cent for example you are looking at a true piece of history, one that President George Washington would have admired, a coin that was newly minted by the two-year-old United States Mint in Philadelphia.'

I sat and listened.

'Coins are also miniature works of art that exhibit a style and beauty all of their own and then there is the rarity, the challenge of competing to find and to own the rarest coins, a worthwhile investment whose value will only increase over time,' she paused, took a sip of tea, 'coins date all the way back to the 6th or 5th century BC, Mr Stewart, and as their accepted usage grew they were increasingly used to communicate not just their individual worth but slogans, propaganda, images of emperors, gods or heroes of the state that produced them. Some scholars say that Emperor Augustus Caesar collected coins, you know, although coin collecting only really gained wide popularity in the 1800s when middle-class individuals had the means, the time and the interest to collect them.'

I nodded.

'A good recent example is the "50 State Quarters Program" launched in1999 in the US. This program recognised each state by issuing a separate coin and each quarter was only produced for ten weeks. Lots of people got so engaged in the idea of collecting the whole set that it became quite a fad. So you see, Mr Stewart, the area of coin collecting is very far ranging and quite complex.'

For a novice like me I wasn't sure this was helping.

'So what would your advice be to someone like me, in my predicament?' I asked.

She thought for a moment.

'I think one of the most important things is not to pretend to know more than you actually do,' she said, 'if he's a serious collector he'll be able to see through you pretty quickly. On the other hand, as you know his area of interest is North American coinage you could gen up on these types of coins, their denominations, the presidents, the rarer years, then at least if he asks you a question you have the chance of giving an intelligent answer.'

That seemed good enough for me. I said so.

'Wait a minute,' she said, 'I might have something to help you.'

She got up and walked across to one of her bookshelves letting her eyes run across the titles on the spines, 'now let me see,' she said to herself, 'ah yes, here it is.'

She reached out a moderately thick volume and brought it across to me.

'Here,' she said, 'you can take this, I can easily replace it.'

'Thanks,' I said, 'that's very kind.'

'There is another strategy of course,' she said, 'you could always deflect any questions into areas he probably knows little about but that you could do some cramming on, ancient Roman or Greek coinage for example. Do you want me to find you some books?'

I raised my hand.

'Too risky,' I said, 'I don't know what he's not interested in and if I get it wrong by trying to pass off a thin veneer of information as deep knowledge I could look a real idiot. I'll stick with plan A.'

'Yes, I see what you mean, that's probably a wise choice in the circumstances.'

I was just leaving Amanda Harker's apartment block when I got a call. When I looked at the screen I couldn't believe who it was. I found a convenient spot to stand and answered,

'Sir?'

He must have picked up the surprise in my voice.

'I have a few moments between meetings,' said AB, 'and I wanted to hear how things stood, from the horse's mouth as it were.'

I started to tell him...

'I know, I know,' he said impatiently, 'what I really want to know is how long do you intend to wait before you start chasing?'

This took me off balance. AB knew better than most that at this stage of a negotiation patience was the thing. We had actually made good progress so far. Whatever Toni Malguzzi and others had done to set up the deal before I got involved had obviously whetted the appetite of Lejon Vandla and his daughter, Sky. The first meeting had gone okay as far as I could tell and now we were at the critical moment of decision. Would both parties want to proceed to close the deal or not? For either side to show over enthusiasm at this point would immediately raise the suspicions of the other. Sky had told me to wait and that's what I was doing.

AB was showing an unhealthy level of interest in this assignment, it could not possibly be the most important thing he was dealing with. I just couldn't understand why I was getting this level of attention.

'I think we should wait awhile yet, sir,' I said, 'after all we're in no giant rush.'

There was an uncomfortable silence.

'It is your call,' he said, 'keep me up to speed.'

Click.

I think what he meant was; don't dawdle, don't cock it up, and if anything does go wrong it'll be your fault.

Some calls are motivational. This one wasn't.

Teresa, my daughter, AB, Logan, Officer Jones, Toni Malguzzi... bloody hell, have you ever just wanted everybody to leave you alone?

Chapter 25

I lost my wife to cancer. No one meant it to happen it just did.

You can't replace a loss, you can't get over grief. All that happens over time is that you cope, you learn how not to show your grief, how to have a parallel life free of enough grief for enough of the time to keep you sane. It just isn't possible to grieve at the same intensity all of the time, it has to ebb and flow. Trivial things that you've encountered many times can suddenly, for no good reason, strike a chord and dredge buried feelings back, still raw, to the surface. The recurrent, insoluble emotions of guilt, sadness and loneliness form a hole, a hole in your being that can't be re-filled.

Although some days are better than others.

She'd taken a lot on when she'd married me. I'd been in the armed services too long.

It's not difficult being in the armed services, what's difficult is when you come out.

In the armed services you know your job, you have some appreciation of the risks, you think you're doing something worthwhile, you support your mates, your mates support you. Whatever situation you're in you've been trained to deal with. No matter how precarious, you're in your chosen element.

When I left I didn't know what to do. I'd jumped from a life of comparative clarity, order, discipline and teamwork, into a world that didn't seem to want me.

The shock of being back on civvy street can throw you off. The simplest tasks; shopping, socialising, become impossible to manoeuvre. You start to flounder, way out of your comfort zone, while the people all around you are in theirs and unable to comprehend why someone who has coped with what you have coped with cannot cope with what they take for granted as mundane and every-day.

You crave and avoid in equal measure the company of other military personnel. You don't want them to see you when you're feeling out of control. You don't want to expose your weaknesses to those who relied on your strengths.

Finally I was rescued by joining "The Store". There are worse outcomes, worse obsessions, and worse jobs. I was one of the lucky ones.

You can look a lot more dispassionately at other people's problems than you can look at your own. Other people's problems can provide an interesting intellectual exercise, a diversion, an opportunity to share the wisdom you've acquired from your life experience. Your own problems are an entirely different matter, they're personal, they're problems whose depth and width other people could not possibly understand and, in the main, their advice is unwelcome.

If I'd have wanted any advice I'd have asked for it.

I sometimes wonder whether this is more of a

man's perspective. Women seem to me to be much more open about themselves and their issues, to discussing and sharing them, which is probably, in itself, therapeutic. Women seem more sensible. For as long as I can remember I have always believed that women are superior to men in lots of ways with emotional intelligence being top of the list.

Everyone has regrets but you can't live your regrets, it would squeeze the life out of you.

I do my work out of the limelight. The more successful I am the more invisible is my handiwork to all but a select few. Let others be heroes. I'm content with the way things are … or I thought I was.

To productively use up more waiting time I'd made another appointment to see Meredith-Taylor. On my way to the AGO I took the offending friendship bracelet into a jeweller's that I had found on the internet and talked to over the phone, discussing alternatives. I also popped into a liquor store that sold an acceptable range of Scottish whiskies.

Meredith-Taylor sat behind his desk and leaned back in his leather chair a familiar paper cup within easy reach. I almost lost sight of him behind the piles of papers and books that were scattered and piled all around us.

'You ask me about art forgery,' he said, 'it's a touchy subject in the art world.'

'I'd just like your opinion,' I said.

'What is a fake and what is an original?' he said, 'let's say a fake is something that is not what it purports to be. If it declared itself as a fake then it would, in fact, be an original,' he took a swig from his paper cup, 'if you see what I mean?'

'I think so,' I said, not really sure whether I did or not.

It was a welcome relief to pass some time with Meredith-Taylor. He was one of the few people I'd met who didn't seem to want anything from me or hold me solely responsible for something significant.

I settled back to listen to him with coffee in my cup, not brandy.

'If somebody sat in front of, say, the Mona Lisa,' he said, 'and painted a copy of it then that wouldn't be a fake would it. No, that would be a copy and more than that it would be an interpretation of the Mona Lisa and as such an original work by the artist, with his or her own brushstrokes, his or her unique touch. It may be a work of value in its own right, but no one would ever confuse it with Leonardo Da Vinci's painting.'

'Again, if the artist were to claim that their painting was, in fact, the original they would be laughed out of court because the original is there, hanging on the wall in the Louvre, for everyone to see. So here are the lessons for a faker, Michael; a faker must choose a lesser known work to fake or, even better, they should fake a work that has never existed.'

'Once a clever faker has done his research, chosen his quarry, then they must deliver it convincingly on a technical level by carefully following the style of the chosen artist, choosing a theme or a subject that their artist is known for, matching the colours, the pigments and the substrate surface; canvas, or card, or wood or paper, and then, when it's finished, they have to find a way to slip it surreptitiously into the art world somewhere, at an exhibition, or at an auction, or by passing it through the hands of an art dealer, always accompanying it with a believable, but fictitious, provenance. And then they have to wait, the stone has been thrown into the pond, the ripples will surely follow. Don't push it, that's the important thing, let the cognoscenti discover the painting, absorb it, take it in, take credit for its discovery.'

Meredith-Taylor paused and smiled.

'There is a famous case of a known faker who stepped forward to own up to his fakes which by that time were hanging proudly on gallery walls, accepted as the real thing, only to find that his claims to fakery were rejected! The paintings were defended as genuine by the so-called experts, the current owners, and the auction houses that had handled them and achieved high prices.'

'But they were fakes?' I asked.

'Almost certainly,' said Meredith-Taylor, 'but nobody likes to be made a fool of, particularly when your livelihood is solely predicated on your reputation as an expert. Or then again as an owner you don't want your taste to be brought into question, you could become a laughing stock and what's more the value of your hitherto worthwhile investments may fall through the floor.'

I reached down and handed him my earlier purchase.

'What's this?' he said.

'I noticed that you quite like a drink,' I said, 'so I've brought you and example of the real aqua vitae, the waters of life, transported all the way from my own native land to the streets of Toronto.'

He opened the bag, took out the bottle and held it up so that the daylight played through its amber contents, making it sparkle.

'Edradour, a Scottish single malt whisky' I said, 'Gaelic for "between two rivers" probably the smallest distillery in Scotland. Every bottle has that personal touch and is not sullied into sameness by the routines of mass production.'

'That's very generous,' he said, 'although brandy is my drink of choice...'

I'd noticed.

'...but it would be churlish of me not to try this.'

He got up and retrieved two new paper cups, opened the bottle and poured a generous portion into each. He handed one to me.

'You must join me, Michael,' he said.

Single malt out of a paper cup, I thought, what is the world coming to.

'Thanks,' I said.

I lifted the cup to my mouth and took a sip, the taste was full and rich on the tongue, a hint of honey and buttered toast, the finish was spicy, warming and carried a dry edge.

Meredith-Taylor smacked his lips, 'I must say,' he said, 'it's very warming.'

If that was the best he could come up with then I was never going to convert him to a whisky drinker, I thought.

He paused, moved the paper cup with the whisky in it to one side and went back to his brandy.

'Do you think,' he said, getting back to our task in hand, 'that we will get the chance to examine this painting of yours? We have a very sophisticated conservation and research laboratory here and we could definitely put it under scientific scrutiny.'

'I don't know,' I said, 'right now I'd put the chances at about 50/50.'

'It would be such a shame, after you coming all this way, if we didn't get to see it after all.'

"Shame" was an understatement, I thought, it would be a disaster.

'Yes,' I said, 'these tests, how certain do you think you'll be by the end of them whether the picture is genuine or not?'

He thought for a moment, sipped his brandy, pulled a face,

'As we've discussed,' he said, 'the question is not whether it is a fake or not but rather what it is. Was it dashed off by the hand of Picasso himself? Is it a good copy by a talented hand? Or is it an amateurish affront to the experienced eye?'

I waited.

'If it is the last of these three then we will be able to tell you very quickly,' he said, 'but I would be disappointed if it were.'

And I, I thought, I wouldn't know what the hell to do next.

'If it is either of the first two then we should be able to give a balanced view, a probability one way or the other. After all, Michael, we have no other picture claiming to be the original that we could use for comparison.'

He smiled.

That was true. If the original picture by Picasso had indeed been burned then its ashes were unlikely to re-congeal in an effort to discredit this one. And if it were a good fake, or should I say a talented interpretation by an experienced hand, and give inconclusive scientific results, then it would still stand as unique. Whether disputed or not it would leave us, or rather it would leave Toni Malguzzi, with a choice.

Meredith-Taylor looked at the remaining brandy in his paper cup and then with resolve went back to the one holding the residual whisky and downed the contents in one. He gasped as the liquid took his breath away for a moment and then regained his composure, his eyes watering.

'Let me take you for a bite to eat,' he said, 'in return for your present.'

Why not, I thought, I was feeling a bit peckish.

'Great,' I said.

Meredith-Taylor picked up the phone and got through to the Bistro. After a short conversation he smiled and put the phone down, took out a handkerchief, took his glasses from his nose and polished the lenses,

'It's always a good idea to let them know I'm coming,' he said, 'that way we're sure of a good table. It gets very busy with tourists this time of year, you know.'

Chapter 26

We decamped to the Espresso Bar in the Galleria Italia. The Galleria Italia is a 200 metres long projecting canopy viewing hall within the body of the AGO. Made of glass, steel, and wood its large arcing windows front onto Dundas Street. The galleria was named in recognition of multi-million dollar contributions made by several Italian-Canadian families, none of whom were named Malguzzi.

Meredith-Taylor had managed to secure us a table by the window.

'Please sit down, Michael,' he said raising his hand and summoning a student-aged waiter who wandered slowly over.

'Yes?'

'Donald, this is Mr Stewart, he's a guest of mine.'

Donald nodded at me, 'Hi.'

'So,' said Meredith-Taylor, 'Donald, I would like you to do me a huge favour and pop down to the Bistro for me and get us a couple of their magnificent BLT's, no french fries just salad.'

He looked across at me.

'That works for me,' I said.

'And then get me a latte if you would, and for you, Michael?'

'Just a mineral water with a slice of lemon,' I said.

Donald nodded and left.

I was aware that I was drinking too much caffeine. I could hear Officer Jones' voice in my ear telling me I'd made a wise choice.

'He's a good boy really,' said Meredith-Taylor waving his hand in the general direction of the waiter's retreating back, 'he's working his way through college. We have a lot of students working here on and off although he's not one of the more effusive.'

I'd noticed. We chatted while waiting for the BLT's and I asked,

'The subjective evaluation of a painting, tell me more about how you would go about it?'

'Ah, yes, our little project,' he rubbed his hands, 'I'm quite looking forward to it.'

I wasn't so sure I was.

'Well,' he said, 'it's all about how you look at a painting. Many people just rush past them, they glance at a Degas, they glimpse a Matisse, they... well you get the idea. But what you need to do is to pause, take your time, look...'

Donald politely interrupted his flow to lay the BLT's and the drinks in front of us.

'Thanks, Donald,' said Meredith-Taylor, 'and please make sure it's charged to my entertaining account.'

Donald nodded and sidled away.

'One of the benefits of working for an institution,' said Meredith-Taylor, 'is an entertainment allowance. It's not very lavish but it's useful on this kind of occasion.'

I didn't mind being his excuse for a free meal, it might not be very lavish but it was a lot better than nothing.

'I have told you how important I think art is,' said Meredith-Taylor, 'how it is fundamental, intrinsic to the human condition, and it is because of its importance that I baulk at people who try to tamper with it, people who try to make things out to be what they are not. It is for this reason that I was happy to offer my assistance to you in your venture. I can leave to one side the matter of legality but I cannot overlook the moral depravity of fakery.'

Meredith-Taylor took a bite of his BLT. Chewed. Swallowed. He took this seriously alright. I hoped that come the moment he might also show a little pragmatism. Time would tell.

'The archetypal introverted artist of the 19th and early 20th centuries,' he continued, 'poured their soul onto the canvas, each brushstroke important, never satisfied, no piece ever "finished". So their efforts deserve to be looked at, contemplated over.'

He paused and gazed into space, as if contemplating an invisible painting. His BLT ignored for a moment.

'You know, Michael, I love my job,' he said, 'there are so many interesting things about art. Did you know, for example, that Van Gogh tried to capture sound, movement and mood in his paintings by using colour, different length brushstrokes, more or less vigorously applied paint. But what was he really capturing? Was it the mood of the external environment at the moment of his painting or was it his own internal mood? Did he transpose those moments of inner contentment, however fleeting, onto the scene before him or on other occasions did he use his inner torment, his feelings of anxiety to transpose dynamism and turmoil into a landscape?'

He paused briefly so I had time to grasp the point.

'We view his paintings today detached from his motives. The best we can do is to try to understand Van Gogh's psyche across a vast chasm of time, to try and put ourselves in his position. It's impossible really, we have no chance of accuracy, although so-called experts believe that they can, and if a gaggle of experts agree then they will seek to turn their interpretations into acknowledged fact,' he paused, aware that he was letting his prejudices show, 'and as neither of the Van Gogh brothers, Vincent or Theo, are here to contradict them then they might get away with it if they are loudly convincing enough for long enough.'

He took another bite. I was halfway through my BLT. It was delicious.

'And you know that Van Gogh hardly sold anything whilst he was alive, although he took solace in the thought that he "painted for posterity". In other words he believed that his work was worthy. Now it is worth millions but is it looked at? I mean really looked at. Or is it automatically a masterpiece because it's signed "Vincent". Not all of an artist's output is of equal quality, Michael, that would be impossible.'

His BLT took another hammering. He'd almost finished it.

'That's the important thing to me as a professional appreciator of art. Not how much the piece is worth, but what the artist is trying to say, the quality of the individual piece of art. And to seek that out you need to look, think, contemplate. Spend enough time looking and you begin to recognise the artist's technique, their methods, themes, colour palette, you begin to get into their mind. You come to recognise art that could only have been painted by a particular artist and could not possibly be by anybody else. Even though I said before that a good fake can be convincing if, like me, you are willing to settle for a conclusion that is "maybe" rather than demand of yourself the black or white of a "no" or a "yes" then you free yourself to look, to appreciate, to assess and finally to judge. I have purposely built a reputation that is not so fragile that it must break at the first sign of uncertainty. I have always allowed myself to make mistakes, admit to them and move on. I just wish that my outlook was more the norm and less the outlier, but there we are, c'est la vie.'

He finished his BLT, drank his coffee. To be honest he looked like a man who had found his calling and lived a good life. He was comfortable in his rather outsize skin.

'I know Picasso,' he said, tweaking his glasses, 'he is like an old friend. When I see your picture I will look at it and I will know.'

'You've seen photographs?' I said.

'Yes,' he said.

'And do you think there's a possibility the picture is genuine?'

'Photographs are never good enough,' he said.

'I believe they were quite detailed,' I said, 'how would you assess the chances...?'

I left the end of the sentence hanging. Dr Peter Meredith-Taylor looked contemplatively at his empty plate,

'I think,' he said, 'from what I've seen and the views I have already sought that the chances are as high as ... hum ... let's say ... 50/50.'

Well at least it wasn't zero, I thought.

'And would your judgement be unequivocal?' I asked.

He laughed.

'Of course not,' he said, 'this is the art world, nothing is ever unequivocal.'

I felt better. What I needed was room to manoeuvre. Maybe the deal would have to be made by moving through the cracks. But I needed there to be some cracks to move through.

I thanked him for his time and got up to leave. We shook hands.

'Oh, and Michael,' he said, 'if you are ever tempted to be good enough to consider bringing me another present, please make it a brandy.'

There's just no educating some people.

Chapter 27

Back in the hotel room I picked up my phone and clicked through to the music, turned the volume up to max and lay back on the bed as the first notes of Miles Davis' album "Kind of Blue" struck up. I was just getting into it when I received the call,

'My father would like to meet you.'

It was Sky.

'That's good,' I said, trying to keep the euphoria out of my voice.

'I'll pick you up at 6am outside of Union Station, do you know it?'

It was just across the street. Did she really not know where I was staying? Maybe she didn't care.

'I'm sure I can find it,' I said.

'Good, I'll be driving a metallic blue Mercedes AMG GT do you think you'll be able to spot me.'

Driving a car like that? Even in a big city like Toronto it was a stand-out model, pricey, sleek and powerfully built.

'Yes, I think I'll be able to spot you,' I said and felt like adding, 'and I'll be wearing a red carnation' except of course, I wouldn't be.

'We have about a two and a half hour drive,' she said, 'so come prepared.'

"Come prepared"? What did she mean; make sure you've been to the bathroom, bring a book, have some mints handy?...

'OK,' I said.

'So you'll be going to Kingston,' said Logan after he'd entered the room and settled himself on the sofa. The listening devices were obviously working. 'That's where he's being held in detention. We need to charge him soon or we'll have to let him go,' he paused, 'and if we do that there's a real chance we'll never see him again.'

He explained the rules around visiting and how, because Lejon Vandla was not a convicted inmate, these would be more relaxed in his case.

'Anything else you need to know?' he asked.

I shook my head.

'Now we need tonight's meeting with Toni Malguzzi to go well,' he said, 'this is one time we don't want to see or hear what goes on. Sometimes too much information is a bad thing. What you don't know is easier to ignore.'

He had a point.

'So you'll be in here on your own with Malguzzi. We'll be watching the doors, anything gets out of hand then press this,' he gave me a beeper, 'or press it when you're finished.'

I wondered how long it would take to try and rescue me if Toni Malguzzi decided to attack me. Too long was my reckoning.

At precisely 8pm the door opened and Toni Malguzzi was escorted into the room by the same two be-suited companions that had been with him last time. He was wearing a sharp blue suit, a matching waistcoat, a white open-neck shirt, red socks, and polished brown shoes. He was obviously a man who liked to look after his appearance.

Once he had seated himself on the settee his two companions left. Officer Jones had thoughtfully ensured that a bottle of Jack Daniel's Old No.7 had been placed on the table between us with two glasses and a bucket of ice.

I told Toni Malguzzi about the phone call I'd just had with Sky.

'Good,' he said and poured himself a large drink over two cubes of ice. I poured myself a much smaller one and took a sip. As it hit my tongue I could make out the charred oak bitterness mixed with hints of vanilla. It was nothing like a Scottish single malt but it was OK. I added a couple of ice cubes. Malguzzi smacked his lips.

'Do you know. Michael, I was the capo di tutti capi, a part of the family, I ate at their table, I dealt with their worries. I was part of a team. The Vandlas could depend on me and I thought I could depend on them. But things change. I'm not a part of that team anymore. I'm fine on my own you understand. I don't need to depend on anyone else.'

I felt like he had more to say. I was right.

'We built the business together. Without me it would have gotten nowhere. I moved 'em into protection. It meant we didn't have the hassle of running prostitution, drugs, gambling and all that. We just creamed off a percentage in return for keeping any dogs or wolves away from the doors, you know what I mean?'

I wasn't sure that I did. I wasn't sure that I wanted to.

'It was a good business we had it ticking over just nice and then, what do you think? Lejon decides to pack it all in, to walk away from all that and put himself out to grass. And when things broke up do you think I got a fair share?'

I shrugged. It was a rhetorical question. To me he was starting to sound like a broken record, using me as some kind of sounding board, a captive audience he could vent his spleen to without fear of being interrupted. Like it or not I had to work with this guy so I had to listen.

'No siree,' he paused to empty the contents of his glass down his throat, refill it from the bottle and add some more ice.

'I had some bad luck,' he said, 'anybody can have bad luck can't they? I started a few things, they went wrong. I was just unlucky. So when I went to Lejon and asked him for a leg up I expected to get it 'cos I'm owed. They should'a remembered the hard graft I done for them and not just show me the door with some kinda meaningless words,' he clenched his fists and the spider tattoo on his left hand stood proud, threatening, 'I gotta believe it was Sky influenced Lejon, without her I'm sure he'd have given me more money. She probably said that I'd only waste it again and keep coming back. But that ain't the truth I was through my run of bad luck, I coulda done good, all I needed was the leg up I was owed.'

He glowered at me as if it were my fault.

'That gal done me bad and I gotta get even. I'm gonna give up the goods on a lotta people, the guys in uniforms are gonna have a lot to thank me for.'

He looked into his glass.

Was he repeating his grudge to help himself to justify his actions? How long can you bear a grudge? I thought as he continued his tirade.

I can't bear one for very long, my memory isn't good enough. After about 2 or 3 weeks I'll have forgotten what it was that so upset me and as bearing a grudge takes effort I'll not be bothered enough to carry it on.

I'm always amazed that there are people who can bear a grudge for years. They nurture it and carry it with them long after the original cause has become obscure, fogged by time. Indeed some grudges can be passed on from one generation to other and converted into lasting vendettas that feed on themselves through reciprocal reprisals. Is the energy required to maintain or escalate an old grudge really worth it? I suppose it could provide a sense of purpose, a reason for being, but at what cost?

Sometimes the reason for holding a grudge is not a directly offending act or event but more a vague feeling of having been wronged. This seemed to be the case for Toni Malguzzi. For him Sky lacked respect for him or maybe even, behind his back, vindictively influenced her father in a way that prevented him from achieving his true potential, and all for no good reason.

Over time Malguzzi would probably have come to see everything Sky did, everything she said, as vindication of his supposition that she was scheming against him. He knew in his heart that it was true but he just couldn't prove it. She was too clever for that, too clever by far. Over the years it must have gnawed at him. He didn't need proof he just needed a way to get back at her. And he could wait.

As grudges go Toni Malguzzi's must cut deep as it was deep enough for him to put aside any loyalty he felt to anybody else and if he had to bring others down to get to Sky then so be it.

As soon as I met Toni Malguzzi, as soon as I shook his hand and looked him in the eye I could see that here was a man who was born to hold a grudge. Such a mixture of arrogant self-confidence and lack of achievement was bound to be somebody else's fault

Sitting in front of me he was still jabbering on.

'But all this wasn't necessary,' he said, 'they forced me to do it. They should have helped me when I asked, like I always helped them.'

If he expected me to feel sorry for him it wasn't going to happen. Toni Malguzzi was a thug and now he'd decided to turn on the hand that had always fed him. The only good thing was that the settling of his own grudge might bring some semblance of overdue justice to others.

I tried to smile re-assuringly.

'Why this painting?' I asked.

I'd asked him this before and he'd given me some rubbish about art appreciation. I thought I'd try it one more time

'It's a trophy,' he said, 'I know how much Lejon likes to collect things. I'm gonna take a part of it away.'

'So the coin is a fake?' I said. Again this was something I'd asked before but I thought I deserved to know.

Malguzzi's eyes blazed, 'Don't you ever accuse me of trading in false goods,' he said.

'But if it's real you're vastly overpaying for the painting.'

'And you think only a fool would do that?' he snarled, his body tensing. I looked to see how far away I'd left the beeper. It was on the table. Too obvious. Too far away.

'No,' I said quickly, 'it just seems strange.'

'I'm gonna put her away for a very long time,' said Malguzzi, 'him too. What use is his collection then? I'll have my Picasso hanging on my wall, Lejon will have a bucket to piss in for the rest of his life.'

'Well,' I said, forcing a smile, 'I'm here to help.'

'Yea, you're my patsy,' he said grinning.

I didn't like the idea of being anybody's patsy, but maybe that is what I was. Maybe the only thing I was good at was being a patsy for people I had some respect for. I had no respect for Toni Malguzzi. I didn't like him and I never would and I didn't like the idea of being his patsy.

'I guess so,' I said.

'You do what I want and we'll keep getting along just fine,' he said, 'but you get out of line and I got a lot of friends,' he brought his fist down hard on the table nearly upsetting the bottle of Jack Daniels, 'and you won't be needing your return ticket, you understand me?'

I got the point, he wasn't exactly being subtle.

I nodded.

His dark eyes set hard and bore into me, his lips were tight and parted in something between a grin and a snarl. He wasn't an easy guy for anybody to like.

'Let's just get on with it,' he said.

'After I visit Lejon Vandla tomorrow,' I said, 'assuming everything goes well, I'm going to need the coin.'

Toni Malguzzi thought about this for a few moments.

'It's in a safe deposit box on the American side of Niagara Falls,' he said, 'you'll have to go and get it.'

'And how do I do that?'

'Get me a pen and paper,' he said. I went to the bureau and returned with the required items while he sat and re-filled his glass. He wrote for a couple of minutes. His handwriting was just readable.

'You go and stay at this hotel,' he pointed to a name, 'you look up a friend of mine called Beni Deschamps, he's the Casino manager there. Then you go across the border to this bank,' he pointed again, 'you ask for this box number, under this name and you use this combination to open the box. You'll also need a key. You'll get it when you tell me your meeting with Lejon was a success.'

He paused, lifted his glass and finished it.

'Enough?' he said.

'Enough,' I said and pressed the buzzer. Toni Malguzzi was a dangerous and unstable man. The sooner I was out of his company the better.

'Would you like to join me for dinner?' I asked Logan after Toni Malguzzi was well gone and I'd updated Officers Logan and Jones as far as I could without saying too much. I remembered his penchant for good food, especially when it was free, and thought it might bring welcome relief.

'Not tonight Josephine,' he said, 'you need your beauty sleep. We'll send something up for you, you need to be fresh in the morning, it's an early start.'

Not just early, very early, I thought, although this was one time when any residual adherence to the UK time zone my body was carrying would work in my favour.

The call from Sky had come through a lot sooner than I had anticipated. They must be keen. Although this was a good thing it meant I had little to no time to do the homework Professor Amanda Harker had recommended.

I found the book she'd given me. It was entitled "North American Coins & Prices". When I opened it up I found it too far ranging, too full of abbreviations and the specific language of numismatists, just as Amanda Harker had warned me. It was too much for me to attempt to pick up any reasonable idea of the subject so I reverted to Plan B; I would be prepared to give Lejon Vandla an open and transparent declaration of my total ignorance of the subject.

I had dinner in my room and tried to call Teresa but there was no answer. If this continued I was going to need help.

Chapter 28

Logan was in my room at 5am. He was going to start rumours if he wasn't careful.

'Are you ready?' he said.

'Just,' I answered brushing the errant flakes of a fresh croissant from the corners of my mouth. As I didn't know what the day would bring in the way of sustenance I'd eaten well and was feeling rather full.

'Well,' he said.

'Well what?' I said.

'Well are you going then or not?'

'It's a 5 minute walk,' I said.

'There could be traffic.'

'I'm taking the underground walk through.'

'It's better to be early than sorry.'

I felt under pressure but needed a trip to the bathroom before I left. I told Logan and he snorted.

'Go on then,' he said.

It's not very helpful to have someone hovering around the bathroom door while you're trying to complete your ablutions. When I finally emerged Logan was pacing up and down.

'Do you want me to go?' I asked.

'I think you should.'

'I'll go now then.'

'Good.'

It was for this reason that I had to stand on the sidewalk for over 40 minutes, increasingly attracting strange glances, before a metallic blue Mercedes AMG GT pulled up at the kerb and the passenger door was pushed open.

'Get in,' said Sky.

I gratefully acquiesced.

'Have you been waiting long?' she asked.

'Just got here,' I said, fastening the seatbelt.

Sky was wearing a tailored dark blue trouser suit and a white shirt with the top two buttons open. Around her neck hung the same silver-chained necklace with the large blue stone and diamond surround pendant that she had worn the first time we met. I wondered if she ever took it off.

I don't as a rule dress to impress, my daughter would be with me on that, but on this occasion I'd thought it important to make a good impression on Lejon Vandla and was actually wearing a deep red coloured tie, white shirt and dark grey suit. I'd kept the socks striped; red, yellow, and blue on a black ground. A man's got to have some show of individuality.

There were only the two of us in the car.

'No Spike today?' I said.

'I didn't think I would need him. Was I wrong?'

No, I thought, but I would have liked the opportunity to have a chat with him about my watch.

We drove for about 30 minutes in silence before Sky said, 'The other offers we got were up to $3m cash for the painting, you know.'

I didn't. I didn't even know if this was the truth.

'The reason we're taking your offer so seriously is because my father is intrigued with the idea of a trade,' she paused, concentrated on the road for a moment or two.

'My father wants to meet you because he wants to know if he can trust you. That's the way he operates. Its old school I know but if he doesn't trust you then you could offer him the Cullinan diamond and he still wouldn't be interested.'

'But I'm only the go between,' I said.

'For a client who wishes to remain anonymous,' said Sky, 'that's suspicious enough wouldn't you say?'

'I've explained the reasons,' I said, aware that my explanation was pretty thin.

'Hmm,' she said, 'let's put it this way, this anonymous client chose you to represent them so his judgement is that you are trustworthy. Now we'll see if my father thinks the same.'

After another few moments of silence she said,

'My father is currently incarcerated.'

I knew this but tried to look surprised.

'Wrongly imprisoned,' she said, 'held against his will on nothing more than groundless accusations. It is an example of Canadian justice at its worst, Mr Stewart.'

I nodded although I wasn't sure that this was a widely held belief.

'He will, of course, be released soon, exonerated of any and all wrongdoing, but the timing of your visit is unfortunate and rather than delay he has decided that we should talk now and let the discussion reach its own natural conclusion.'

I wasn't sure what that meant but the fact that this was happening at all had to be a good sign.

'I had been wondering,' I said, 'why your father had backed away from fronting the negotiations himself. This explains it.'

She bristled.

'My father has never backed away from anything in his life. He is not a man who backs away. He would never choose to back away.'

I'd obviously hit a nerve.

'I only meant…'

'I do not care what you meant,' said Sky, 'I hope I have made myself clear.'

Crystal, I thought.

We traveled on in silence.

Our journey took us along the eastern bank of Lake Ontario, on to the beginnings of the St Lawrence River and close to the area known as "Thousand Islands" that emerges from the northeast corner of the lake and stretches 50 miles downstream, straddling the Canada-US border. The name is actually an understatement as the area contains over 1,800 islands ranging in size from over 100 square kilometres through smaller islands occupied by only a single residence to uninhabited outcroppings of rock.

Finally we turned inland and parked outside what looked like a very large Canadian Chateau with high walls running out from its flanks.

'This is a multilevel correctional facility,' said Sky.

'I'm sorry I don't understand,' I said.

Sky tutted.

'It means that it is made up of a number of different areas that each operate at their own level of security ranging all the way from minimum to maximum.'

The main building would not have been out of place in a fairy tale with its towers, steeply pitched red metal roofs and symmetrically projecting dormers. The resemblance faded however when Sky mentioned that there was a history of unrest, sometimes fatal, between the more violent inmates. This facility was definitely not built for pleasure.

Before we moved to enter through the main entrance, the "visitors" entrance, Sky went around to the back of the car, opened the trunk, swapped her driving shoes for black high heels and took out a brown paper parcel tied up in ribbon, which she tucked under her arm.

Once inside the cavernous entrance hall Sky took control and registered our names and our appointment details at the reception window. We were suitably checked-off and underwent airport-like security, our phones and watches being taken from us "for safe keeping". One of the guards picked up Sky's carefully wrapped package after it had been through the security scanner and handed it back to her.

'Again?' he said.

'My father needs mental stimulation,' she said.

The guard smiled.

'He's a lucky man,' he said.

Not so lucky, I thought, he's in here.

Another guard then escorted us through the main building, doors being unlocked and relocked as we went until we found ourselves back outside and standing in an open courtyard with paths leading off to the various areas of the complex.

The guard chose our path for us and lead us through more locked gates and on towards a long single storey building that was separated into chalet-size slices. He unlocked the door of the first of these.

'This is one of our private family visiting units,' he said, 'they are normally reserved for longer family visits including overnight but you can use this one for the next two hours. I'll lock the door as I leave. If you want to leave earlier than the two hours you can use the phone that's in there to contact us.'

Good to his word the guard left us to it. I could hear the lock clunking home behind me. For a correction facility it all seemed pretty relaxed to me, professional but relaxed. I was impressed.

The unit we were in was comprised of a lounge, an adjoining kitchen, separate toilet/bathroom and a bedroom. We made our way into the lounge.

Chapter 29

Lejon Vandla was already there. He was sitting on the settee wearing bright orange overalls. He looked small and frail, not at all as I had imagined him from the photographs I'd seen.

'My father demands that if he is to be treated like a prisoner then he will dress like one,' said Sky.

Lejon Vandla rose as we entered. His daughter rushed over to him and engulfed him in a hug that almost knocked him backwards.

So this was the man who had terrorized several Toronto neighbourhoods for decades. He certainly didn't look like he could do it now. His face was deeply lined and contoured like a three dimensional road map drawn on parchment. His complexion was pale and pasty and he'd obviously lost weight. He looked like a size 12 man in a size 16 skin. This effect was further exaggerated by the oversized orange overalls he was wearing. His eyes however were ice blue and his gaze had an intensity that demanded respect. I got the distinct impression that to underestimate him would be a very dangerous thing to do.

There were two armchairs across a low coffee table in front of the settee and I sat in one and Sky in the other.

'I've brought you a present,' said Sky to her father and put the package she had brought on the coffee table in front of him. It looked most likely to be books and the brown paper wrapping was lifted by the red, white and yellow striped ribbon that held it together. There was even a neat bow tied on the top.

Lejon Vandla took the package and ran his boney fingers over the surface.

'My daughter always brings me books,' he said, 'to keep my brain ticking over. Books on Psychology, Physics, Poetry and so on and always beautifully wrapped in brown paper and this signature ribbon.'

Sky smiled shyly. For a moment she was a little girl again, a little girl being complimented by her father.

Then he turned to me,

'Do you know why you're here?' he asked.

It was a surprising question.

'To represent my client,' I said, 'to offer you a trade.'

'Why you're here,' he said, 'is because of what you're offering. I wanted to sell this painting for cash, to the highest bidder. But I've shelved all of that to see you. Do you know why?'

I stayed silent. I had the feeling he was going to tell me. I was right.

'Are you a collector?' he asked.

I'd been asked this question before. This time I gave it a little more consideration. I thought of my love of well-engineered watches. I used to have one but had lost it so I didn't think that that would count. I couldn't think of anything else that might qualify me.

'No,' I said.

'Then you probably won't understand,' he said, 'although I guess the person you represent would. As you know I am a numismatist, a coin collector. For me a coin has a history… what has it bought? what has it sold?… it has a presence, it has a value, and above all, it is a survivor,' as he said this Lejon Vandla held his hands out in front of him, moving his fingers as if manipulating an invisible coin, turning it over, running his fingertips across its surface.

'Of course some coins are more valuable than others,' he said, 'and this is where the investment angle comes in. The value of a rare coin will far surpass its face value or the value of its metal content, and for as long as there are rich men who want to hold rare things then the price of these coins will rise. It is not fashion like in the art world where an artist can fall in or out of favour and prices can take off or crash. No, a coin is a more stable investment and if it's rare then it's sought after and its price keeps going up.'

He paused, his breathing was laboured.

'If you're collecting a series of coins and you're missing a certain year then you'll pay over the odds to plug that gap. Know your buyer that's the important thing. How much does your buyer want to buy. How deep are their pockets.'

I nodded. I knew most of this already from Professor Amanda Harker and the book that she'd given me. I was pleased I had chosen to adopt the option of Plan B; a declaration of total ignorance in the field of numismatics. It was allowing him to talk and me to listen. Perfect.

'My client is an avid collector,' I said, 'as I told your daughter, his current passion is Picasso.'

'Ah yes, Picasso and the harlequin, the alter ego, the trickster, the lover, the acrobat, perhaps there is a little of the harlequin in us all eh, Mr Stewart?'

'Perhaps there is,' I said, 'and please call me Michael.'

Lejon Vandla smiled. It seemed to give him pain.

'And I am Lejon,' he said, 'tell me, Michael, why would your client be interested in buying a painting that no longer exists?'

His directness took me off guard. Was he admitting the painting was a fake? Or was he challenging me to respond?

'Well,' I said, 'although we may, I hope, agree to proceed towards a trade the one thing that we are all sure of is that this painting was stolen. It was taken out of the possession of its legally rightful owners.'

He smiled, it was like the grin you would get on a corpse, 'So?'

'So,' I said, 'any stolen Picasso is normally too hot to handle, the hunt to recover it is never called off,' I paused, 'but if it has been destroyed then who in their right mind would continue to spend time and money still looking for it.'

'So it makes it an ideal acquisition?' said Lejon Vandla.

'For a collector like the one I represent...'

Sky interrupted to say, 'A collector who makes his money through crime.'

'…a collector who wishes to diversify his investments and follow his passions,' I said, 'a collector who wishes to collect works by Picasso and have them, hold them, enjoy them without any fear of unwelcome guests hammering at his door in the dark of night,' I shrugged, 'a collector like that may not care too much about whether all of his possessions were rightfully acquired in the first place.'

'And?' said Lejon Vandla.

'And in any case he will insist that the picture be put through a thorough authentication process before completing the trade.'

'Ah ha, and how does he propose to do that?' asked Lejon Vandla, coughing.

'You will set the location and the time and bring the painting. I will bring the experts and their equipment. We will put them together and see what conclusions we reach.'

Lejon Vandla stroked his lower jaw. I could see the veins tangled like blue spider's web beneath the translucent skin. He was not a well man and the way he moved, carefully, stiffly, painfully, brought back memories that I would rather had stayed pushed back, hidden away, in the darker recesses of my mind.

'I don't mind that,' he said glancing across at Sky, 'I'm confident in the picture.'

Sky smiled.

Was he overconfident, I wondered, or did he know

something that I didn't.

'And the coin?' I asked.

'Ah yes the coin, the item that no collector of North American coinage could ignore,' he paused, 'it is almost as though your client knew exactly what carrot to dangle in front of me in order to get what he wanted. It is almost as though he knew me.'

This was a dangerous comment. Why would an anonymous buyer living in Europe know Lejon Vandla? Unless, of course, I was lying about who my client was. I kept my face deadpan, my reply matter-of-fact,

'It's easy to track someone's online purchases these days,' I said, 'once my client knew you were the seller he did a little homework. My client is not a coin collector himself, he got this item in settlement of a large debt, he knows what it's worth but if it buys him a Picasso, particularly a Harlequin, particularly one with an interesting history like this one, then he's happy.'

'He is a very generous man,' said Lejon Vandla.

This deal was set rolling long before I was involved so I just smiled and nodded, pretending a level of knowledge that I didn't have.

'He likes to get what he wants,' I said.

'At any cost?'

'At almost any cost,' I said.

'Hmm,' said Lejon Vandla, 'it's hard to believe that someone would be willing to make such a poor deal…'

'But you more than anyone must understand the passion of the collector,' I interjected.

He thought for a moment, each breath coming as an uncomfortable gasp.

He looked at Sky. She shrugged. Lejon Vandla tried to smile.

'My daughter,' he said, 'she would rather I take this chance than we sell the Picasso for cash and she have the money in her pocket.'

'But we would of course have to ensure that the coin is genuine,' said Sky, 'we would need to complete our own analysis before any exchange of goods was possible.'

'And do you know what would need to be done to give you that reassurance?' I asked, 'My client is happy to allow all reasonable measures to be taken. He realises that this is the holy grail and has anticipated that this transaction would require verification... on both sides.'

I paused for effect and then continued.

'My client would like to make this deal. Indeed, if he were not in earnest then I would not be here.'

'Just so,' said Lejon Vandla.

'So, I have to ask, what is your position?' My mouth was dry. I hoped I didn't sound over-eager.

Sky looked at her father.

'I want to talk to my daughter,' he said, 'alone.'

The guard was summoned. I retrieved my watch and phone on the way out and less than 5 minutes later found myself waiting outside, sitting on a bench, hoping it wouldn't start to rain, and hoping that I hadn't unintentionally said or intimated anything that was going to scupper this deal.

If I had I knew I was going to be in big trouble.

Chapter 30

I soon got tired of sitting and walked back and forth along the front façade of the main building and its adjoining walls, always keeping the main door in view, always waiting for Sky. If the CCTV was picking up my movements they must be wondering why I had decided to add a new patrol routine to their rota without asking their permission first.

It was a warm day, a few cottonwool clouds meandered slowly and purposelessly across the overhead blue. It was uncomfortable walking all dressed up in this hot and windless atmosphere and I could feel the tension in my shoulders. After a while I returned to the bench and sat staring fixedly at the main entrance. It was surely only a matter of time before a uniformed guard came out to ask me what the hell I was doing.

To an idle passerby I could have been just another tourist, although an overdressed one, just taking the opportunity to sit and mull over life's foibles. However I didn't have the patience for mulling over anything right now. What I felt was under pressure and increasingly out of control.

I was relieved of my station when Sky finally reappeared. She walked briskly past me and hardly gave me a glance,

'We can do business,' she said, making her way purposefully to the car, high heels clacking on the concreted surface of the car pack. I got up and followed behind her, in her wake.

Had I heard her correctly?

I'd been waiting for what felt like days but my eco-watch told me it had been less than an hour. I tried not to appear too excited as she changed back into her driving shoes and we prepared to leave.

'Let's go,' she said.

We manoeuvred our way through the Kingston byways and onto the 401 heading back towards Toronto.

I said nothing. I could see that it was taking Sky some time to relax. Whatever the conversation with her father had been it had visibly upset her.

'Did he like the books?' I asked eventually, trying to make a crack in the newly formed layer of ice that lay between us.

'He always likes his books,' she said.

'I hope you don't mind me saying,' I ventured, 'but your father did not look a well man.'

The car swerved involuntarily. My attempt at small talk had severed a nerve and knocked her off course.

'What do you mean?' she said.

It had been playing on my mind, my subconscious making connections. I hadn't meant to say anything but it was the first thing that came into my head. Well, I'd opened the can of worms now so I may as well see it through.

'I'm afraid I've seen that look before, my wife died of cancer.'

I knew I was jumping in at the deep end, both taking a risk with our fragile relationship and, to some extent, guessing. I hoped I wasn't about to snatch defeat from the jaws of victory. I did have experience though. I had watched my own wife proceed step by step through her own fight which she eventually lost. Memories of the ups and downs of both the disease and the effects of the treatments were still raw and when prodded were an easy wound to re-open.

Sky said nothing for a long time. I could see I'd guessed right. Lejon Vandla had cancer. I could also see that Sky was battling with her own emotions.

'What kind of cancer has your father got?' I asked.

Eventually she said,

'Pancreatic cancer. Diagnosed too late. It wasn't until the abdominal and back pain, the loss of appetite, the fatigue and weight loss became too oppressive that he sought help. By then the cancer had spread to other organs.'

She was talking automatically, as if she was reading aloud from a medical report, trying to distance herself emotionally from the fact that it was her father, not some other stranger, that was suffering. She was trying to cope.

'I've looked into possible treatments; surgery, chemotherapy, radiation therapy or some combination, but it's incurable at this stage and my father has accepted that and just wants palliative care.'

'Although he was doing his best to hide it I thought that he was probably on painkillers,' I said.

'After you left I was talking to him about the latest prognosis. He was reticent to discuss it and is very pragmatic about it himself, but it is not good.'

I knew what she was likely to see her father go through. I did not envy her that.

'I've long wanted a different life, Mr Stewart,' she said, 'I am my father's daughter in many ways but not in his chosen way of life. I've witnessed too much, seen too many things happen to too many people. I've wanted out for a long time. My father knows that and has accepted it. We were making our plans to leave Toronto when my father was arrested.'

'And where are you planning to go,' I asked, I thought it was at least worth a try.

'Far away,' said Sky, 'very far away. Canada is a big country, the West coast is very different from the East for example, the distance between here and Vancouver, where I went to school and college, is over two and a half thousand miles. So there are many alternatives we could consider even without leaving the country, which, of course, is another option.'

Her look made it clear that that was all she was willing to say on the matter.

So if anyone was going to nail Lejon Vandla they'd better do it quick. Logan, Officer Jones and all the other interested parties were just in time. Toni Malguzzi had come forward just in time.

I decided to re-direct the conversation back to the thing that had brought us together.

'I've got to be sure,' I said, 'what can I tell my client? Do we have the makings of a deal?'

She laughed, more out of relief than amusement.

'I told you already, my father would like to proceed and make the trade…'

Although these were the words I had been longing to hear they somehow sounded hollow.

'…we also recognise that there will need to be a process of authentication on both sides but my father wants it done and completed as quickly as possible.'

The reasons for this were only too obvious but "quickly" was what I wanted too.

'The coin is worth 5 to 10 times the value of the Picasso,' said Sky, 'why wouldn't we want to trade?'

Yes, but it's illegal to own it, I thought, the FBI have an open case to track down any remaining examples, repossess and destroy them.

'Value is only what someone will give,' I said, 'my client has no use for the coin, he's happy to exchange it for something he wants.'

'You mean he's happy to make it somebody else's problem,' said Sky.

I remained deadpan.

'Give it to somebody who appreciates it,' I said, 'someone who is happy to have and to hold.'

'A collector,' said Sky.

'A collector,' I said.

'But your client is trading one problem for another,' said Sky, 'the Picasso is stolen goods. We freely admit that, Mr Stewart, it comes with a health warning.'

'But it's not hot,' I said, 'and it's in my client's sweet spot. It makes sense. All it has to be is real.'

She rankled at this challenge.

'I have been educated in art,' she said.

I knew that already but tried to look surprised.

'Really?' I said.

'Yes, and of course we covered the work of the 20th century icons including Picasso, Pollock, Matisse, Mondrian, Dali, Kahlo, Rothko, Warhol and others. I have studied their works closely, Michael, and none more closely than Picasso. I would recognise a poor fake easily. Let your experts evaluate the picture, we have no fear of the outcome.'

Interesting that she'd chosen to say "no fear" rather than "no doubt", I thought.

'But I would still like to know more about your client,' she said, 'It is always good to know your enemy.'

'Enemy?' I said.

'Just a saying, Michael, probably too strong a word in this case,' said Sky, 'but what I mean is every negotiation is a competition, a trial of strength, and it is not easy to make a deal when one of the contenders is sitting hidden behind a black curtain.'

'But this negotiation is so straight forward,' I said, 'it is a trade, a bartering of one thing for another. The outside world may judge that the items have different values but as long as you and your father and my client are satisfied then nothing else matters.'

'Quid pro quo,' said Sky.

'A what?'

'A favour for a favour, a picture for a coin, an agreed equality of trade.'

'That sounds about right,' I said, 'and as long as this equality holds in the eyes of the trading parties then nothing else matters.'

'Hmm,' said Sky, 'there are always hidden depths to deal-making. It could be like an arm wrestle, a trial of strength,' she paused, 'or a way of getting even for previous perceived wrongs.'

This was all getting too close. Was she teasing me? Did she know Toni Malguzzi was at the back of this, that it was his face behind the black curtain?

'I think,' I said, 'that I would rather see this as an opportune meeting of minds. Five years ago my client would not have been in a position, would not have had the means, to be interested in the Picasso. His interest would not have been piqued by the history of the picture, the risk of whether it is genuine or not. A risk that he is now willing to take.'

'A risk assuaged by authentication prior to exchange,' said Sky.

'He may be audacious,' I said, 'but he's not a fool.'
She smiled.

'Trust no-one,' she said, 'I think we share the same outlook. This was the cardinal rule in my father's business but it is very rare to achieve results working entirely on your own. You have to rely on a few others at some time or other. They have to play their part, however trivial,' she paused, 'Choosing who you can trust is an important thing, it is the difference between success and failure, sometimes it is the difference between life and death.'

'Do you trust Spike?' I said.

'A good example,' said Sky, 'I trust that as long as Spike's interests and ours remain sufficiently aligned then he will continue to play his small part?'

'Do you think he is loyal?' I asked.

She seemed surprised at the question.

'What is loyalty, Michael? At what point does it break? Is it through loyalty that you would be willing to do or say, or not do something that normally you wouldn't even consider? Or is it through self-interest? Loyalty is not respect, Michael, loyalty is not the same as family,' she paused, 'After all, as I've said, I don't require much from Spike, so what's he got to lose by doing as he's told?'

'What has he got to gain?'

She shrugged, 'He stays close to us, my father and I, so he knows something of what we are doing. Who knows that might be valuable information to someone, and,' she added, 'he gets paid by us, he gets paid more than he's worth.'

Sky clearly wasn't a big fan of Spike's, he was a necessary evil. I wondered whether the Vandlas appreciation of Malguzzi's position had been the same back in "the good old days". Toni Malguzzi may well have thought that his importance to the Vandlas was more than it was.

'We've had many people working with us over the years,' said Sky, as if reading my thoughts. I had to be careful, 'some who we came to treat as almost family. But you must always watch your back, Michael. Family is blood and blood cannot be substituted. Do you know what I mean?'

I thought I got the point she was trying to make but I remembered some of my colleagues in the armed forces. There were definitely some of them that I trusted with my life, and they to me, and circumstances in which I would trust them more than I would be able to trust any family member. They were trained to protect me, and I them.

I explained my point to her.

'Yes,' she said, 'in the short term maybe, under certain circumstances. But in the long term it's always family that matters most. It's always family you fall back on in the end.'

I was sure this wasn't universally true but I could see it was true for Sky.

'It is true what you said earlier,' said Sky, musing, 'five years ago my father would not have gone near this trade either. He has always believed that if something seems too good to be true then it probably is.'

'But now?'

'Now, he thinks that if he doesn't take this chance then he never will. The pull of owning, perhaps only for a short time, something he's always longed for is too strong. Sometimes you can regret the things you don't do more than the things that you do, the missed opportunities that were there for only a fleeting moment and can never come again.'

For some reason this made me think of Teresa.

'Our original objective of freeing up some cash can always be achieved in a different way. There is always more than one way of skinning a fish.'

'Skinning a fish?'

'My father is not a young man, not a well man, and he does not enjoy spending his time incarcerated. At each visit he seems to me to be more frail,' she paused, 'When I was young my father taught me how to fish for salmon. There is lots of good fishing in Canada and it is one of the few things that I remember us doing together when I was young. He taught me how to choose the right brightly coloured artificial fly as bait; a bait so enticing that even though the salmon did not want to feed it was too much of a temptation and it would take it. He taught me how to choose the right place and the right time, and he taught me the patience to wait and to persevere. And when the bite came he taught me how to strike and how to play the fish, how to net it and land it. So you must forgive me my allusions to fishing, Michael, they were happy times. My father taught me how to fish. I am a father's girl.'

The truth as I saw it was that it was Toni Malguzzi who was doing the fishing and he was doing it to score some kind of a personal point, a final game of one-upmanship. The coin couldn't be genuine could it? If it were fake then there was the buzz for Malguzzi of trading Lejon Vandla a fake coin for an original Picasso. That must be the poke in the eye Malguzzi was pursuing before proceeding to shop Lejon and Sky Vandla with his information, getting them put away forever and then swanning off somewhere with the luxury of witness protection.

'So we're going to trade a stolen Picasso for an illegal coin,' I said.

'Yea,' said Sky, 'we'd better be careful.'

For some reason this felt like a veiled threat. I just hoped against hope that Toni Malguzzi wasn't setting me up. Please let the coin pass muster.

There was no talk for a while, the low hum of the powerful engine, the rumble of tyres on the hard road surface eating up the miles to Toronto were the only sounds. I was content. I didn't need to say any more. I didn't need any more to be said.

It was Sky who spoke again.

'I know something about making deals, Michael,' said Sky, 'I've been doing it all my life.'

If she was using this personal sharing to throw me off my guard then she was getting close. I recognised, I hoped not too late, that I needed to be careful, I needed to keep my distance, this was business not pleasure.

'You've got my father hooked into this one,' she said.

'My client is also hooked,' I said.

She looked at me. Her blue eyes set to piercing.

'With the greatest respect, Michael, I don't give a shit about your client.'

That had the advantage of clarity, I thought.

'What I care about is my father and the fact that he wants this coin. Like I said he's hooked and if anything should go wrong it would be really upsetting.'

I think I was getting the message.

'And if he's upset then I'm upset and do you know who we'll be upset with?'

I wracked my brains, who could she possibly mean?

'You,' she said.

I'd guessed as much. Thanks for the confirmation.

'I'm going to do my best to get this deal done,' I said, meaning it, 'and quickly,' I added, meaning it even more.

'Then let's just hope your best is good enough,' said Sky and turned on the car radio.

As luck would have it the track that was midway through playing was "It's impossible", not the original Spanish version written and recorded by Armando Manzanero in 1968 but the first recording in English sung by Perry Como.

Chapter 31

Sky dropped me back at the same place as she'd picked me up, just outside Toronto's Union Station. She'd asked me if there was anywhere else that I'd liked to be dropped off but I'd said that this was as good as any.

'I will let you know the location we've chosen,' she said as I was getting out, 'and the date and the time. In the meantime, Michael, get ready, do not let us down.'

Was there nobody in this whole messy business that did not hold me somehow responsible for the successful delivery of their intended outcome? It didn't seem fair.

As soon as Sky was out of sight I took my tie off, it had begun to feel like a noose. I needed time to absorb what had just happened so before returning to the hotel I went into the station and found a coffee bar.

I'd missed my lunch so I got an Americano, a tuna panini and a chocolate chip muffin. Not the healthiest of combinations but I was sure it would hit the spot. I took the tray, found an out-of-the-way table to sit at and tried to mull things over.

So Lejon Vandla had terminal cancer. It would have been nice to have been forewarned. He wanted the coin. Good. We wanted the picture. Good. Each side was willing to let the other authenticate their piece before completing the trade. OK. Although this was necessary it was complicated and full of potential pitfalls, for example the Picasso might be a fake, the coin might be a fake, somebody might change their mind at the last minute.

I did't think Sky or Lejon Vandla knew who the real buyer was for sure. I didn't really know if they even cared, but there had been some awkward moments.

Lejon's cancer added urgency to the completion of the deal so although tragic it worked in our favour.

Sky would let me know the place and the time they had chosen to try and complete the deal.

Overall things seemed to be going Malguzzi's way, which meant they were going Logan's and Officer Jones's way, which also meant, most importantly, that they were currently going my way too.

What I needed now was to get my hands on the coin otherwise I'd be left with nothing to trade and that was unlikely to make me very popular. I had to trust that the coin actually existed, that Toni Malguzzi knew just where and how to get hold of it and that he would give me the wherewithal to go and get it.

All I had to do now was to keep all these plates spinning and complete the deal.

What could possibly go wrong?

I thought about my relationship with Teresa, AB's unusual level of interest, my new-mother daughter, my almost unknown granddaughter and my missing watch.

Hmm, life is never easy, I thought. A memory of what my own father used to say to me flashed into my mind "Son, if you can't get it right then at least get it done."

Just as I was entering the hotel lobby I got a call from the jeweller I'd dropped the friendship bracelet off with to say that he could do what I wanted and by tomorrow as long as I paid a premium, he mentioned the sum,

'Phew,' I said and then, 'OK.'

He wanted payment up front and I didn't blame him. We swapped details and I made the payment electronically and sent him a copy of the receipt. Within 5 minutes he'd texted back "Thanks".

I was annoyed with Officers Logan and Jones and I was determined to let them know it. They'd sent me into a dangerous situation lacking critical information. That's not what you do to someone who's on your team. Back in my hotel room they sat opposite me eager to be briefed on my meeting with Lejon Vandla. But before they got that they needed to hear my beef,

'You didn't tell me he had cancer,' I said, trying to keep my voice even.

They looked at each other.

'We thought it was something you didn't need to know,' said Officer Jones her face a picture of concern. She looked at Logan hoping for support.

'How did you find out?' he asked unapologetically.

'It's not difficult.' I said, 'the effects of the illness are etched on his face, in the way he holds himself, in the way he moves.'

'You're an expert then are you?' said Logan continuing his unfriendly tone.

'And Sky told me,' I said.

'We didn't know if it would come out or not,' said Officer Jones uncomfortably, 'Lejon Vandla is very sensitive about his condition and anyway we thought that if you did know you might betray the fact and that would have put you in a very awkward position.'

I thought about it. Yes, I could see that.

'So,' continued Logan jumping onto the same bandwagon, 'if you didn't know and it came out, like it has, you could react genuinely surprised, like you have.' He open his arms wide as if he had just revealed what a master plan it had been for them to say nothing and that my own reaction had proven them right. They had done me a good turn.

There was perhaps some truth in this version of reality but I still felt like I'd been sent naked into the lion's den.

'Does Toni Malguzzi know?' I asked.

'Hell no,' said Logan, 'we don't want him to know. As far as he's concerned he's getting even with the Lejon Vandla that he remembers; fit, powerful…immortal.'

I could see why letting Toni Malguzzi know was a bad idea. Anything that reduced his resolve to spill as many beans as he'd got was exactly not what Logan, Officer Jones and their colleagues wanted.

I decided to let it go. No point holding a grudge. I'd survived so all's well that ends well, I thought.

'Are there any other secrets you've got up your sleeves?' I said.

'No,' said Logan, too quickly.

'I don't think so,' said Officer Jones unconvincingly.

I spent the next 30 minutes debriefing them on the meeting and its outcomes.

'Now I have to go and get Malguzzi's item of trade,' I said.

'You mean he doesn't have it?' said Logan.

'I mean he doesn't have it but he knows where he's put it,' I said.

Logan snarled, 'Are you trying to wind me up?'

'Why would I do that?'

'Just don't,' he said.

'I need to meet with Toni Malguzzi as soon as possible,' I said, 'to tell him about my meeting with Lejon and to fix up some things.'

'Some things?' said Logan.

'Some things you don't want to know about,' I said, 'and then I'll need to go off grid for about 48 hours.'

'You're kidding,' said Logan.

'We'll need to check on whether that's possible,' said Officer Jones wrinkling her nose and not looking at all happy.

'Be quick,' I said, 'I need to leave tomorrow.'

Chapter 32

After they'd gone I called Samantha and gave her the same update.

'I'll pass the good news on to AB,' she said, 'when I can.'

'What do you mean "when you can"?', I said surprised.

'He's taken a few days leave, he's calling in intermittently. The next time he calls in I'll let him know.'

'That's not like him,' I said.

'No it's not,' she said. I could hear the undertone of concern in her voice.

'Are you worried about him?' I asked.

'Worried,' she said, 'about AB? No, of course not.'

She was definitely worried.

It was less than 20 minutes later that there was a knock at my door. I opened it and found AB standing there. It was a complete surprise. My mouth must have fallen open.

'Hello, sir,' I said.

AB was smartly dressed as usual in a navy blue jacket, white shirt open at the neck, cream slacks and brown brogues. I'd showered and changed into a pair of black casual trousers, checked shirt and grey socks but I immediately felt under-dressed. At least I was clean shaven and had recently brushed my teeth.

'Can I come in? Not disturbing you am I?' said AB, 'or are you just going to stand there with your mouth open?'

I closed my mouth. AB had a way of unsettling people and it always worked on me.

'Sorry,' I said for no apparent reason.

AB strolled over to the sofa and sat in the middle of it. He gestured to me to sit opposite. He'd already taken command of the room.

'Nice room,' he said.

'I've been in a lot worse,' I said, and a lot of them were your doing, I thought.

AB smiled, as if I'd tried to be amusing and he wished to condescendingly recognise it. Sometimes it's better to keep your mouth shut. I wanted to ask 'What are you doing here?' but I didn't.

'How are things going?' asked AB, 'I've asked our friends next door to kindly switch off their surveillance equipment whilst I'm talking to you so feel free to say anything you like.'

I glanced up at the cameras, the little red lights were out. He obviously also held some authority over this side of the pond.

'Now tell me from the beginning what has been going on,' he said.

I knew that he'd have heard most of it already so he was presumably cross checking to ensure accuracy. I gave as accurate and succinct a summary as I could, missing out only Teresa's visit and the muggings.

'It's fair to omit your personal visitors,' said AB, 'but I'm surprised you omitted the altercation that followed your first meeting with Sky. It would be hard to believe they're not related.'

As always it was evident that AB knew a lot more than I'd imagined. By "personal visitors" he was clearly referring to Teresa. That was too sensitive a point to press so I told him as much as I could about the unprovoked attack instead.

'Probably a Ketamine injection,' said AB, 'although the individual response depends on the dose the effect can be rapid, just like yours, also your nausea and confusion fits. You were lucky it wasn't more severe.'

I didn't feel lucky.

'Yes,' I said, 'probably.'

'Do you know who and why?'

I had my suspicions.

'Not yet,' I said.

AB nodded, content to leave that as my business.

'As you know, my days of being in the field are over,' he said in a surprise move towards a level of personal sharing I wasn't used to from him. It made me feel uncomfortable, 'I'm now either stuck behind a desk, or in meetings, or at dinners, or in front of a computer screen, or on the phone. You should count yourself lucky, Mark, being in the field gives you a lot more personal freedom than I've got.'

I thought about how I'd already been mugged twice. I looked at AB's immaculate appearance, his custom-made tailoring, and thought about the plushness of the environments he normally inhabited. I found it difficult to feel too sorry for him. To me he'd always seemed comfortable in the world he inhabited, calm and in control.

I said nothing.

'I thought I'd get out a little more,' he said smiling, 'stretch the legs, dip my toes back in the water.'

I wasn't convinced but there was little I could do about it. Rather than pushing back I decided I may as well take what advantage I could from his presence and influence.

He returned his attention to the meeting with Lejon Vandla.

'Cancer,' he said, 'any idea how severe.'

'If the outward symptoms are anything to go by it looked pretty severe to me,' I said.

'Hmm,' said AB, before adding, 'I'm obviously delighted that we appear to have agreed a transfer of goods. Did Sky give any indication of how long we're expected to wait for them to specify the time and location?'

'No,' I said, 'other than they want it done quickly.'

'As do we,' he said.

'There is one thing though,' I said, 'Toni Malguzzi does not have the coin. I have to go and collect it.'

'Yes, I understand that,' said AB.

'And to do that the way he wants me to I need to go off grid, untracked, for about 48 hours,' I said.

'An unpopular request,' said AB.

'But one for which I need consent granted quickly,' I said.

AB considered for a moment.

'Do you know,' he said, 'that there are now completely undetectable GPS trackers?'

'Really?' I said with no idea of why he should bring this up now.

'When I say undetectable I do of course mean that they are miniaturised and can be remotely put into a sort of deactivated "sleep" condition. It is while they're in this state that they avoid detection. They can then be remotely reactivated at any time.'

'Clever,' I said.

'Yes,' said AB, 'put that together with the fact that solar cells can now be produced in the form of threads and you've got the makings of a very sneaky device.'

'But you wouldn't do that to me would you?' I asked.

'Of course not, wouldn't dream of it,' said AB.

I wasn't completely reassured.

He then sat gazing out of the window for a few moments.

The silence was uncomfortable.

When he finally spoke he said, 'I'll see to it that your experts are available when you need them. Just let me know when and where.'

It wasn't at all certain that we would get that far but I just said, 'Thank you sir.'

He rose to leave.

'Anything you need, call it in,' he said, 'and see its marked for my personal attention.'

The door closed behind him, the latch slipping back into place with a soft "clunk".

I'd never been honoured with such a visit in mid-assignment before. It was not without a degree of personal risk for both of us. AB knew that. What was he doing here? What justified the risk?

I felt I was missing something, something important.

Chapter 33

Good to her word Officer Jones had arranged for Toni Malguzzi to pay me another visit. When he arrived he settled himself on the settee. The room surveillance was again turned off and we were alone together. He was sitting where AB had sat not long before although the contrast in personality, in social worth, was extreme. Malguzzi was visibly delighted with the news that the deal was set to proceed to completion.

'And she brought him books,' he said, 'wrapped in brown paper and tied with a ribbon. That is so Sky, plain and over-the-top at the same time. So did they seem close?'

'Very,' I said.

'She has such an enormous influence on Lejon, always to her advantage and to other's disadvantage,' he said.

It was clear whose disadvantage he was thinking of.

'How did she look?' he asked.

I wondered which Sky he meant, the well dressed, attractive blonde in a trouser suit, the self-confident young woman smart enough to hold her own in any company, or the girl who doted on her father, or the girl who battled to control her emotions when talking about his illness. It was a mixed bag.

'She seemed fine to me,' I said.

'Good,' he said, 'that's how I want her to feel. I want her to believe that she has the upper hand. I want her to think that things couldn't be going any better.'

He grinned, showing his gold teeth.

'And then after we've completed the transfer, when she's still on a high with what she thinks she's done for her father, then, at that point, it will be my pleasure to bring her down,' he glared at me, his eyes sparkling, 'without her bad influence my life would not have taken the unfortunate twists and turns it has. She got in the way and treated me as if I had no value. All I had done for her father over the years she just treat with contempt. It was a contempt I did not deserve.'

I had no idea whether it was justified or not. It didn't matter to me. I just had to do my job and move on, the quicker the better.

'Oh yes, I owe Sky,' he said, 'she's got it coming.'

I didn't tell him about Lejon Vandla's cancer. I didn't think it would help the situation.

He took a plain brown envelope out of an inside pocket of his grey silk jacket.

'The key to the safety deposit box I told you about is in here along with everything else you need,' he said, 'including a direct line to me, use it when you have to.'

I wondered whether he'd got clearance to give me that as it bypassed all the witness protection and safe house protocols. I decided to go for broke and gave him my direct number in return. Now it was my turn to keep a secret from Officers Jones and Logan.

'When you open the safe deposit box,' he continued, 'you'll find only two things inside. The second of these is C$50,000 in cash. You can use some of this for your expenses but don't overdo it. The rest I want you to give me when you get back. Give it directly into my hands. Do you understand?'

Be good to me and I'll be nice to you, but not too nice, was the underlying message.

'I understand,' I said.

As he had a captive audience of one and was clearly short of conversation Toni Malguzzi then chose to regale me once more with a series of stories about his life, his sacrifices, the stresses and strains he had had to cope with, the toll it could have taken on a weaker man.

I tuned out after the third or fourth sentence and just nodded occasionally. Unfortunately that only seemed to encourage him. From the file I'd read in London I knew that Toni Malguzzi was a man who never started a fight without first ensuring he had the upper hand, be that in numbers or in armaments. As far as I knew he wasn't prepared to step into a ring he wasn't sure of stepping out as the winner. From the death of a young tourist girl to his latest suspected murder he'd always been able to keep one step ahead of incarceration either through lack of evidence or through witness intimidation. He was proving to be a hard man to like and I wasn't willing to put in the effort.

'You look like a pen-pusher to me,' he said after he'd got tired of bigging himself up.

I kept my peace. He was wrong. I've actually been in what they euphemistically call "action". It is no fun when you can no longer depend on the ground under your own feet, when the shuddering noise, the tremors of impact set everything in motion and all you can do is fall on your face and hold on, completely out of control in a world consumed by the uncertainty of when and from where the next explosion is going to come. The only thing you do know is that it will come. It will come. That's one of the reasons you don't talk about it with anybody outside of the "club", if you haven't experienced it for yourself then there is no possible way you can understand.

'You're right,' I said, 'I'm happier in front of a computer screen than behind a gun.'

He laughed, reached over and slapped me on the back.

'I like you,' he said, 'you don't pretend to be anything more than you are.'

I couldn't reciprocate his feeling of bonhomie but I tried my best not to shrink back from his touch.

'Thanks,' I said attempting to force the semblance of a smile. I had to work with this guy and if he didn't intensely dislike me then maybe it would make it easier to endure.

'There is one more thing,' said Malguzzi.

'Yes?' I said.

'I been nice to you so far haven't I?' I nodded, he hadn't hit me so I guess that meant he'd been nice, 'but I don't want you to get the wrong idea. I don't want you to think you can be a wise guy. I mean if you were to think of crossing me at any point then, you know, I wouldn't if I were you.'

Such a course of action was very far from my thoughts. All I wanted to do was get my job done, get out of Toronto and never see Toni Malguzzi again.

He leered at me, saliva moistening his grinning mouth. You could tell this grin wasn't meant to be friendly. He didn't need to get all threatening with me but I guess he didn't know that. He was only doing what came naturally to him, out of habit.

'You know what I mean?' he said, clenching his fists, the spider tattoo on his left hand looking ready to pounce.

I knew what he meant. He probably still had plenty of "friends" out and about that he could point in my direction if I misbehaved.

'I'll remember,' I said, hoping that would do.

'You just make sure you do,' he said, 'I don't like no wise guys.'

I didn't feel it was the right time to point out his inappropriate use of the double negative.

Even though the room was air conditioned I felt the sweat starting to trickle down my spine, making my laundered shirt sticky.

So here we were again. It was all up to me. If things went well it would be just like it was always supposed to be. If they went badly it would be all my fault. Where had I heard this before? Oh yea, from everybody else and from all directions. Great, there's nothing like being caught in the middle to keep you on your toes. This assignment was just getting better and better.

Toni Malguzzi got up to leave. His be-suited guards appeared at the door ready to escort "mister nice guy" away. I was delighted. I'd spent more than enough time with my friend the psycho.

'Be seeing you,' he growled as he exited, 'you just remember what I said.'

How could I forget, I thought.

Chapter 34

I went down to the bar on the third floor and got myself a Molson Canadian lager beer and a bowl of salted peanuts. I was hoping that because my location could be traced through my phone I'd be pretty much left alone.

I was wrong.

No sooner had I sat myself down in a comfy seat, in a quiet spot, than a clearly-part-of-the-surveillance-team person casually, too casually, entered, saw me and camped himself on a barstool.

There was a mirror at the back of the bar and he positioned himself so that he could keep an eye on me through that.

So be it. I was clearly too important to risk losing sight of. Letting me go off grid for 48 hours wasn't going to be any easy decision for them to make.

At least I still got to make my call in some semblance of privacy.

My daughter picked up on the second ring.

'You're lucky,' she said, 'she's just gone for her nap.'

'How's she doing?' I asked, trying to picture my granddaughter, Amelia, remembering how beautiful she was.

'Wondering when her granddad is going to visit,' said my daughter.

It was a fair point, so far in her life I had been a lousy granddad. I'd only seen her once or twice and the last time she'd thrown up on me. It was just what I deserved. When this assignment was over I resolved to turn over a new leaf. I told my daughter.

'Really?' she said, 'Again! Another promise? You're running out of time dad.'

I wanted my daughter to know that I was being serious. I wanted her to know what I'd been thinking about and told her that I realised that I'd not been the best dad and not the best husband either.

When I left the services I carried too much baggage with me. I knew I couldn't talk about it and I knew it was gnawing at me, affecting my behaviour. What I'd seen, what I'd done, dehumanised me. It had to if I was going to survive. I wasn't perfect in the first place but now I had more and deeper flaws.

The nightmares would recur but inconsistently. I could be good for a month and then bam! I couldn't control it. That was one of the worst things, the loss of control. Something had control over me, something that lived inside me, that teased and tormented but couldn't be seen. I told my daughter some of this, not a lot, just a little, and then said,

'Your Mum stuck with me when I didn't deserve it. I don't know why...'

'I do,' she said.

'...and I don't know how.'

'It must have been tough,' my daughter said, 'I just saw the two of you as my mum and dad. Two big people who looked after me, told me off, but more than anything were there for me. Just like she was there for you.'

It was a strange comparison but maybe apt. My wife had been there for me when I needed it most but I lot of the time I'd done my best to reject it.

We all lie. The difference is in the frequency, the severity of the consequences and the apparent veracity of the delivery, the ability to adhere confidently to a fallacy.

'Hello… dad…?'

Silence, then she said,

'Mum loved you,' she said.

I know, I thought.

'Even when you argued, fell out over something trivial or something serious. She had faith in you.'

And me in her, I thought.

'Remember when she threw that blancmange?'

'How could I ever forget,' I said, 'I had to have that suit dry-cleaned.'

Funny how things that annoy you at the time can make you smile when you remember them. It was good to hear her laugh. It was still a little girl's laugh to me and hearing it had broken the tension.

The conversation wandered away to other memories. I don't always like thinking about the past but I enjoyed recalling these shared intimacies with my grown up daughter. We traded stories.

It was a jolt when she dragged me back to the subject.

'She always trusted your judgement, dad. And I trust your judgement now.'

'She won't talk to me,' I said, knowing my daughter knew who I was talking about, knowing that she probably knew that this was one of the reasons I'd called.

'How hard have you tried?'

I gave her the rundown of the number of times that I'd attempted to call Teresa, her lack of pick up and lack of response. I ended with,

'So maybe I should just stop calling?'

There was a pause.

'She's upset.'

'I know but if she won't take my calls….'

I let the problem hang. She let it hang too.

'So what can I do?' I said eventually.

'Call her again.'

'And if she doesn't answer?'

'She will. I'll talk to her.'

'And what do I say?' I asked.

She thought about it, and then she said,

'Dad that's really up to you.'

It wasn't a great answer but I could see it was correct.

'OK,' I said, 'I'll call her tomorrow.'

'You do that,' she said.

'And thanks,' I said.

'That's OK, dad, that's OK.'

After a lonely dinner I went back to my room. It had been a long day. To relax I did what I always do; I listened to Maria Callas. I chose a live recording of a recital in 1952. Although it was re-mastered you could still hear a muted crackle of background static but it didn't matter because her voice transcended it, her delivery at once passionate and serene. After that I took a shower and hoped for a good night's sleep.

The subconscious is a pain in the ass. You wake up in the middle of the night knowing something is not quite right, a vague flock of doubts circling your head like carrion crow, your sleep disrupted while at the same time you're too tired to be properly awake.

Something was bothering me about this assignment and I knew what it was. The pieces of this jigsaw did not fit together, the picture that was emerging was vague and fuzzy. I wasn't sure whose game I was playing or what side I was on. The sooner I got this job over with the better. I had a feeling there would be losers but wasn't sure that there would be any winners.

I struggled to get back to sleep. In a nest of vipers it's difficult to know which one to befriend.

With an effort I switched my thoughts to Teresa, leaned across and switched on the bedside radio for comfort. I finally fell asleep to the strains of Elvis Presley singing "It's Now or Never".

Chapter 35

After a bad night my body needed a shake up to get the muscles moving and my head clear. I was already on the treadmill in the hotel gym when Officer Logan arrived expecting to join me for breakfast.

Begrudgingly he borrowed some shorts, a pair of trainers and a t-shirt from the hotel store and started up the treadmill next to mine at a slow walking pace.

I ignored him. My earphones were tuned to Callas and my mind was focused on putting one foot in front of the other and building up a sweat.

He tapped me on the shoulder. When I glanced over he was already perspiring. I slowed my machine a little, took out my earphones and said,

'Do you come here often?'

He didn't seem to appreciate my wit and to show me the kind of stuff he was really made of he ramped up his treadmill to a brisk walk. The various ways in which parts of his body started to move told their own tale. He needed this work out a lot more than I did.

'You've got your permission,' he said, '48 hours off the grid and no more. You won't be bothered, you won't be followed or tracked.' As he spoke I could see he was getting more and more out of breath.

'What else do you need?' he asked.

As he'd delivered such good news I decided to go easy on him.

'Nothing,' I said and started to slow my machine in preparation for departure, 'I hear that Smitty's do a great breakfast,' I said, 'let me treat you.'

'I'll book a taxi,' he said stopping his machine dead and starting to towel the sweat from his brow.

The taxi took us out to Lindsay. The trouble was worth it. Logan was in his element ordering from a packed menu.

'Always good to have a feed after a tough workout,' he said, 'makes it feel like it was worth it.'

What tough workout, I thought.

Logan ordered first,

'I'll have the Meatlover's Skillet,' he said. From the menu I could see that this consisted of diced sausage, bacon, ham and back bacon topped with shredded cheddar cheese served over hash browns with toast. He was obviously on a diet.

I ordered two fried eggs over easy, bacon and sausage which I thought was lavish enough. We both ordered black coffee to drink.

'Is that all?' asked the waitress.

'Have you tried Poutine?' said Logan.

I answered in the negative.

'Give us a side order of Poutine,' said Logan, 'lots of gravy.'

We ate and talked at the same time.

'Wasn't easy swinging it,' said Logan, his mouth full, 'letting you out of our sights for 48 hours ain't exactly plan A. However we got to look at the bigger picture.

What we're doing here isn't exactly normal. We think we can trust you and the powers that be want what Malguzzi's offering. Cleaning up so many cases in one go ain't exactly normal either, so…'

I wondered if AB's presence had had anything to do with swinging things my way. I'd probably never know.

'Now you gotta try this,' said Logan pointing to the Poutine, 'it's French fries topped with cheese curds and a special gravy. Delicious!'

He took a fork, dug in deep and filled his mouth.

I took a smaller portion. It looked like a heart attack on a plate but it tasted good, really good. I took a second helping. Logan smiled,

'We'll turn you into a Canadian yet,' he said.

I could think of worse things, I thought, and tried some more.

By the time we got back to the hotel we were friends again.

I returned to my room and noticed that the surveillance cameras were still switched off. Good. I took a long hot shower followed by a colder one, had a second shave, and re-cleaned my teeth, enjoying the sharp spearmint bite of the toothpaste. Then I completely changed my clothes and sat down by the window. Although Teresa couldn't see me I was glad I'd made this effort. I picked up my phone and dialled her number.

I knew this was going to be awkward. I'm not very good at begging. As I placed the call I could hear my daughter's voice in my head saying 'It's up to you.'

'Yes.'

Not a promising start judging from the tone, but at least she had answered.

'It's me.'

'I know who it is.'

'Well Teresa, you see, I've been thinking...'

'Nice to know you sometimes do, especially before opening that big mouth of yours.'

Ooh boy, Teresa was definitely not in the mood to make this easy for me.

'Right, yes, you see I've talked to my daughter about ...'

Wrong, wrong, wrong.

'I know!'

Pause.

Longer pause.

I held my breath, if she started speaking Spanish I'd know I was in deep trouble.

'And what did she say?' she asked.

At least she was speaking English. Be thankful for small mercies, I thought. But I still had to tread carefully.

'She seemed to suggest I was an idiot.'

Another pause.

A really long pause.

Laughter from her end, relief at mine.

'She knows you very well.'

'All her life.'

I thought it was better to strike while the iron had thawed to scalding.

'Where are you?' I said.

'New York.'

'OK.'

'OK, what?'

'Listen Teresa, I need your help. Can you fly into Toronto Pearson International Airport later today?'

'Is that an apology?'

'Sort of, when I pick you up you can come join me in Niagara for a day or so. We can talk, you know, face-to-face.'

I was getting used to awkward silences. When she broke it she said,

'You mean you want me to just drop everything and come, at your beck and call, to Canada, to help you with your assignment?'

Didn't sound too good when she put it like that.

'It's the only way I can think of to see you soon and I want to do that. I want to see you. I really do.'

I waited. It was like waiting for the judge to pronounce sentence.

'It's stupid, it's ridiculous but I'll do it,' she said, 'I must be loco.'

Excellent.

'I'll book the tickets straight away and text you the flight number and arrival time.'

'Excellent,' I said, 'I'll come and meet you at the airport and I'll reimburse you for the cost.'

'You better had,' she said.

I couldn't imagine what my daughter had said to Teresa but this was a much better outcome than I'd expected. Yahoo!

'I'll see you later,' I said.

'Yes,' she said, 'I'll see you later.'

Within half an hour she'd texted me her flight details.

As well as being delighted that Teresa was coming to see me there were other benefits. She was now an American citizen although she had had to work hard and long to get it by making all the right applications, securing a green card, proving a residency of 5 years, passing English Language and Civics tests, attending a citizenship ceremony, taking an Oath of Allegiance to the US, and finally applying and receiving her US passport. I'd helped her with this a little bit, maybe pulled a few strings to help it go a bit faster but she had still had to put in the effort, she still had to pass all the tests, there were no shortcuts there. When she finally got her US passport she was so proud. I was proud too but of her, not the passport.

So with Teresa's passport and American driving license and my British passport, visas and IDP, or International Driving Permit, we were in a great position to pop back and forward across the Canadian/USA border at Niagara. Indeed the fact that there were two of us, a man and his woman, going across the border to experience the American side of the Falls couldn't be more commonplace. Who would give such an excursion a second thought and if, while we were on the American side, we stopped off to do a little additional visit well I mean, who needed to know or care?

I now needed to make the remaining preparations for the trip. I leapt into action. First of all I booked a taxi to take me from the hotel. I wanted to make it difficult for anybody to know where I was going so taking a taxi was a good choice. Second I checked I had everything I needed from Toni Malguzzi; names, addresses, instructions and most importantly his key to the safety deposit box. Third I changed phones leaving behind my trackable phone and taking the pay-as-you-go I'd bought when I first arrived in Canada, about a 100 years ago.

Moving to the hotel bar and using this phone I then pre-booked a hire car that I would pick up at the airport. I booked it under joint names and joint drivers as hopefully Teresa would be with me by that time. Lastly I rang the hotel in Niagara that Malguzzi's mate worked at and using his name as a reference made sure they had my booking and then upgraded it to a room for two people with a kingsize bed and a view of the Falls. I could always sleep on the floor if things didn't work out.

Having sorted all this out I grabbed a coffee. I had to keep my caffeine levels up no matter what Officer Jones might say about it.

On the way back to my room I stopped off at reception. As I'd hoped there was a small package from the jewellers. I checked the contents. All seemed to be satisfactory although experience had taught me that my judgement of what was and what was not satisfactory in the jewellery stakes was sorely lacking.

Chapter 37

Back in my room I packed a bag but before I could leave I got two surprise calls.

The first was from Toni Malguzzi. Before I answered I checked the security cameras. The lights were off. Now we were in direct contact Malguzzi was obviously going to make the most of it.

'I had to ask,' he said, 'you got everything you need?'

'I think so,' I said.

'You give Beni Deschamps my regards,' he laughed, 'he's a slippery customer, Michael, but a good friend.'

Was that some kind of warning?

'And don't forget,' he said, 'you come back here safe... and quickly. You got that?'

That was definitely a threat. Running off with the goods was not my plan. I shook my head. There'd be too many people tracking me down for me to get away with something like that. He had nothing to worry about. Maybe he was just nervous by nature or lived every day by the "trust no-one" adage.

'I won't forget,' I said.

'You look after me, I look after you,' he said.

There was one loose thread he might be able to help me with. I took a chance.

'Do you know a guy called Spike,' I asked, 'he was with Sky when we first met, tall, skinny, red hair.'

Malguzzi laughed. It was a harsh, guttural noise.

'His hair, it's been through the rainbow, white, yellow, blue, red, he likes to change it about. We called him Mr Peppermint,' said Malguzzi, 'he has this addiction to peppermint mouthwash, uses it like four times a day. I asked him once why he did it, told him it couldn't be doing his health any good and he just said something about a clean mouth meaning a clear conscience. I didn't get it. I think he's crazy. Let's put it this way I never turned my back on Spike.'

'Sky seemed to rely on him,' I said.

This clearly rankled.

'I wouldn't rely on Spike,' he said, 'like I said he likes to play all ends at once does Spike.'

He thought for a moment.

'Do you like him?' he asked.

I thought of my watch.

'No,' I said, 'I think I can safely say that I'm not his greatest fan.'

Malguzzi grunted.

'Then you'll be pleased to know he's on my list,' he said, 'Some of his robberies were aggravated. That's the problem with Spike, he doesn't know when enough is enough, when doing nothing is better than doing something.'

Yea, I thought, like for instance there was no reason for him to attack me. I was no threat to him.

But I am now.

Malguzzi laughed again, it was even more humourless than the last time.

'I'll tell you something about Spike,' he said, 'he collects souvenirs.'

'Souvenirs?'

'Yea, little mementoes of his misdemeanours. I warned him about it. He said it was a harmless hobby, said anyway he hid the stuff away so it wasn't a problem.'

'And is it a problem?'

'It's only a problem if someone knows where he keeps the stuff and what it's about.'

'Hmm.'

'I don't like Spike,' said Malguzzi. He was probably one of the many that Malguzzi didn't like, 'like I say he's on my list. If you get back from Niagara safe and sound then I'll tell you were to look for his stuff and I'll tell you a coupla places he picked up some of them pieces too.'

'That would make him unhappy.'

'Yea, what a shame. He's going to have to say goodbye to his hair stylist,' said Malguzzi, 'for a long time.'

'I feel for him,' I said.

'Who, the hair stylist?' said Malguzzi.

'Yea, the hair stylist,' I said.

Malguzzi's laugh was no more attractive than it had been before. I'd made a deal with the devil, it had been so easy. But Spike had annoyed me and I wanted my watch back.

The second call came shortly after and was from Sky.

'We want to meet with a view to exchange tomorrow,' she said.

Wow! And I'd been worried this whole thing would take forever. Unfortunately this was a timescale I couldn't live with.

I told her and started to give some kind of garbled explanation, she cut me off.

'I don't care about your explanations,' she said, 'when can we meet?'

'I need some time,' I said.

'We don't have much time,' said Sky.

'Authentication is going to be a big thing for my client. I need to get the experts on board.'

'For us too,' said Sky, and then quietly, menacingly, 'you really had better not be leading us along, Mr Stewart. So when?'

I didn't know whether I was or not. It wasn't in my hands.

'Day after tomorrow,' I said, with my fingers crossed.

'OK,' said Sky, 'I'll text you the details.'

True to her word the text came through. I read the details. Phew, this was going to need some organizing and I was going to be off grid for most of the time. I needed help.

I called Logan and sent him a copy of the text.

'You must be joking,' he said.

'I'm deadly serious,' I said.

'They really want to meet out there?'

'They do.'

'It's crazy,' he said.

'It might be crazy but it's their choice,' I said.

'OK, what do you need?'

I told him.

'That's a hell of a lot to organize in one day,' he said, 'what if the people you want are not available?'

'I'm sure you have ways of making them available,' I said.

He didn't sound confident.

'I'm sure you're up to it,' I said, 'Oh and by the way Professor Kieran Lansbury will need a first class ticket from Manchester, UK.'

I ended the call before he could object.

Chapter 37

I checked online during the taxi ride to the airport; Teresa's flight was on time. As a distraction I talked to the taxi driver about life, the universe and everything, the way you do. He had two daughters who he was putting through college, a wife who didn't understand him and a brother who owed him money. We discussed the state of the world, it's just getting worse and worse apparently, and who the next Canadian Prime Minister should be. By the time we reached the airport we were talking about sport. I tipped him well and we shook hands.

Looking at my watch I had a little time so I used this to sign-in for the hire car, pick up the keys, pay for the damage waiver and locate the right bay in the parking lot. I put my bag in the trunk and made my way to the Arrivals Hall.

Pearson International Airport is a glass and steel architectural marvel, the Arrivals Hall is cavernous but doesn't seem like it because of the crowds of people constantly milling to and fro. I looked up at the electronic arrivals board and found Teresa's flight. It was due in just about now. I went to stand at the rail so that she would be able to see me as soon as she came through the sliding doors. First impressions are important and I'd made an effort although I wasn't wearing a tie. If I had been I'm sure she would have thought that something was badly wrong.

Her plane landed.

Passengers streamed out of baggage collection and customs clearance into the Arrivals Hall. I scrutinized every face and after a while I'd scrutinized so many that my visual perception was on overload and I wasn't sure whether I could have recognized my own mother any more.

But then she was there.

She was wheeling a trolley with two large suitcases on it. I thought about my small bag. It was quite a contrast.

I waved.

She saw me.

The mass of other people seemed to part as she walked towards me. I wondered whether I should attempt a polite kiss on the cheek or just offer to shake hands.

She waited until she was about 3 feet away and then threw herself at me in one giant hug. I'm not heavily in to public displays of emotion but in this case I thought I would let it pass and returned the favour.

'You're here,' she said.

'I said I would be,' I said.

'The internet's a wonderful thing,' she said, 'I thought you would keep a check on arrival times just in case the plane was delayed.'

'You're on time,' I said. I found I was smiling.

We kissed. Sod the rest of humanity, I thought, let them look if they wanted. I didn't care.

'It's good to see you,' I said.

'It's good to see you too, Mark,' she said using my real name, 'by the way where's your luggage?'

'I've put it in the trunk of the hire car,' I said, 'by the way I'm travelling light.'

She glanced down at her suitcases.

'I was in a hurry,' she said, 'I didn't know what to pack.'

So you brought everything, I thought.

I looked into her big brown eyes, her body was lightly touching mine. She dragged my head down to hers and planted another big fat kiss smack bang on my lips. For a moment I forgot all about the assignment, Malguzzi, Sky, Lejon, Logan… and was just happy to be alive.

30 minutes into our 90 minute drive to Niagara I found I was laughing. I can't remember what she said to spark me off, it probably wasn't anything that remarkable. But it was genuine laughter, no shamming, not out of politeness. It surprised me. I hadn't realised how long it had been since I had laughed, properly laughed. It's like not missing something until you've found it and then realising you've been hoping and hunting for it all along. I didn't want the feeling to stop but it was only a second or two that it lasted, genuine joy doesn't last that long. I could feel my eyes moistening. This was going too far. I glanced across and into Teresa's deep brown eyes, and cleared my throat.

'Thanks,' I said.

'For what?' she said, crinkling her nose.

She knew what.

The female of the species is more savvy than the male.

'For being here,' I said.

And I meant it, in every sense.

Chapter 38

When we reached the hotel a porter took our bags. At reception instead of checking in I asked for Beni Deschamps. The receptionist was surprised but picked up the internal phone, dialed, spoke for a few seconds, listened for a few more and then asked us to go and wait in the hotel lounge bar.

'Remember when I used to work in one of these?' said Teresa.

I did. It was actually how we met. It already seemed a lifetime ago.

Our reminiscences were interrupted by the arrival of Beni Deschamps. He was a man who you instantly felt would be at home as a circus ringmaster. A natural extrovert he flowed across the room, threw his arms around me and kissed me on both cheeks. To say this exuberant exhibition of bonhomie from a man I'd never met before took me by surprise would be an understatement. His smile was from ear to ear and his teeth shone white in contrast to his tanned complexion. The tan looked like it was out of a bottle.

'Ah, Michael, it is so wonderful to meet you, and who is this beautiful lady?'

I introduced Teresa. I'd already told her that on this assignment I was "Michael". She'd got used to my chameleon-like identity changes.

'Come let me show you around,' he said.

'Our bags, our room?' said Teresa.

'Do not worry it is all taken care of. Once I have shown you around a little I will take you to your room myself.'

He took me by the arm and led Teresa and I on a whistle-stop tour of the casino, past row upon row of chattering slot machines, the green felted roulette and blackjack tables, and on past the hallowed grounds of the Texas Hold'em alcoves. He was a fast walker and his talk was no slower.

'Any friend of Toni's is also a friend of mine,' he said, leaning close and talking to me confidentially.

After the whirlwind tour he took us to his office. It was at the back of the casino through a door marked "Staff only". For such a lavish hotel his office was a disappointment. It was on the pokey side and rather messy. The most notable pieces of furniture were his desk with chairs on either side and a large safe. I pointed at it.

'It is a casino,' he said shrugging, 'a lot of money changes hands and I need somewhere to keep it.'

A casino, that would mean more money coming in than going out, I thought.

'Would you like a drink?' he said nodding towards a whisky bottle. It was a Talisker. I was tempted.

'No thank you,' said Teresa, 'could we see our room now.'

As good as his word Beni Deschamps escorted us up to our room. Our bags were already there waiting for us. Mine looked pitifully small next to Teresa's luggage.

As I'd hoped the room was spacious with a kingsize bed, separate toilet and shower and a lounge area. The best feature of the room however was undoubtedly the wall-to-ceiling windows that gave a bird's eye view out and over Niagara, the Falls steaming powerfully in the distance.

'And we also have a room safe,' said Beni Deschamps, opening one of the wardrobes and pointing to it, 'so that any treasured belongings that you might have can be kept in here. You set the pass code yourself and no one can open it without that.'

It was true that no other guest could open it but I knew every hotel had a kind of master key. They had to because otherwise they couldn't retrieve the passports and other belongings of guests who had managed to forget their pass code.

I was quite relieved when Beni finally left us. He had an overpowering presence and the room seemed a lot bigger and quieter after he'd gone.

It's only polite to draw a veil over the next few hours. Suffice to say we ate in our room and I got the distinct impression that Teresa still liked me. The time flew past and I think it would be safe to say that our relationship had been rekindled and that whatever my daughter had said to Teresa to get her to give me another chance had definitely paid off.

Chapter 39

The next morning after a late breakfast Teresa and I drove over the Rainbow Bridge that spans the Niagara River and separates Canada from the USA. Teresa had not put any pressure on me about the status of our relationship and I was grateful for that. I felt my daughter's influence in the background. Maybe I was wrong but I wondered whether she had attempted to give Teresa an in depth tutorial on the vagaries of my personality. Whatever the case we were both in good spirits as Teresa drove over the bridge. With her American Passport and driver's license I was sure that passing through the Canadian/US border controls onto the US side would be a doddle. I would just act the annoying British tourist hanger-on in the passenger seat.

As it happens I was right and we sailed through without a hitch and drove down Prospect Street towards our target destination.

When we arrived Teresa pulled into the bank's visitor car park and I went inside alone.

Approaching one of the tellers I made my request and she asked me to wait.

Within two minutes a young clerk came out to meet me.

'How can I help?' he asked.

I repeated my request.

'Follow me,' he said.

Inside his office he pulled down a ledger from a large bookcase and ran his fingers through the pages and down the columns. In these years of digital-everything I was quite pleased to see such archaic practices.

'Box number?' he asked.

I told him.

'Letter of authority,' he said.

I handed it over.

He read it over twice and then filed it.

'Password,' he said.

'"Retribution",' I said.

He smiled.

'I assume you have the key?'

I nodded.

'Then please follow me.'

He led me down a series of grey concrete steps into a basement which housed the vaults. He stood in front of one of the heavy armoured doors where he put in the combination and then took out an impressively heavy key to open it. Once the key had released the lock he pulled hard to swing the door open on its greased hinges. We went inside.

As I followed him in the lights came on automatically and I couldn't help noticing the ceiling-mounted security cameras.

Security boxes of various sizes were arrayed from floor to ceiling on the three facing walls; largest at the bottom, reducing in depth as they climbed upwards. In the centre of the room was a metal table. On the table was a metal hooded area open to only one side. Everything was polished and free from dust, grime or fingerprints.

The bank clerk worked his way around looking at the numbers until he came to the appointed box. It had two keyholes and a rotary combination lock. He took a key from his pocket, placed it in the left hand keyhole and rotated it through 90 degrees. Then he stood back.

'Thank you,' I said and moving forwards I put a second key in the right hand keyhole and turned it. Then I rotated the six numbered dials to the combination Toni Malguzzi had given me and pulled on the handle on the front of the safety deposit box hoping that this would not be one of Toni Malguzzi's little jokes.

The box slid smoothly out. I tried not to let my relief show. I then withdrew the safety deposit box from its cavity completely, carried it to the table and placed it within the hood.

'I'll leave you to it,' said the clerk, 'when you're finished please replace the box and press the red button here on the wall by the door.'

'OK,' I said, 'what about the cameras. I don't want to be watched.'

'We need to leave the cameras active but they cannot see within the hood,' he said, 'you can inspect the contents with privacy and we can maintain our vigilance on behalf of all of our customers.' He'd started to speak like an advertising leaflet. This was a bank built on its reputation and their reputation was reliant on the security and privacy they offered to their customers.

'Should you ever require greater security,' he said, 'we do also offer facilities that use biometrics, retina recognition, finger print recognition, voice recognition, and/or facial recognition.'

The deluxe version of security no doubt, I thought.

Sales pitch over he withdrew and left me alone.

I waited a couple of minutes and then lifted the metal flap that covered the top of the security box. I looked at the contents, there were only two.

One was a brown paper envelope stuffed with C$100 bills. I counted them quickly and came to C$50,000. I transferred the envelope into my jacket pocket. It made a bulge.

The second item in the safety deposit box was a small square red leather box, about 4 cm a side and 1cm thick. I lifted this out and opened it. Lying in a formed circular depression in the centre was a transparent plastic capsule and within this lay a single gold coin, the deal-maker. I re-closed the lid of the box and for a moment held it in the palm of my hand. It seemed too small to be the cause of so much trouble. I put it into my trouser pocket.

'How did it go?' asked Teresa as I got back into the car.

'Fine,' I said.

Teresa started the engine.

'Hold on just a minute,' I said.

I got out of the car and went around to the back and opened the trunk. I took the envelope full of Canadian dollars out of my jacket and thought about where to hide it. The spare wheel compartment was too obvious. I closed the trunk.

'OK,' I said.

When Teresa wasn't looking I slipped the little red leather box down the back of my passenger seat.

Now it was time to act the tourist.

There is little doubt that the Canadian side is the best side from which to view the Falls but that does not mean that the American side has nothing to offer. On the contrary it is the place where you can get immersed in the American Falls whilst remaining on solid ground.

Teresa drove into the Niagara Falls State Park where we left the car on Goat Island and took off on foot. She had dressed casually for the day in beige slacks, a white blouse and sensible shoes. I was overdressed in my jacket, seamed trousers and blue shirt. It was a warm day, the sky was blue, the clouds wispy and fleeting so I threw my jacket into the trunk of the car before we set off.

Teresa had brought a camera, a fairly lightweight Canon EOS 650D, and we spent an hour or so walking around paved pathways, moving between the observation points of the river rapids and the rim of the American Falls and Bridal Veil Falls. She took about a million photos and I marvelled at just how much one SD card could hold. One black squirrel happened across our path and was the subject of a photo call frenzy and is now, Teresa tells me, an internet sensation.

We then braved "The Cave of the Winds" taking an elevator 175 feet down into the Niagara Gorge. Clad in the bright yellow ponchos and footwear provided, we wound our way over a series of wooden walkways to the so-called "Hurricane Deck". Standing next to the railing you are conscious of being very close to the powerful waters of the Bridal Veil Falls. On the day we were there it was like standing in the middle of a storm, the rushing waters looming above us and soaking us in their spray. Our ponchos were little protection and our hoods were blown back. We got properly wet.

The boardwalks were slippery so we held on to each other. It was no good trying to talk, the water was too loud. Teresa pointed. A rainbow danced in the watery mist thrown up from the thundering waters.

When we got back in the car we dripped all over the seats. Neither of us had thought of bringing spare clothes. This was especially galling for Teresa as she thought of just how much clothing she had spread throughout our hotel room.

We were still soggy when we passed back across the border. The border guard took one look at us and said,

'Been raining has it?' then he looked up into the clear blue sky and scratched his head before returning our papers to us.

We both smiled because if an official makes a joke its best to humour them and because we knew we must look like the most amateurish of tourists even though he must have seen more than a few of them in his time.

Chapter 40

Back at the hotel we took off our wet things and put them in for laundering. When Teresa was showering I took the envelope of money out of her bag, it had been in the trunk of the car and my idea had been to hide it in plain sight. Although it had worked it hadn't been free of risk and I was pleased I hadn't told Teresa, I wouldn't have wanted her to worry.

I'd also recovered the little red leather box from the passenger seat and I took both to the room safe and generated a code "4039". I then pulled a hair out of my head, wetted it, and laid it across the join of the safe door. I did the same with a bedside table drawer and a wardrobe.

Once we were re-cleaned, re-dried and re-dressed we took a quick lunch in the hotel bar and headed out to explore the Falls from the Canadian side.

I wanted Teresa to get another experience of the Falls. Not just wet again but this time from the water. As the queue for the "Voyage to the Falls" boat tour slowly wound its way towards the kiosk I told Teresa of some of the crazy daredevil stunts that had been attempted over the years. I told her about Charles Blondin who, wearing pink tights and a yellow tunic, was the first to walk across the Falls on a tightrope, 1100 feet long and two inches in diameter, a feat he performed 160 feet up in the air, witnessed by over 5,000 spectators. I went on to tell her about how he repeated this experience many times over the course of a year or so with variations like doing it blindfolded, or with his manager on his back, or sitting down midway to cook an omelet, or pushing a wheelbarrow across while dressed as an ape. Then there was Annie Edson Taylor, a 63-year-old schoolteacher, who in October 1901 was the first person to take the plunge down the Falls in a barrel and survive. But these feats are dangerous and I told Teresa that of the 15 people who had tried their hand at going over the Falls by various means between 1901 to 1995, 5 had died in the attempt. In conclusion I explained to her that trying to go over the Falls on either the American or the Canadian side is now illegal and if you were to try it and survive then your prize would be to face criminal charges and hefty fines. I'd done my homework. Teresa looked fascinated as I passed on the benefits of my learning. Or at least that's what I interpreted her look to mean. What she actually said was,

'Are we ever going to get on this boat?'

Just think how much more frustrated she'd have been without my historical commentary.

Finally though we got to and past the ticket kiosk and were issued with the same type of transparent plastic poncho that we had had on the American side except that those had been yellow and these were red. I wasn't sure which colour suited me best.

I asked Teresa.

'Neither,' she said.

We walked obediently in single file onto the boat, listened to the safety announcement about holding on, the roughness of the water, the slipperiness underfoot, the need to hang on to your cameras and other personal belongings and the declaration that the boat company would accept no responsibility for any injuries or losses sustained.

Thus reassured we cast off and sailed past the American and Bridal Veil Falls, seeing them from below this time.

However the best was yet to come.

As we approached the Horseshoe Falls the boat started to rock about from side to side and the noise rose to a shuddering roar. The inherent power of the water that raged around us was amazing and we were covered in spray and surrounded by rainbows.

Never mind Ms Taylor, I had felt over a barrel these last few days so, I reckoned, there was no better place for me to take the plunge than here.

The deck was slippery with water.

What I was about to do felt as dangerous to me as going over the Falls in a barrel. I got down on one knee. The spray was everywhere, the noise of the Falls was thunderous.

'Teresa,' I yelled, 'Will you...'

Teresa was too engrossed in the noise and the spray, the way the boat was being thrown around by the turbulence of the waters, the joy of the moment. I don't think she heard me. I got up again and tugged at her poncho. She didn't feel it. I tugged a bit harder. Her head turned.

'Isn't this marvellous,' she shouted.

'Yes,' I yelled.

I went down on one knee.

Teresa had a worried look.

'Are you alright?' she shouted, removing one hand from the ship's rail and bending down to help me up.

With her head closer to mine I had a better chance of being heard.

'Teresa will you marry me,' I blurted out at full volume.

In her surprise she let go of the rail as another wave hit us and was propelled into my arms. Locked together I struggled to get the ring out of my pocket.

I finally succeeded and looked into the soaking wet face that was so close to mine. It was wet I thought with more than just the steaming waters of Niagara Falls.

She put her mouth to my ear and whispered,

'Yes.'

I slipped the ring onto her finger before I dropped it. Teresa lifted her hand and looked at the ring. It was covered in spray, little rainbows dancing about in the refracted light.

'It's beautiful,' she said.

'I'm glad you like it,' I said making a mental note never to mention its previous incarnation. The jeweller had done a great job of converting a bracelet into a ring.

The rest is a blur...

The boat trip only lasted about 20 minutes but it had changed the course of our lives forever. That probably sounds a bit over dramatic but, hey, that's how it felt at the time.

Chapter 41

When we got back to our room Teresa said she needed another shower. I looked at the drawer and saw that it was undisturbed, the hair was still in place. I opened it and could see that the envelope full of money was still there. The cupboard was also undisturbed but I didn't need to look inside because there was nothing there. As soon as I looked at the safe however I could see that it had been tampered with, the hair had gone. I opened it up and saw that the box had gone. There was only one person I could think of who could have been both interested in what we'd brought back and had the means to act so quickly. I told Teresa I was just popping out for a minute,

'Don't be long,' she called from the bathroom.

I entered Beni Deschamp's office without knocking. The place was in disarray. A suitcase was on the floor. The safe was open. Beni was sitting at his desk with his head in his hands. The little red leather box was alongside him. Open. Empty. I put my hand into my left hand outside jacket pocket. My fingers found and traced the circular plastic of the coin's protective outer case. Who would be stupid enough to keep such a valuable coin in his pocket instead of using the security of the room safe. I guess that would be me.

'Beni,' I said, 'Beni, Beni, Beni.'

He looked up. He had tears in his eyes.

It would have been difficult not to feel sorry for him if it were not for the fact that his actions, had they been successful, could have got me killed.

'I'm sorry,' he said, 'it's just that...'

It's just that it had been too tempting, I thought, you saw an opportunity, you took me for a mug.

'I've been thinking of moving on,' he said, 'I don't want to stay in this job forever...'

His explanation was pathetic.

'Toni is going to be so upset,' I said.

He looked up at me, his big blue eyes like a puppy dog's, pleading.

'Is there anything...' he wailed, 'I wouldn't want Toni to think...' he trailed off and just shrugged his shoulders.

'...that you were trying to rob him?' I said.

Beni's eyes opened wide and he put his finger to his lips.

'Ssh, ssh,' he said trying to force a smile and failing, 'do not joke. The walls, the floors, the ceilings, they all have eyes, they all have ears.'

'Hmmm,' I said.

'I wonder,' said Beni Deschamps, 'I wonder if there is anything...?' He shrugged again.

'Well,' I said, 'it would be nice if our stay here was completely complimentary.'

'But of course, but of course,' he said, 'for any friend of Toni's it is nothing but a pleasure. If you had not asked I would have offered.'

'And,' I said.

'And?' echoed Beni.

'We may play in your casino tonight. Blackjack.'

'Ah, excellent choice,' said Beni, 'I wish you luck.'

He smiled, feeling for solid ground.

I removed it.

'Yes,' I said, 'luck, it can be such a fickle mistress. I wonder how many people leave your casino as winners?'

The shrug returned.

'I would like to,' I said, 'what a thing to tell Toni. I'm sure he would be pleased.'

I'd dropped the penny in the slot.

He pulled the lever.

'It is such a lottery,' he said.

The wheels were spinning.

'I wonder how many people win say, C$50,000?' I said.

'Not many,' he said, 'but it's possible...'

The wheels were slowing.

'Or C$100,000?' I said.

He gulped.

The wheels had stopped.

'OK,' he said.

Jackpot.

Before I went back to the room I made a couple of calls, the first was to Toni Malguzzi.

'I've got it,' I said without preamble.

'Good,' he said, 'don't lose it.'

I nearly had and I almost told him but I didn't. No need to worry him.

'How is Beni?' he said, 'is he looking after you?'

From now on I had the feeling he was going to be looking after me very well indeed.

'He's fine,' I said, 'he sends you his regards.'

'Let me know if he misbehaves,' said Toni Malguzzi.

'It's OK,' I said, 'everything's fine. I'm going to call Sky now. Confirm that we're ready to go.'

I could hear him grinding his teeth.

'I hope she's well,' he said, meaning the exact opposite.

When I called Sky she picked up immediately.

'I just wanted to confirm we're ready to go,' I said.

'And we still are,' she said sarcastically.

'Then I'll see you tomorrow,' I said.

'Yes, Michael, let's get this done.'

Click.

I decided not to call anyone else. I'd left people to make the arrangements and I was going to trust them to do it. If they were making a mess of it then there wasn't much I could do from here anyway. Keeping my fingers crossed seemed like as good an interim strategy as any. Besides I had a night out with Teresa to look forward to.

Chapter 42

When I got back to the room Teresa was on the phone. It was a video call and she was talking to my daughter!

'He's back,' said Teresa.

'Congratulations dad,' yelled my daughter, 'nice move to propose on an unstable boat and in the face of such deafening waters.'

I decided to take that comment at face value although you can never tell with my daughter.

I could hear some noises in the background.

'Teresa's been talking to me about bamboo nappies,' she said, 'she saw the mess I got into last time she visited.'

Last time she visited! This relationship had grown much closer than I'd imagined.

'Oh,' I said.

'I just googled it,' said Teresa, 'Amelia is such a cutie but apparently some babies pee more than others and adding boosters can sometimes help.'

Teresa thought my granddaughter was a cutie! I needed to get my ass into gear. I was missing too much.

'Yea,' said my daughter, 'I'll give it a go, it's worth a try, just like us to have a daughter that's full of p...'

I tuned out. How did I get involved in a discussion about my granddaughter's bladder movements. Was being able to produce huge quantities to be applauded or was it a symptom of something more serious?

'What do you think?' asked Teresa looking at me.

What did I think of what? I'd stopped listening.

'There's no point asking him,' said my daughter, 'he'll have no idea when a baby's smile is through face recognition instead of just wind.'

She was right there.

'So anyway,' she said, 'I've been thinking, we need to be making plans.'

'We?' I said.

'Yes, of course,' said my daughter, 'when are you planning to get married, how long have we got?'

This was all a bit presumptuous, I thought.

'We haven't decided,' I said and looked to Teresa for support.

She didn't say anything which wasn't too helpful under the circumstances. I quickly thought through my options. Before I could get my thoughts into any order however my daughter said,

'When is your favourite time of year?'

'I like the start of autumn,' I said, 'when the leaves are starting to change colour but it hasn't got too cold yet.'

Teresa bit her lip. Had I said the wrong thing?

'That doesn't give us long, just two or three months,' she said, 'but best to strike while the iron's hot I suppose.'

I hadn't meant this autumn!

But it was too late, the ladies had already sidelined me and were talking about making lists and setting budgets. I had this vision of do-it-yourself wedding guides, online searches for venues, menus and dresses appearing out of nowhere. All I thought I'd done was to propose marriage and been thankful that miraculously Teresa had said 'yes'.

I looked at Teresa, listened to my daughter and once the initial shock had worn off the idea of an early ceremony started to appeal to me. After all why wait? I would have probably have got around to thinking about this sometime anyway.

'Good decision dad,' I heard my daughter say.

'Hmm,' I said.

Had it really been my decision?

After the call Teresa went off to get changed. I switched my phone off and put it into the room safe creating a new combination. I didn't want our time to be interrupted. The coin I decided to keep with me. Other than a couple of hundred dollars I took just in case I needed it I left Malguzzi's envelope of Canadian dollars in the drawer untouched. Even though we live in the age of the credit card and electronic money I still feel better if I have a bit of cash to fall back on. I thought about how Teresa had shown off her engagement ring to my daughter; a Canadian solitaire diamond that had once adorned a friendship bracelet. It was a nice stone and the conversion had cost me a fortune. I liked the idea of love and friendship wrapped up together although I wasn't ever going to tell Teresa just in case she took it the wrong way.

I'd just finished sprucing myself up when Teresa came out of the bedroom. An old friend of mine once told me 'If you can't say anything positive don't say anything at all'.

Teresa smiled, threw her arms wide and did a twirl.

'What do you think?' she said.

I obeyed the rule. I tried to hold a neutral expression and said nothing.

Her smile faded.

'You don't like it?'

'I didn't say that,' l said sheepishly, avoiding eye contact.

'I thought you'd love it,' she said, starting to pout.

'Well it's just that it's a little...,' I tried to stop myself. I could see the hole I was about to dig and I didn't want to fall into it.

'It's a little what?'

She wasn't going to give it up.

'Go on, it's a little what?'

'Well,' l said apologetically, 'it's just that it's a little...'

'Yeeees....'

I struggled for the right word. 'Tarty,' I said at last, pretty sure I'd chosen the wrong thing to say.

'Tarty!' she repeated

'Weeeell, yes .... tarty.'

She turned her back to me. I could see her shoulders starting to shake. This wasn't going well.

She broke the silence with a noise. Oh God, I'd made her cry. What was I thinking.

She turned towards me, there were tears in her eyes… tears of laughter.

'You're an idiot.' she said.

Who was I to disagree.

'This is a night dress, it's for later.'

I looked again.

'Wow!' I said, trying not to drool, 'Wow.'

In this new context her outfit was exceptional and I told her so.

'That's better,' she said and kissed me on the forehead, 'good boy.'

I reached out my arms.

'Now, now,' she said, 'I have to get ready to go out.'

Do you have to? I thought

Her smile was broad. She twirled again.

'I thought you didn't like me like this,' she said.

'That was when I thought others were going to see you… now I know it's meant for me I'm overjoyed.'

I could see by her face I'd said the right thing at last.

We went to a neighbouring hotel for dinner. I'd noticed that it had a Blues Bar and that tonight "Bad Dog and his Blues Band" were playing. I told Teresa and she agreed it was worth a shot. We ate in the restaurant first. We were both ravenous so we kept to the simple but copious options. I had steak with pepper sauce, Teresa had chicken with a creamy mushroom sauce, we both took fries and onion rings.

I had a glass of red wine, Teresa had white. Over the meal I said I was sorry it had taken me so long to propose. We talked about our pasts and started to dream some hopes for the future.

'I thought we'd honeymoon in Scotland.' I said.

'Where it's cold and wet? What a romantic,' said Teresa.

'God's own country, the sights, the smells, the whisky...'

'The midges, the strange accents, the bagpipes...'

'The neeps, the tatties, the haggis...'

'Yea, I'm sure I'll love it,' she said, 'and you'll have to spend some time in Costa Rica. There's a lot of people there I want you to meet.'

'You mean where it's warm, with sun kissed beaches… and leafcutter ants,' I said.

'And spiders, and snakes, and mosquitoes,' she said.

'Ah, mosquitoes,' I said, 'it'll be just like home.'

The Blues bar was full. Most people were standing and we joined in the crush at the bar.

'This takes me back,' said Teresa, 'I had some good nights when I was serving at the hotel bars.'

I wasn't sure I wanted to know.

Around us men and women were wearing Bad Dog t-shirts; white lettering on black that read "Let me in the Dog House", "Bad Dog Sings The Blues", "Bad Dogs Growl". They were obviously up for a good night. We got a bottle of Molson Canadian lager beer each and found a space where we could see the stage.

'You sure know how to treat a woman,' said Teresa pressing closer to me to avoid being trampled.

The atmosphere was steamy and Bad Dog arrived fashionably late.

He was a big guy with lots of hair. The band struck up a beat that was so bass you could feel it through your feet. Bad Dog zig-zagged lazily between the tables, high fiving fans, saying 'Hi' to regulars, in no rush, his movements exuding cool.

He wore a jacket perched only on his shoulders and when he got to the stage he turned around to face the audience and shrugged it off. There was a cheer. One of the band members caught it, folded it carefully lengthwise and laid it over the back of a wooden chair that was placed, presumably for that purpose, next to the drums.

The band picked up the pace. Bad Dog took hold of the microphone,

'Hi folks,' he growled, 'Bad Dog's here to sing ya'all some blues.'

There was more cheering and shouts of 'Sing it Dog', 'Yea man, you the Dog'. I wasn't convinced we would hear anything even if he did start singing.

Bad Dog raised his hands.

'Waal ladies and gents, aah jus' wanna say it's great fer me an' my band to be back here in li'le ol Ni-ag-ra,' whooping from the bar, 'an' we hope ya'all have a gud time.'

With that the band stopped. The whooping quietened. Bad Dog stamped his foot. The band struck up again and Bad Dog started growling his version of "Hound Dog" into the microphone. It was nothing like the brilliant version sung by Big Mama Thornton or the better known version by Elvis Presley but it was his own take; raw, rough and "tear your heart out" blues. I loved it. The crowd loved it. I looked at Teresa. Seemed like she was loving it too.

The next hour was magical. Bad Dog growled and yelped, barked and howled his way through classics like "The Thrill is Gone", "The House of the Rising Sun", "I Got My Mojo Working" and many more. He then introduced one of his own songs it was called "Bad Dog Blues"

I'm a Bad Dog baby,
that is just my way
I'm a Bad Dog baby,
an' that's how I'm gonna stay
You can't teach me no tricks
I just need ma guitar licks
Yea I'm a Bad Dog baby,
if I was you I'd run away

You don't want no Bad Dog baby,
best be on your way
You don't want no Bad Dog baby,
I ain't asking you to stay
I need a woman who understands me
a woman who'd let me be
(Oh yea, baby, I need someone real special)

Cos I'm a Bad Dog baby,
if I was you I'd run away

Yea that's what I'd do
if I was you
I'd run away
an' never come back, ya hear me
cos I'm a Bad Dog
yea, a Bad Dog baby
jus' a Bad Dog
an' I ain't ever
no I ain't ever
I ain't ever
gonna change my ways

I'm just a Bad Dog
Baby.

It went down a storm. Somebody even threw a pair of knickers onto the stage. Bad Dog picked them up, used them to wipe the sweat from his brow and then threw them back. Here was a man who knew his audience.

I tapped Teresa on the shoulder,

'I know this is great but do you want to skip out before the end so we don't get trampled in the rush?'

She pouted but nodded her head. We listened to one more, it was Bad Dog's version of Mighty Mo Rodger's "Picasso Blue" a nice slow one for us to depart to and a title that was almost too apposite. I didn't want to think about my assignment until tomorrow so I tried to shut out the thoughts that it begat.

The band had a box out front with a slot in the top and a big white label that said "TIPS". I pushed a C$100 note into it.

'And now?' said Teresa.

'How about the casino?' I said, 'we might catch up with Beni there and anyway I'm feeling lucky tonight.'

'Sounds good to me,' said Teresa, 'but let's set a limit. I don't want to lose too much.'

I had a feeling we weren't going to lose at all but I just said,

'OK let's say C$4,000.'

'That's a lot,' she said.

'It's OK,' I said thinking of Toni Malguzzi's envelope stuffed with C$50,000, 'I'm on expenses. It doesn't happen very often, in fact this is the first time, so we may as well make the most of it. It's unlikely to ever happen again.'

'I still think it's too much,' she said, 'just think what we could do with that money. We have so many things to plan for. We'll set our limit at C$100.'

I couldn't fault her logic and I couldn't tell her about her imminent run of luck. This was going to be more difficult than I'd thought. I was proud of her frugality though, it made my Scottish heart soar.

We got back to the hotel around midnight. Beni Deschamps spotted us as soon as we entered and came bounding over. He'd obviously been looking out for us.

'Buenas noches, good evening,' he said, 'Oh Teresa you look so beautiful tonight, what a fabulous dress.'

I thought this was a bit tacky and over-the-top but Teresa didn't seem to mind, in fact she seemed to enjoy it.

'Tonight it is your last night here?' he said, looking at me.

'It is,' I said.

'Oh but what a shame,' he said, although his look was one of relief.

'We thought we would just risk a little in your casino,' I said, 'before turning in for the night.'

'Ah si, but of course, what would you like to play?'

'I thought Teresa could try her hand at Blackjack,' I said.

'Pefecta, a good choice, a game that appears so easy but has so many twists and turns. As your luck would have it we have just opened a new table. Perhaps I can show you the way.'

Beni Deschamps led us into the bowels of his casino. If I hadn't known the truth I would have thought him carefree and full of good cheer. When we reached the table there was a dealer but no other players.

'Here we are,' he said pulling out the central player's seat for Teresa.

'And as a little thank you the casino will advance you C\$1,000 to do with as you will.'

Teresa was shocked. I was relieved.

'Really?' she said, 'are you sure?'

'Of course, of course,' said Beni, handing Teresa some chips, 'now I will leave you alone, enjoy, have fun.'

I stood behind Teresa. Beni had withdrawn but was still keeping an eye on things. I could see that some of the casino staff had been tasked to ensure that there would be no other players joining us at the table, deflecting them away to other tables with whatever kind of excuses were necessary.

Blackjack really is a simple game. You place a bet based on how confident you're feeling at beating the dealer's hand and then you get dealt 2 cards which you flip over so everyone can see them. The dealer's two cards are also on view. The object of the game is to get closer to a total of 21 without going over than the dealer does. If you do go over then you're "bust" and you lose the money you've bet. If you have two low cards, a 3 and a 5 say, then you need more so you tap the table, this is called a "hit", and the dealer gives you another card face up. If you want another card then you "hit" again. When you're happy with what you've got then you wave your hand over your cards to "stand". There are other complicating factors but these are the essentials; get closer to 21 than the dealer and win twice what you bet, draw with the dealer and get your money back, go over 21 or less close to 21 than the dealer and you lose the money you bet. The only other thing to mention is that all cards count at their face value, a 3 of diamonds counts 3, an 8 of spades counts 8 etcetera, and all picture cards, Jack, Queen and King, count 10 and an ace counts 11. That's it. Simple. It's winning that's the problem.

'How much should I bet?' asked Teresa.

'Go for broke,' I said, 'it's free money.'

'This could be the shortest game ever,' said Teresa confirming her bet.

The dealer dealt Teresa two cards, an ace and a Queen.

'21!' she said.

'That also increases your effective bet from C$1,000 to C$1,500,' I said, 'good start.'

The dealer had a 10 and a 5 and then dealt himself a 7; so 22 and bust. Teresa clapped her hands and the dealer pushed another C$3,000 worth of chips her way.

'Let's stop now,' she said, 'that's enough for me.'

Normally I would have agreed, but not tonight.

'Go again,' I said, 'put it all in.'

Teresa was shocked. I bent down and whispered in her ear, 'Go ahead, trust me.'

In went the C$4,000 and Teresa was dealt two 10's.

'Split them,' I said.

'What?'

'It's a special rule. If you get two cards of the same value then you can split them and play each as a separate hand,' I said.

'You must now place the same bet on each hand,' said the dealer.

'But I have no more…' started Teresa.

I waved Beni over and explained the situation.

'It is OK,' he said to the dealer, 'please continue. Assume there is C$4,000 bet on each hand. I am sure my friends are good for it.'

Teresa was visibly shaking.

On the first hand of 10 the dealer put a 9.

'I'll stand,' said Teresa.

On the second hand of 10 the dealer put a 4.

Teresa looked at me. I shrugged.

'Hit me again,' said Teresa.

A 7 flopped on top of the 10 and 4; 21!

The dealer had an ace and a 4 which was 15. He dealt himself a 3. He tutted, he had no choice but to go again. The next card was a 5. His total was 23. He was bust.

Chips to the value of C$16,000 were pushed towards Teresa. She now had C$20,000.

On the next hand she was dealt a 7 and a 4.

'Now is the time to double down,' I said.

'What's that?' said Teresa.

'You double your bet and agree to stand after a third card is dealt to you, whatever it is.'

Beni Deschamps had stuck around.

'If you wish to do that,' he said, 'I will advance you the second C$20,000 but that must be repaid.'

'Let's not,' said Teresa, 'we've won enough.'

Beni Deschamps looked hopeful.

'Just one more,' I said.

His face fell, 'Deal,' he said to the dealer.

It was a King. Teresa had 21.

The dealer's cards were a Queen and a 2; 12. He dealt himself the next card, it was a King; 22 and bust.

Unemotionally he counted out the chips and pushed C$80,000's worth over to Teresa.

'With the C$20,000 you must give back to the casino,' said Beni Deschamps, 'that takes your total winnings up to C$100,000.'

'That's enough,' I said.

'Thank god,' said Teresa.

'Thank god,' whispered Beni Deschamps.

The three of us took the winnings to the teller.

'Would you like cheque or cash?' he asked.

'Neither,' I said, 'I'd like the funds electronically transferred immediately to this account. Please transfer it in US dollars we'll take the hit on the exchange rate.'

I read out the details.

'But that's my account,' said Teresa.

'Well they're your winnings,' I said.

It took a few minutes. Teresa used her phone to confirm that the funds had been received.

'Thank you,' I said.

'You leave in the morning?' said Beni, he looked drained, even his tan had paled.

'Yes,' I said.

'Then I do not think I will see you again,' he said.

'No, I don't think you will,' I said.

He nodded.

'It was nice to meet you, Teresa,' he said, 'have a good night and enjoy the money.'

'What a nice man,' said Teresa as we walked to the elevators, 'and what an extraordinary evening. I've never won anything like that before, and so quickly.'

'It's easier to win when that's what everyone wants,' I said.

She looked at me quizzically as the elevator doors opened and we made our way back up to our room.

I just hoped that come tomorrow there'd be another situation where everybody was able to win.

Once back into our room Teresa changed into her night dress. All thoughts of cash and coins and paintings evaporated. Let tomorrow bring what tomorrow would bring.

Chapter 43

The next morning we breakfasted lavishly from the hotel buffet and then packed our bags, which was an easier job for me than it was for Teresa. I put all the money back into Malguzzi's envelope. He'd get his full C$50,000. I didn't want any of it. The all-important little red box I kept on me at all times. If anyone was going to get it from me then they would have to physically take it.

The drive back to the airport went too quickly. On the way Teresa used my phone to text my daughter a question. Something we'd both agreed upon. As I was pulling into the airport drop-off zone the phone pinged.

Teresa read the message.

'She's agreed,' she said, clearly delighted.

'That's good,' I said.

I helped her with her bags, we kissed and then I watched as she disappeared into the depths of the Departures Area. We'd see each other soon. But soon didn't seem soon enough.

I then took the hire car back and went through the Arrivals Hall to the taxi rank. It was time to get back on the grid.

On my way back to Toronto I called Logan and organised to meet with him and Officer Jones in my hotel room in an hour. I then called Samantha and gave her as good an update as I could with an eavesdropping taxi driver sitting next to me.

'OK, good, give me more details when you can,' she paused, 'I understand AB is in Canada.'

'I know,' I said, 'I've seen him.'

'I see,' she said, not seeing at all.

I spent the rest of the journey discussing the chances of Manchester United ever winning the Premiership again with my talkative taxi driver. He was surprisingly knowledgeable about English football but he wasn't overly optimistic.

The location Sky had chosen, presumably aided and abetted by her father, was an island in the middle of the St Lawrence River within the "1000 Islands" region, a location not far from where her father was incarcerated. The island in question had only one dwelling on it but two jetties, one on the upstream side, one on the downstream. It was a good choice of location with plenty of space for two different groups, a high degree of privacy and a perimeter that was easy to control.

'Welcome back,' said Officer Jones, when I'd got back to my hotel room in Toronto 'we've missed you.'

'Yea,' said Logan, 'Did everything go according to plan?'

'If you mean did I pick up the item that Toni Malguzzi is offering to trade for the Picasso then the answer is yes,' I said.

'Good,' said Logan.

'So are we ready to go?' asked Officer Jones.

'Yes,' I said, 'I've already told Sky Vandla we're on for this evening. Did you make all the arrangements I asked for?'

'I took the lead on that,' said Officer Jones, 'I've got the two experts you asked for; Meredith-Taylor from the AGO and Professor Kieran Lansbury from Manchester, England. He flew over late yesterday and is staying at this hotel.'

'Very good,' I said.

'I've booked a meeting room on the 19th floor for you to use for your briefings. I've also hired you a car, an SUV in fact, to get you to Kingston and I've then got a boat organised to ferry you to the island and back.'

Officer Jones stopped and looked at me.

I smiled.

Officer Jones glowed. Logan sighed.

'I've written all this down and included copies of all the bookings and other information you might need,' she said, 'just so you have it to hand.'

'Thank you,' I said, 'your thoroughness reminds me of somebody I know called Samantha.'

'Is that a good thing?'

'It's a very good thing,' I said, 'Samantha is one of the most organised and professional people I've ever known, although if you ever meet her please don't tell her I said that.'

'OK, OK,' said Logan, 'enough with the appreciation society. Is there anything else you need from us?'

'No, I don't think so,' I said.

'OK then we'll see you again when you're out the other side.'

It was a good idea for Officers Jones and Logan to now stand back. It mitigated the risk of any overzealous observer perceiving a connection between me and the Canadian police. That wouldn't be good at this late stage, or any stage for that matter.

'You mean after the deal is complete?' I said.

'Or not,' said Logan.

He's a glass half empty kind of guy is Logan.

I asked Officer Jones to get my team assembled and in the meantime exchanged my pay-as-you-go phone for my more familiar one and then had a shower and a change of clothes just to freshen up. By the time I'd finished Officer Jones had texted that the team were waiting for me.

I took the elevator to the 19th floor and the first face I saw on entering the meeting room was Meredith-Taylor's. He had arrived from the AGO and stood out because he looked a little flushed. It was near the end of the day and presumably there was a brandy bottle somewhere that was short of a substantial portion of its contents.

'I will do my best,' he said, 'I believe I can reliably identify the hand of the master.'

Sitting next to him was Professor Kieran Lansbury. Although he had freshly flown in from Manchester he looked none the worse for it. I knew him from our service days, he had the constitution of a buffalo and was hardly touched by the vagaries of jet lag. It was a talent I'd always envied. He'd reacted immediately to my call as I knew he would.

'I've brought the handheld equipment with me,' he said, 'no point taking any chances. Divil of a job getting it through security. Don't think I could have done it without help.'

'Help?'

'It was my pleasure.'

The voice came from behind me. I knew who it was before I turned around.

'Sir?' I said.

AB smiled.

'I'm on leave,' he said, 'and I thought I'd just pop by to see how things were going.'

I had never known AB to be this personally interested in any one specific assignment. He prided himself on his objectivity and to maintain that he normally kept his distance.

'You're welcome of course,' I said, a little off balance.

'That's kind of you,' he said, 'I'm going to join your little expeditionary team if that's alright with you. I hope it won't be an inconvenience. I'll put on a lab coat and simply observe if you like.'

'Of course, sir.'

'And you'd better stop calling me sir, it's a bit of a giveaway.'

'Er, what should I call you, sir?'

AB thought for a moment.

'Call me Doctor or Alexander,' he said, 'it's your choice.'

'Doctor it is then,' I said, Alexander was far too familiar for the superior-subordinate relationship that existed between us.

So there we were, a team of only four. All ready to go.

Chapter 44

The car that Officer Jones had booked for us, a Volvo XC90 SUV, had plenty of room for passengers and equipment. We loaded up and set off for Kingston.

I drove, AB sat alongside me in the passenger seat. The conversation en route was muted and after about an hour AB said,

'I know I am amongst professionals and that you will do your analytics with thoroughness and precision. What I must insist on however is that you do not share your findings with anyone outside of this group. Indeed I want you to report them to me first,' he glanced across at me, 'Michael here will be with me but let me be clear, nobody is to know of your findings, interpretations or views until I know what they are and have considered their relevance. Do not gossip,' he looked directly at Meredith-Taylor when he said this and I could see in the rear view mirror that my ebullient friend had shrunk down in his seat as a result, 'do not do anything other than you've been asked to do. Do I make myself clear? If not please speak now. I want no possible errant behaviour once we're out on the island.'

There were only nods, no questions. From that point onwards the conversation was even more muted and it wasn't long before I heard two sets of gentle snoring, one the result of an excessive intake of brandy, the other to jet lag.

I switched on the car radio and tuned into a Blues channel.

We arrived in Kingston harbour around 6pm.

Meredith-Taylor and Kieran Lansbury had both woken up about 30 minutes earlier. They appeared refreshed and had spent the time getting to know each other. From the unforced laughter it seemed to be going well.

A boat was waiting for us. The captain was a woman called Olivia Waters, an appropriate name owned by a lady who exuded self-confidence. She welcomed us aboard.

The sky was still a flawless blue with a crisp feel to the air. It was ideal weather to make a deal. The boat took us up the centre of the river flirting with the Canada/USA border, passing islands of all sizes some of them even straddling the border, the western part in Canada and the eastern part in the USA. This was obviously an area impossible to police, to the historic delight of bootleggers, kidnappers, lovers and runaways, a perfect place for smuggling liquor from Canada to the USA during the prohibition era.

The island that Sky had chosen was shaped like an elongated oval. It had a jetty at each end and a house in the middle with lawns to the front and rear and a few fir trees to the eastern side. The house itself was relatively large and of colonial design with two floors topped by a metal roof that was painted a dark blue. The second floor was balconied. It must have been time consuming, expensive and difficult to ship all the building materials out to the island and complete the construction.

Captain Waters cut the motor and we coasted the last few feet to the upstream jetty. I could hear the shush and slap of the lapping river water on the sides of the boat. If it had been under different circumstances I'm sure that I would have enjoyed the setting, the evening, the slight but not uncomfortable chill. But our purpose tainted the air with the anxiety of uncertain outcomes and I was tense.

Captain Waters berthed and tied up the boat securely. She would stay with it and would do her best not to get too bored. Boredom was unlikely to be a problem the rest of us would have. The presence of AB was unprecedented. Whatever his reasons he was here and I decided to view it as an opportunity rather than a threat.

We collected our equipment and made our way up a graveled pathway to the house.

We had arrived first.

Sky had made all the arrangements for the use of the island and the house. I didn't know who the owner was or how she had done it, that was her business. What mattered to me was that the upper floor was for our use whilst Sky and her team would occupy the ground floor.

We made our way in and went directly upstairs. The house was airy and large windows filled it with natural light. A petrol generator was running to supply whatever electrical power we needed.

The stairs creaked as we made our way up. The top floor consisted of two rooms and a small bathroom/toilet.

The room to our right, originally a bedroom, had been reorganised for us to use as a lounge/kitchen with a kettle available for making tea and coffee. An old fashioned telephone sat on the counter. On a larger table by the windows a buffet of sandwiches, cold meats, salads, fresh bread and butter and, of course, the 1000 island dressing that originated from these parts, had been laid out for us.

The room opposite was set up as a makeshift laboratory with a central metal table, side tables and chairs, a sink and cupboards. This room had large windows in the outside wall that gave views over the river and access to the balcony.

Meredith-Taylor and Kieran Lansbury immediately got to work. They each took one side of the room and laid out their equipment, plugging in their laptops ready for use.

I made the coffee and tea and after the set up was complete we tucked into the buffet. There was very little talking, it had all been done. We were as prepared as we were ever going to be and now we were ready to carry out our various roles.

Sky and her party arrived about 20 minutes later and went directly to their rooms on the ground floor. I knew that both floors were organised on the same general plan although I'd seen from information that Sky had provided that one of their rooms had been purpose-built as a kitchen/dining area.

It wasn't long before the telephone rang. It was an internal line. I answered it. It was Sky.

'We are ready,' she said, 'I assume you will follow the rules; no guns, no intrusive sampling of the goods, no second chances, the trade either happens now or not at all.'

There had to be a degree of mutual trust at this point. No frisking, no turning in of phones or watches. At any sign of misbehaviour the other party could simply walk away. The deal would be off, the trust irreparably broken. If we wanted to make a deal without any bad aftertaste, like a retributive manhunt for example, then it was in all our interests to follow the rules.

'We're ready,' I said.

This was the agreed process; we would each bring our respective item to the other's examination room, each of us would leave one person in attendance whilst the other's team of experts carried out their tests, this person could ask questions but the questions need not be answered. Once the examination was complete each party would take their own item back to their rooms, discuss their own results and decide whether they wanted to complete the trade; yes or no.

I went out to meet Sky as she came up the stairs, she was again wearing a trouser suit, this time in navy blue. Her slim figure was accentuated by the fit and her blonde hair cascaded down her back. Her pale peach coloured blouse had the top three buttons undone and, as always, she was wearing the silver chained necklace from which hung the blue stone surrounded by diamonds. She was carrying a package under her arm that was wrapped in brown paper and tied with red, white and yellow striped ribbon.

'I have the picture,' she said, 'I'll stay with it to observe your authentication processes. It would be a shame if anyone tried a switch or a snatch at this late stage.'

I smiled.

'I've brought two experts and their equipment,' I said, 'There will be a third person in the room but that is only to represent me and observe what is going on. After all we don't want any unfounded recriminations to surface later do we?'

She smiled.

'We think as one,' she said, 'will you stay with the coin?'

'I will.'

'Then you'll be in the room downstairs with my two experts; one is there to authenticate aesthetically all the markings, indentations, mint marks etcetera the other to validate the coin physically; the dimensions, weight, metal content etcetera.'

I thought she'd finished but instead she added,

'And Spike will be there to ensure there are no malpractices or surprises. I'm sure you'll recognise him although today his hair is coloured green.'

From her relaxed attitude I was sure that she did not know about his attack on me. That was interesting. Her whole demeanour seemed genuine. If this were the case then Spike had acted on his own initiative. That made things so much simpler.

I escorted her along to our makeshift laboratory, her heels beating rhythmically on the polished wooden flooring. I held the door open for her. She walked in.

Inside were the three white coated figures of Meredith-Taylor, Kieran Lansbury and AB. They were each wearing white gloves and were looking very intense.

The expensive looking equipment that Kieran Lanbury and Meredith-Taylor had brought lay organised on the various surfaces; the central metal-topped table, the two side tables and on some of the shelves in the wall-mounted cabinets. The room was amply lit with natural light augmented by laboratory grade strip lighting that would keep the light levels high as the natural light faded. It was like a stage set.

I introduced Sky to each of the three in turn remembering that AB was "Doctor Alexander". She nodded to each of them simply to acknowledge their existence and then turned to me.

'All the analysis we subject the picture to will be non-invasive as agreed,' I said, 'we will examine it under visual, ultraviolet and infra red lighting. We will use X-Rays to extract characteristic substrate, board and pigment profiles. All of these results will be compared to those from known works by Picasso from the same period. In addition we will examine the picture stylistically and against archive images taken before it was so unfortunately "mislaid".'

Sky nodded again.

'How long will it take?' she asked.

'Most of the tests are a matter of minutes. The time we need is mainly for the assimilation and analysis of the data and the consequent discussion we'll need to have in order to reach a conclusion.'

'Decision by consensus, how democratic, we could be here for days!' said Sky, her blue eyes sparkling.

'We'll know in about 2 hours,' I said reassuringly.

Sky smiled, 'Well now, Michael, you can leave me to watch your experts play with their toys,' she said, 'please take the coin downstairs and observe our work. Spike is waiting to welcome you.'

I was impressed by Sky's calmness, her apparent lack of concern was admirable considering the knife-edge nature of the current state of play. Maybe it was only me who was stressed out.

I turned to go.

'Good luck, Michael,' Sky said to my retreating back.

With Toni Malguzzi as my guarantor of the coin's authenticity I felt that it wasn't luck I would be needing it was more of a miracle.

I went downstairs.

Chapter 45

When I got to the ground floor Spike was nowhere to be seen so I went to the door that mirrored the location of our own upstairs laboratory and knocked.

Spike answered.

'Good, you're here,' he said.

I followed him inside trying not to feel like a condemned man.

Their analysis room was identical in size and shape to the one upstairs but it was more sparsely furnished. Two elderly men in white lab-coats and wearing white gloves were standing expectantly at the central table.

Spike shrugged.

'No invasive analysis as agreed,' he said, his breath smelling of peppermint, 'I understand that these two guys will measure the metal content, impurities and contaminants, as well as checking physical and artistic details whatever that means. They'll use some standard references we've been able to acquire for comparison.'

It was almost as if Spike had been reading the words from a card so well-rehearsed did it sound. I wanted to ask how they'd come by references but I guessed that wouldn't be part of his script and I didn't want to antagonise him. It was none of my business anyway. As long as what they did gave a satisfactory outcome that was all that mattered. I was about 30% confident. I tried to act 99%.

'And...' I started to ask.

'Between 2 and 3 hours,' he said, guessing the question correctly.

The two whitecoats reminded me of a couple of witches about to go and cackle over their caldron, cooking up chaos.

'Any questions?' asked Spike.

Lots of questions I thought, like what happens if you find a problem, in particular, what happens to little old me? On the basis that every question deserves an answer but not every answer is deserved I decided that discretion was, in this case, the better choice.

'No, no questions,' I said.

'Well then,' said Spike, 'give the guys the coin and we'll have a coupl'a hours to kill.'

'Sounds good to me,' I said.

As with the room upstairs this room was well lit with large windows looking out onto the St Lawrence river. I moved to the table in the centre of the room and took the small red leather box out of my pocket and handed it to the first of the white coats. He took it reverentially.

'Thank you,' he said.

I returned to where Spike was leaning against the wall.

'I guess you'll be leaving Toronto soon as this is over,' he said.

'Yes,' I said, 'no matter how it works out my job will be over as soon as both sets of results are in and the decisions are made.'

'Good,' he said, 'very good. Best not to stay any longer than you need to, eh.'

To look at him, this skinny, pale skinned skeleton of a man you'd be forgiven for thinking him an overgrown teenager, someone whose body hadn't yet caught up with its growth spurt, someone who hadn't yet outgrown the experimental 'What colour shall I dye my hair today?' stage. But Toni Malguzzi had led me to believe that Spike dragged a chain of wrongdoings behind him longer than Jacob Marley's ghost although thus far it hung only lightly on his conscience.

Looking at him I could imagine how unpredictable he could be, maybe he became more so under pressure, and I could imagine that that unpredictability could lead to unnecessary displays of aggression.

I tried to imagine him in a fair fight but could only see him weaseling his way out of it but when I thought of him in a situation where he held the upper hand, either because he held a weapon, or because he was in a position of strength, then I could see him lauding it over a terrified victim, yes, under those circumstances I could see him puffing out his chest and acting the big cheese.

My thoughts left a bad taste in my mouth so I turned my attention away from Spike and towards the work the white coats were doing. I tried to read their reactions from their faces but I couldn't, they were inscrutable. The two of them just quietly and methodically carried out their analyses, made notes, occasionally cross-referenced each other's results.

'What's that?' I asked one of them.

'It's a portable x-ray fluorescence spectrometer I'm going to use it to scan the coin,' he said, holding out something that looked like a taser, 'it will give me the elemental composition down to parts per million.'

The second whitecoat joined in.

'And I'll use a laser scanner to scan for surface detail,' he said.

'Thanks,' I said and then stood back to watch as they started to analyse the hell out of the coin. Unfortunately they seemed to know exactly what they were doing. We were unlikely to get away with anything much.

I continued to watch as they first measured overall weight, diameter and thickness before moving on to do their scanning.

The laser scan was converted into a precise 3D image from which surface detail, including depth and positioning of the engraving could be electronically compared with whatever standards they'd been able to acquire. Once satisfied with his modeling one of the whitecoats retreated to a side table, sat in front of an open laptop and started tapping away at the keyboard. The laptop screen was turned away from me so I couldn't see what he was doing.

It wasn't long before Spike got fidgety. He kept looking at his watch. When he saw me looking at him he grinned,

'It's a Rolex,' he said.

'I can see that,' I said.

'A GMT Master II, they're very sought after.'

'Yes, I bet they are,' I said.

He pulled up his sleeve so I could inspect the watch. As it caught the light I could see the black face, the bi-coloured black/blue cerachrom bezel and the finely polished stainless steel strap that held it to his wrist. More importantly however I could also see that the watch glass was scratched, just one scratch, a straight line running from above the 2 on the dial and down to the 5. It's always the imperfections that are distinctive. The bastard was flagrantly wearing my watch and had the arrogance and audacity to show it off to me.

'Didn't you have a watch something like this?' he said, he was obviously enjoying this game of "taunt the victim".

'Yes,' I said, 'I did.'

'But you ain't got it no more?' he said.

'I loaned it out,' I said, 'I wanted to try out one of these solar powered watches.'

I held out my Citizen eco drive for his inspection with its elegant simplicity, deep blue dial and matching bezel, a date window and a stainless steel case and bracelet.

He grinned. He didn't say anything. He just grinned and smelled of peppermint.

He probably didn't know that he was on Toni Malguzzi's grass list. I glanced at him. He was playing with his green hair. Play on Spike, I thought, play on while you still can.

I turned back to watch as the whitecoat with the handheld x-ray fluorescence spectrometer was midway through scanning the coin. I could see the spiky readout on the back of the instrument. This was the analysis I feared most, it was like taking a fingerprint. If they had managed to get a content profile of the real thing, although how they could have got hold of that I had no idea, then this test would be conclusive. You might be able to laser sculpt and replicate all the surface detail to a near microscopic level but you couldn't fake the material fingerprint. It would be the trace impurities that gave it away. The whitecoat completed his readings and retreated to a second side table and opened a second laptop. The screen, as with the first, was turned away from me.

I was very aware that if these analyses did not go well then it would be my probity that would be called into question, with unpleasant results. I focussed my mind on the object under scrutiny. I knew that beneath the eagle was inscribed "In God we Trust" and I tried to keep the faith.

After a long two hours one of the white coats put the coin back into its plastic sleeve and placed it in the recess within the red leather box. He brought it over to me with the lid still open so that I could see that the coin was there.

'We're finished,' he said.

I took the box and closed the lid.

'You can go now,' said Spike.

God, he was another example of a tough guy to like.

Chapter 46

The results were in.

AB, Meredith-Taylor and Kieran Lansbury were gathered around the makeshift laboratory table alongside me. AB allowed me to take the lead. I asked Meredith-Taylor to go first,

'First of all,' he said, 'I brought with me a full-sized acetate of the original picture that was produced by amalgamating the best archival image references we could find of Picasso's *Tête d'Arlequin*. It is a fairly minor work so there was not a lot to go on but we digitally layered a number of images on top of each another to try and ensure we got as representative an image as possible. We then produced a 24 x 33 cm transparent actetate which is the same size as the original picture.'

'We?' I said.

'The AGO conservation department helped me with this and they are world class,' he said.

Kieran Lansbury nodded his head, 'They are renowned,' he said.

'They also constructed a metal frame for me,' continued Meredith-Taylor, 'so I could place the transparency physically on top of our supposed Picasso without risk of actually touching the surface. All the techniques I have used are noninvasive. So, once I had the transparency in place I played with the lighting and examined the resulting match both manually and digitally. Here I'll show you.'

At this point Meredith-Taylor fired up a laptop, inserted an SD card and played with the keypad. We all gathered round the screen as he scrolled through some images,

'Here,' he said, 'is a photograph of the acetate only and next is a photograph of the Picasso in question. If I scroll them back and forwards you can see that superficially they're very similar.' We could indeed see that, 'and now here is the transparency and picture overlaid. I examined this very closely and can confirm that there are no significant discrepancies in any areas, either in line or in colouring. It remains a very good match.'

'So what does that mean?' I asked.

'It means,' said Meredith-Taylor, 'that the rest of our tests and analyses are not a waste of time. From this visual analysis the Picasso is either genuine or a very good copy. If it were a poor fake then I would have picked it up immediately.'

So far, so good, I thought.

'I then analysed the picture stylistically and looked carefully at the mark making. For this I used an old-fashioned magnifying glass and also, on the laptop, digitally zoomed in and out of our high resolution images. This is a later work by Picasso drawn in 1971 only two years before he died. It is produced with pen and brush using indian ink, pencil, oil pastel and chalk on thick brown wove paper. Picasso's final works were a mixture of styles, his means of expression in constant flux right up until the end of his life. He was 90 years old when he produced the *Tête d'Arlequin* and it was during a period in his life when he was creating a torrent of paintings, drawings and copperplate etchings. Like most 20th century artists Picasso painted quickly. You can't produce as many pieces of art as he did by working slowly!'

'The face of harlequin in this picture is a melancholy double of Picasso who embodies loneliness and fragility. The image is distorted, disturbing, powerful and troubling. It both looks out and through the observer, challenging them to look into themselves. Here there is nothing content or comfy about harlequin, he is an old man, the ravages of life, experience and time are carved into the deep fissures of his face. It is a damaged, no longer handsome or beautiful visage, he is a shadow of the acrobatic trickster full of youth and vigour. As you can see his shoulders fall away, the shoulders of an aged, skeletal body. Here is both the subject and the artist, harlequin and Picasso, introspectively staring with trepidation into an unstoppable future. As I said it is drawn at speed and with the confidence of an experienced artist. There is passion in the mark-making, the application of pen and pencil. It is that which is most difficult to fake. You can't produce a vigorous brushstroke by applying the paint slowly or carefully, the marks left on the canvas are just not the same. How long do you thing it took for Picasso to complete the *Tête d'Arlequin*, a week, a month?'

I shrugged. Professor Peter Meredith-Taylor was in his element.

'He may have been thinking about it for some time, he may even have returned to it several times, though I think not, but the time he spent on the picture itself? Minutes, Michael, minutes not hours, he drew and painted quickly, with passion, that's a big part of what made him who he was. He was supremely confident in his own abilities. He therefore drew and painted at speed and rarely with corrections, especially when producing the kind of picture we have here. You could almost call it a sketch.'

He paused, took a deep breath.

'So I have done the best that I can, although, conscious of time, I have had to rather rush my analysis. Even so I'm fairly confident of my conclusions.'

'And what are your conclusions?' I asked.

Each step of this process was like encountering a trip hazard.

'I have studied Picasso quite carefully over the years,' he said, 'I helped curate an exhibition of works from his "Blue Period" at the AGO for example, assembling pieces from all around the world and hanging them side by side, choosing interesting juxtapositions. It was one of the few occasions that this has happened since Picasso's death. Therefore I feel I can speak with some authority.'

'That's why I invited you to help us,' I said, and then repeated my question 'and what are your conclusions?'

'My conclusions are that I cannot, in all good faith, be absolutely certain and I would like to defer my final judgement until after I have heard the scientific evidence,' he nodded towards Kieran Lansbury, 'but prior to that I would say that this second part of my analysis has reinforced my first, that this is either an original Picasso or a very well executed fake.'

So far, so good, I thought. At least there was nothing catastrophic so far.

'Thank you,' I said and then turned to Kieran Lansbury, 'well Professor it's over to you.'

'My analysis was limited in two ways,' began Kieran Lansbury, 'firstly because all my analysis needed to be non-invasive I was prevented from taking scratch, small or particle samples and so could not use microscopy or Gas chromatography – mass spectrometry for chemical analysis.'

'Secondly the equipment I used needed to be portable which ruled out Large area micro X-ray fluorescence spectrometry which could have analysed the whole picture in one go.'

'So much for the bad news, the good news is that I was able to use Infrared reflectography which is a great way of looking under the surface of a painting. It is particularly good at detecting any under-drawing as it detects carbon based materials like graphite, charcoal and ink. From what Peter has already said

Picasso drew fluently so we wouldn't expect to find a preliminary outline or multiple revisions.'

Prof. Peter Meredith-Taylor nodded, 'Kieran showed me his results and we agreed there was little evidence of under-drawing or revision,' he said.

Good, I thought.

'Secondly I took a Multispectral scan, it's basically a very high definition photograph at over 240 million pixels using 13 different light filters. Again you use this to see "through" the picture and identify pigments. Thirdly I used X-ray fluorescence to analyse the pigments used. I'd be surprised if they didn't use this same technique on the coin.'

'They did,' I said.

'So with Peter's help I cross-referenced these results with results from pigments we know Picasso used during this period. Portable XRF devices are popular and convenient for people like me. And fourthly and lastly I carried out the best Thread count analysis I could on the paper. Basically I tried, by handheld microscopic analysis to characterise the paper filament structure and again compare this with accepted standards from Picasso's work at the time.'

Again this was the set of analyses I feared most. Kieran had taken a fingerprint of the picture.

'And what did you conclude,' I asked.

Kieran Lansbury stuck a USB memory stick into the side of the laptop.

'Let me show you some of the analysis first,' he said.

We gathered around once more as Kieran led us through a number of screens explaining clearly the meaning of the data we were seeing and the process of analysis and comparison to known standards he had undertaken. After he'd finished the run through he said,

'We've had a very limited time to inspect the painting and I'll now leave Peter to summarise our agreed outcome.'

So here we go, I thought. I knew Kieran would be thorough and professional. Had he been too thorough?

'You must understand we cannot say that these conclusions are definitive,' began Meredith-Taylor. Then he paused, getting his thoughts together. This was very far from the easy-going, brandy drinking man I'd first encountered. This was his profession and in this he was focused and serious. 'From our combined analysis of style, technique, brush and pen strokes, rudimentary pigment analysis and comparisons with historical data ...'

He stopped.

I waited. He sat looking at me.

'Yes?' My heart had started to thump, I could hear it in my ears.

'You must remember that this painting has been reported as being destroyed, literally burnt to ashes.'

Oh God, I thought, let this not be happening.

'I know that,' I said, more sharply than I'd meant to, it wasn't their fault, 'but what do you think?'

'Well,' said Meredith-Taylor, 'it's most surprising but we can find no definitive evidence that this picture is not genuine.'

I let this sink in for a moment, unraveling its meaning.

'So you think the painting is genuine?'

'The truth is, I, we, don't know,' he said, 'it is either genuine or a very well done copy. You have to remember that the standards we have used are the best we could come up with. Picasso was prolific and the *Tête d'Arlequin* is a comparatively minor work, it has never been studied in detail.'

I wanted to shout hallelujah. This far from ringing endorsement was not a rejection. A rejection would have given me severely difficult decisions to make.

'So,' I said, 'if I can summarise. We have found nothing that would immediately and conclusively conclude that this picture is not an original Picasso,' my two experts forgave me my double negative and nodded in agreement, 'on the other hand we have not enough confidence to confirm that this definitely is an original Picasso.' Again the nods. I turned to AB.

'Then there we are then,' he said, 'that's good enough. We are not being taken for fools, that's the most important thing. Well done everybody. We should now move to conclude the trade.'

This was my assignment! This should have been my decision but I didn't mind in the slightest that AB had taken the responsibility from my shoulders.

'Assuming of course,' AB continued, 'Sky and her experts find the coin to be acceptable.'

There's always a hitch, I thought.

We went back into the lounge area, sat around and waited. There was nothing more to say and we were each immersed in our own thoughts.

After a wait of 10 minutes, that felt like 10 years, the internal phone rang.

'I would like to talk to you,' said Sky.

I had a sinking feeling.

'Of course,' I said, trying to keep my tone light, 'where?'

'Outside,' she said, 'I'll meet you in 5 minutes.'

Chapter 47

Standing outside the main entrance to the house waiting for Sky to emerge I looked out at the river that flowed steadily past without a care in the world. I lifted my head and my gaze travelled up to the horizon and then on, to sky above.

I thought about the sky, that ever changing elemental canopy, with its differing moods, tones, textures and tempers. It could be calm, clear blue, transparent, mild and forgiving. It could be glowering, crackling with electricity, threatening. It could weep tears from mizzly to torrential. It could hold steady for days or change completely within an hour.

Sky exited and came to stand beside me. She'd changed her clothes and looked cool and refreshed in a light short-sleeved cream blouse, black loose fitting trousers and red stilettos. Her eyes were a deep blue and I wondered if this Sky were as changeable and temperamental as the one above me. Chances were I was about to find out.

So here we were, we had finally reached the critical moment. Sky and I faced each other. I was very aware that she had the upper hand. I was on her chosen turf, on her terms. I knew that we wanted the deal but I didn't know if she did.

'Do we have a deal?' I asked.

'From your side,' said Sky, 'are you happy?'

Happy? Oh, deliriously, I thought.

'Yes,' I said.

She paused and looked out across the river.

'My father does not have long left to live,' she said.

I kept silent.

'When your wife was close to the end,' she said, 'if she wanted something would you have given it to her?'

'If I could,' I said.

'No matter how difficult?'

'If I could,' I repeated.

'Yes,' she said, 'I think most of us would.'

I waited. Whether we had a deal or not seemed inconsequential for a moment. But only for a moment.

'We are satisfied,' said Sky.

'I'll go and get the coin,' I said.

'We'll complete the handover in the lobby,' she said.

And with that we turned and walked back into the house. Sky walking two steps ahead.

I couldn't believe it.

Toni Malguzzi could not possibly have found a genuine gold $20 1933 Double Eagle could he? And if he had would he be stupid enough to trade it for a picture worth a tenth of the value? It was all too much for me I was just grateful for this unexpected outcome. When I told AB, Kieran and Meredith-Taylor they took it in silence. There was no euphoria, no cheering.

I took the coin and with AB one step behind me went back downstairs.

Sky was there on her own, no Spike. On seeing this AB hung back.

There was a small table in the lobby presumably used for mail or keys or a indoor plant. Today it had an open metal suitcase lying on top of it.

'Come see,' said Sky.

I went over and saw that the framed Picasso was lying in the open suitcase within a nest of plain brown paper and coloured ribbon.

'I wanted you to see the picture before I complete the wrapping,' said Sky.

I bent over to take a closer look. The harlequin seemed to stare accusingly at me. I moved away.

'OK,' I said.

Sky's hands moved dextrously for the next few moments; it was mesmerising to watch. Corners folded, shaped and taped, the piece de resistance being the red, white and yellow striped ribbon that she looped around it and completed in a bow.

'It is traditional in my family,' she said, 'important things should be presented well. And although this is not exactly a gift it is nevertheless an important thing that I give into your hands.'

She closed the suitcase, picked it up by the handle and held it out to me.

'Yours I think,' she said.

I took the little red leather box out of my pocket and held it out to her.

'And this is yours,' I said.

I took the suitcase with one hand at the same time as she took the little red leather case from the other.

I stood and waited as Sky opened the red leather box and examined the contents.

'So be it,' she said, closing the lid and slipping it into her pocket.

'Sorry I didn't gift wrap it,' I said.

She smiled.

'Never mind,' she said, 'I will wrap it before I give it to my father.'

'So that's it then,' I said, 'we've been to a lot of trouble to complete this deal. If we'd been able to trust each other we could have done it a lot quicker and easier.'

'It's difficult to trust when you don't know who the other party is,' said Sky. Fair point, I thought, 'and when what you're exchanging is either stolen, illegal or non-existent.' Another fair point, I thought, maybe this trade had gone as well as it possibly could have under the circumstances.

I was amazed we'd completed it.

'We'll leave first,' said Sky, 'please give us 30 minutes before you go.'

'We'll do that,' I said and reached forward to shake her hand. For a fleeting moment I held it, it was dry and cool, firm and assured. It was only in the back of her eyes that I thought something flickered; something more of sadness than of joy.

I turned towards the stairs.

'Safe journey,' said Sky.

I turned to look at her one last time, realising just how little I knew or understood her.

'Safe journey,' I said.

Chapter 48

I carried the case to the bottom of the stairs, held it out and gave it to AB. He exhaled slowly. How long had he been holding his breath? I wanted to ask him why he was showing such an interest in this assignment but knew that now was not the right time.

I went back upstairs with AB in the lead. We didn't immediately go back into the lounge, instead we walked through the lab room and out onto the balcony. From there we watched as Sky, Spike and the rest of her party departed, walking down the graveled pathway, past the greenery and protruding rocks and onto the wooden jetty at the downstream end of the island.

The engine of their boat kicked into action as they stepped aboard and soon the propeller was churning the water white as their boat backed away, turned and started on its journey back downriver.

Over in the west the sun was setting in glorious reds, yellows and purples. Somewhere far off a bird, a Great Northern Diver or loon as it's more commonly called, wailed piercingly. A shiver ran down my back and I suddenly felt a chill.

None of Sky's party looked back.

I turned to AB.

'I think this is my last assignment,' I said, 'it's time for me to move on.'

AB didn't flinch.

'Everybody has their limits,' he said, 'the work we do is not for everybody.'

'Or not forever,' I said.

'Things change,' he said.

'Yes,' I said.

'Think about it,' he said, 'you don't need to decide immediately.'

'OK,' I said, 'I hope you don't mind but I have some calls to make.'

'Of course,' said AB, 'I'll go and tell our two friends the good news. Do you mind if I take this?' he said motioning towards the metal suitcase.

'Go ahead,' I said. If I couldn't trust AB who could I trust.

After he'd disappeared inside I took another moment or two to gaze out at the river, the flickering lights on the boats reflecting the movement of life as the river flowed on. The plaintive cry of the Great Northern Diver echoed once more across the water adding a haunting note.

I took out my phone and dialed.

'Yes?' Did Toni Malguzzi's voice always sound threatening no matter what the circumstances?

'The trade is made,' I said.

I could feel him tense. I'd got his attention.

'Any hitches?'

'None.'

'When can I have it?'

'Tomorrow,' I said.

'Good, I'll bring you the present I promised.'

I was pretty sure that by "present" he meant the information he had on Spike and his "souvenirs".

'OK,' I said.

Next I called Officer Jones and asked her to invite Logan onto the line as part of a conference call.

'Thanks for the arrangements,' I said, 'they all fell into place. We're still on the island but I'm sure getting back will be similarly smooth.'

'Never mind that,' growled Logan, 'how did it go?'

'How did what go?' I said.

'This is not the time,' said Logan, 'just put us out of our misery.'

He was probably right, it wasn't fair to tease, it was too easy.

'We've made the trade,' I said, 'I have the picture, I think we should pass it over to Toni Malguzzi tomorrow.'

'Oh my,' said Officer Jones.

'Are you shitting us?' said Logan.

It was a fair question, I'd not always been as straight talking with Logan as I could have been.

'Logan,' I said, 'I promise I'm not shitting you.'

'Phew,' he said.

'Wow,' said Officer Jones.

'Can you organise the meeting with Toni Malguzzi?'

'Yes,' they said in unison.

'Anything else?' I asked.

'Just one thing,' said Officer Jones.

'Go on,' I said.

'I was just wondering if there was a possibility you guys might be going to celebrate a little.'

I didn't know and I said so.

'Well, just in case I'll book you a driver, he'll drive you and your Volvo XC90 back from Kingston to Toronto.'

'OK, thanks,' I said, she was getting more and more like Samantha. I appreciated her help and foresight.

I decided to text Samantha rather than phone her. She had complained to me about waking her up at odd hours but the real reason was that I didn't want to engage in conversation with her, I was bound to let it slip that I was going to resign. I didn't expect a reply but got one almost immediately.

'Good. Let me know when passed over to M. I'll inform AB.'

So she didn't know he was right here.

Nice to have a 'Good' though. 1 felt like I'd just received a merit from the teacher.

Back in the lounge the suitcase lay on top of the main table. All four of us sat around it. There was a strange atmosphere in the room. Rather than euphoria it was closer to anticlimax. It was Meredith-Taylor who spoke first,

'Is there any brandy in this place do you think?' he said.

He was well on the way to a wasted liver but at this point his enquiry was welcome.

'Wait here,' said AB.

He disappeared across the corridor and into the makeshift laboratory returning a couple of minutes later carrying a bottle in each hand.

'I asked Officer Jones, a very capable officer by the way, to provide some alcohol just in case we were in need of it, either for celebration or to drown our sorrows.'

So that's how she knew to ask whether we would be celebrating or not, I thought, she was a clever as well as a thoughtful lady.

I started to relax, a glass of something did seem to be called for. AB put the bottles on the table.

'I have one bottle of brandy,' he said, 'a Remy Martin Louis the thirteenth.'

If the bottle was anything to go by it was an expensive one. Meredith-Taylor's eyes lit up,

'My goodness,' he said.

'And one bottle of whisky, a Macallan 25 year old single malt,' said AB.

I knew this was a good one and that it didn't come cheap.

'Now if someone could bring over some glasses, I'll get on with opening the bottles,' he said.

I had never imagined that Meredith-Taylor could move so fast, his body was not built for speed but he made a good fist of it.

We took our drinks outside onto the veranda were there were chairs and a low table. The evening was beginning to cool but not unpleasantly so. AB had poured healthy portions of liquor into large tumblers and after one or two refills we were in animated conversation about life, the universe and almost everything.

Chapter 49

A while later we packed up our respective gear and carried it out, a little unsteadily, to the jetty. AB allowed Meredith-Taylor to take the remains of the brandy with him.

'I'll treasure the bottle,' he said.

Kieran volunteered to look after the Macallan.

We'd almost forgotten about Captain Waters, but there she was dutifully waiting for us.

We boarded the boat. AB carried the metal suitcase.

Captain Waters started the engines, the noise smashing through the silence of the looming night. Then she loosed the moorings, backed the boat away from the jetty, turned and we sped away.

I had no feeling of satisfaction or even of relief, it could all have gone wrong but it hadn't.

I looked back towards the island, seemingly still attached to us by the umbilical trail of white turbulence the boat's engine churned up in the river water behind us. I watched as this wake melted back into the river, breaking our connection and releasing the island to disappear slowly into the distance, the house disappearing into the gloom, merging with the coming night.

Soon the island, the jetties and the house would settle back into the hibernation from which they had briefly been roused, our visit nothing more than the fleeting memory of a dream.

Our conduct on the return journey was not something that any of us will remember with pride. The liquor had had some effect and for some reason we thought it would be a good idea if we sang our way back to Kingston harbour. I could see that Captain Waters was not too impressed with our rendition of "I've been a wild rover…" but we thought it was fantastic and that our voices blended well together. We even toyed with the idea of releasing it as a single. I'd never seen AB behave like this before. It was a revelation. He was almost human.

Captain Waters poured us out at Kingston harbour and the driver Officer Jones had organized helped us carry and load our equipment into the SUV.

'See,' said AB, 'how very capable this Officer Jones is, she thinks ahead, an excellent officer, she should go far.'

I slept most of the way back to Toronto. I think the others did too. When you're tired enough you'll sleep almost anywhere and I was oblivious to the sharp metal corners of the seat that dug into me.

Before I'd closed my eyes I had seen that AB had the metal suitcase nestled in his lap. So I could relax knowing that it was in safe hands.

Back in Toronto the first port of call was the Fairmont York hotel where I was shaken awake. My throat was sandpaper dry and my body ached from the convoluted position I'd unconsciously adopted. I needed a drink of something non-alcoholic and a wash.

Here AB said his farewells, handed me the suitcase and set off with Meredith-Taylor to the AGO and then onward to I know not where. Kieran heaved his rucksack full of equipment onto his back.

'Thanks Kee,' I said, 'I really appreciate what you did.'

'No problem,' he said, 'do you mean dropping everything and leaping on an aeroplane to get my butt over here in time, or do you mean bringing the right equipment with me, or do you mean the expert analysis done in record time?'

I smiled.

'All of the above you dickhead,' I said. Being in the armed services is like being part of a big family and Kieran was like a long lost brother.

'Very nice,' he said, 'I've had to travel all the way across the Atlantic just to be insulted.'

'And you wouldn't have missed it,' I said.

He laughed.

'And I wouldn't have missed it,' he said.

'Now it's my turn to be a dick,' I said, 'I'd love to find a bar and reminisce all night…'

'You mean get pissed,' he said.

'…but,' I said, ignoring the truth of his assertion, 'I still have work to do.'

'Again not a problem,' said Kieran, 'believe it or not I would have had to take a rain check anyway. I've just got time to pack and then I'm back on a plane to Blighty.'

He looked at his watch, 'In fact, if you don't mind…'

I shook his hand, as always his grip was strong.

'Let's meet up soon,' I said.

'Your call,' said Kieran.

I was welcomed back into my hotel room by Officers Jones and Logan who had obviously been waiting for me. From the disheveled look of the coffee table; used cups, coffee pot, chocolate biscuit wrappers and crumbs, they'd been waiting some time. Logan jumped to his feet,

'Welcome back, man, come and sit here, do you want a drink?'

What had happened to Logan? If I didn't nip this in the bud he'd be calling me "mate" soon. I carried the metal suitcase over to where they were sitting.

'I'm OK thanks,' I said, 'is there any coffee left?'

'A little, but it'll be cold,' said Officer Jones.

'It doesn't matter,' I said, going over and pouring some of the leftovers into a fresh cup. It was lukewarm hotel coffee. Better than nothing and bitter as hell. It made me feel better.

'If it's OK with you guys,' I said, 'I'd like to get this conversation over with as quickly as possible. I'm tired.'

'I can understand that,' said Officer Jones, 'it must have been stressful.'

'It went to plan in the end,' I said, 'that's all that matters. Here is Toni Malguzzi's Picasso.'

I held out the case. Logan took it.

'We'll take good care of this,' he said, 'until we see Malguzzi tomorrow.'

'I'm sure you will,' I said, 'is there anything else?'

'I'm good,' said Logan.

'Is there anything we can do for you?' asked Officer Jones.

'There is one thing,' I said.

'What's that?'

I pointed up at one of the surveillance cameras, its light was back on.

'I think we can dispense with all of this can't we. You've got the Picasso, I'm not the one you need to worry about any more. Even if I ran away it wouldn't matter anymore. Please switch all of this stuff off permanently, it'll make me feel a little bit less like I'm living in a goldfish bowl.'

The two officers looked at each other.

'I think we can do that,' said Logan.

After they'd gone and the camera light had gone out I took a hot shower and put on a complete change of clothes. The crisp, white cotton of the new shirt made my body feel light and cool.

I felt I was now ready to touch base with a different reality. The kind of reality I wanted to major on in the future. I called my daughter.

'Hello.'

'Hello dad, everything OK?'

This sounded more like an accusation than a question. Why does my daughter seem to believe that I only call her when I'm in trouble or need help?

'I'm fine,' I said.

'It's late,' she said, 'you're lucky I'm awake.'

'Sorry,' I said.

'It's OK,' she said, 'good to talk to you.'

After the normal dad, daughter small talk, 'How's Teresa?', 'How's my granddaughter?' kind of stuff I decided to broach the subject that was niggling at me.

'Thanks for agreeing to be my best man,' I said, 'it means a lot to me and Teresa.'

It had only been a quick exchange of texts so I hoped she'd remember that she'd agreed.

'No problem,' she said, 'glad to oblige.'

OK, so far. She hadn't changed her mind.

'I know it's early,' I said, 'but have you had any thoughts on what you might wear?'

There was silence at the other end of the line, I could hear her thinking.

'I have thought about it a little,' she said.

'And...' I said.

'I was thinking of a long pink silk dress...'

She would look great in pink.

'... tight fitting...'

She had a great figure, but this was beginning to worry me.

'...strapless with a low cut neckline...'

Oh shit, oh shit, I could see that this ensemble would certainly attract attention, or more worryingly, distract attention from the bride.

This was what had been niggling me.

If the best man was a man then there would be little to no chance of his distracting attention away from the bride on her "big day". I might be thick headed but even I knew this was important. There'd be photographs and videos and these would be lasting mementos. However as we'd broken with tradition and asked my daughter to be best man there was a risk she'd outshine the bride. Even though I say so myself my daughter is a good looking woman and in the right dress could out shine just about anybody, and if that dress was bright coloured, tight fitting and revealing then…

'…and I thought I'd stick a carnation between my boobs to finish it all off!'

I gulped and stammered. I was dumbfounded. The silence hung like a fog, growing thicker, becoming treacle.

This growingly awkward atmosphere was blown away by the sound of her laughter.

'Oh dad,' she laughed, 'oh ha, ha, ha, I can't believe you sometimes.'

A glimmer, a ray of sunshine pierced through my clouded thoughts.

'You mean…'

'I mean I'm a woman…'

The mental image of her in a tight-fitting, strapless, low cut, pink silk dress left that in no doubt.

'...and I'm not stupid.'

'Ah,' I said.

'So I know that what I wear at the wedding is important.'

'Yes, of course,' I said.

'So what I'm going to do is leave you completely out of it and talk to Teresa. We've had a chat about it already as a matter of fact, about the things we need to get prepared, and of course the dresses were one of those things,' she paused, 'as was your suit.'

'Right, good, very sensible,' I said, and then, 'my suit?'

'You don't think we'd leave that to you do you?'

'And why not?' I asked, a bit peeved.

'Because Teresa wants quite a small, intimate wedding, more casual than formal.'

'She does?'

'Yes, she does, and you would probably turn up in a DJ looking like an hotel maître'd if we didn't sort it out for you.'

How did she know my intentions?

'You might be right,' I said.

'I know I'm right,' she said.

'Good, well I'm glad we've had this little chat, cleared the air, got things sorted.'

Her voice softened.

'Yea, me too dad, I'm looking forward to it, Mum would have been very happy you know.'

Daughters, they know just what to say. When we completed the call I was a much happier man.

To make the most of my newfound freedom I decided to go out for a walk before finally settling down for the night. I needed to walk off some of the residual adrenalin and even though it was late at night it would be nice not to feel like my every step was being monitored. I needed to think, to get my thoughts into some kind of order.

Heading out into the glittering dark I walked down towards the Harbourfront. For no good reason I waved a reassuring hand at two guys tying up a boat. They didn't wave back. Stepping away from the graveled pathway I walked across a small lawn which had a few trees clinging to one side. Under the trees was a bench seat and I sat down to contemplate life, the universe and what the hell was happening to me.

For some time now I'd been going from one crisis to another, either mine or somebody else's. At least I hadn't self-destructed.

I sat staring out across the lake. In this lull in proceedings I was surrounded by relative peace, the stars shone overhead and the Milky Way could be discerned even in these light-polluted skies. The lake waters whooshed and tinkled gently back and forth on the shingle edge. From this distance other people's voices were hushed and indistinct, their murmur blending with the other few animal noises of the night, a dog barking, a rustling in the leaves.

Shit, I was becoming morose. What was it about this assignment that was bringing me down? Why did I have this premonition that there would be no winners in the end?

What I needed to do and what I would do, as a kind of New Year's resolution made at the wrong time of year, was to decide on the things that were important to me, the things that it was not too late for me to do and I would promise myself to do them.

Did these games that I played really matter in the end? Did my role really matter? Had I got my priorities wrong? At the end of the day wasn't it family, friends and partners that meant the most?

Teresa's outburst of a few days ago had shocked me. When she threw me out I hoped she would come back and apologise not leap on the first plane out! I wasn't prepared for her emotion. The whole of my professional training had made me dispassionate, able to stand aside from events and view them from different angles; logical, rational angles.

Teresa had shocked me awake. I didn't want to lose the benefits of that awakening.

My thoughts began to wander. Should I visit and spend more time with my daughter and her family? I seemed somehow distant from the real world, everyone else was living real lives and I was just at the edge, watching. Had it always been like this? Had I always prescribed greater worth to my work than it deserved, had I used it as an excuse to not do the things that I really, in my heart, knew that I should be doing? I started to list some of those things,

Talking more to ageing parents; too late now.

Spending more time with my daughter, watching her grow; too late now.

Holding my wife closer, helping her more as the illness bit home; too late now.

I extracted my personal mobile phone and texted Teresa.

I miss you

I wasn't expecting a reply, it was too late into the night.

Ping.

Miss you too.

Back inside, a single malt rattling in my glass, I no longer cared whether the coin or the Picasso were genuine or not, I only wanted to get this assignment finished and get the hell out of here.

But I knew I still had some work to do first.

Chapter 50

Toronto was yawning itself awake in the murky pink dawn light as I sat by the window eating my fresh croissants and drinking good coffee. A few private cars, early buses, enterprising taxis, and hurrying pedestrians carrying disposable cups and Danish pastries were already about, making their way hither and thither, destinations unknown.

I got a phone call.

It was Logan.

The final transfer was going to take place at Toni Malguzzi's safe house and Toni Malguzzi wanted me to be there. A car was being sent for me and I'd better be ready. Logan sounded gruff as usual but I could also hear the anticipation in his voice. This was a big thing for him. He probably had colleagues that would quite like to see him fail and superiors who would make damn sure that if he did it would be counted as all his own fault and not theirs.

From the moment Toni Malguzzi made his offer to him and Officer Jones they had been living on the edge. Yes, there was the possibility of glory and promotion, of sticking your head above the parapet and not getting it shot off. But there was also the other possibility and with the years service Logan had built up that meant he had a lot to lose. Officer Jones on the other hand was a woman, black and quite early on in her career, all things that in Logan's eyes would have appeared as unfair advantages. The chance of her taking the fall if all this went wrong was minuscule. But somebody would have to. And that meant him.

'I'll be ready,' I said, 'I'll go down and wait in the hotel lobby.'

'And bring nothing with you,' said Logan, 'no phone, no electronic devices of any description.'

This was quite a turnaround from the 'we must have eyes on you everywhere' that I'd become accustomed to.

It was easy to recognise the driver. He was built like an American football player, was dressed mainly in black, had polished shoes and a self-assured look on his face.

'Mr Stewart?' he said.

'Yes,' I said.

'Let's go.'

The windows of the limo were all blacked out. The driver opened the back door and I got in. A screen separated the back of the car from the front, again it was blacked out. There was an intercom for communications. It was like being in the deluxe version of a prison van.

'Ready, Mr Stewart?' the driver's voice asked through the concealed speakers

'Ready,' I said, 'but I'm surprised you didn't frisk me.'

'There's a scanning device built into the doorframe of this vehicle, Mr Stewart, rest assured that if there was anything for me to worry about I would already know about it.'

That was reassuring, I thought. The speed of technology development and its miniaturisation was mind-boggling to me. I remembered a world before smartphones, damn it I remembered a world without the internet.

The driver started the engine and we drove off.

I soon got impatient and politely knocked on the screen that separated me from the driver. He was obviously hard of hearing. I knocked louder. And then louder still.

The intercom crackled into life.

'Yes sir?'

'Where are we going?' I asked.

'About 10 minutes sir,' the voice said politely.

I'd phrased my question wrong, this was of course the best answer I was going to get.

'Just sit back and relax.'

The intercom went dead.

Just out of interest I tried the door knowing it would probably be deadlocked. I was right.

There was no point worrying and taking a more thorough look around I found that someone had thoughtfully provided a couple of small bottles of mineral water within the central armrest. I wetted my throat with the one and splashed my hands and face with the other, pouring a little over my head to keep me awake. The water was chilled and did the trick. I straightened myself up as best I could and waited out the rest of the journey.

Eventually the car stopped and I heard an electronic door opening. The limo slipped through the gap and the door closed behind us. When the car stopped again the driver got out, came around and opened the back door for me.

'We're here,' he said, 'please follow me.'

The 'here' was an underground parking lot, all bare concrete and artificial lights. It was completely nondescript. I could have been anywhere in the city.

The driver shepherded me through a green door, up a stairwell and through another door, a dark blue one this time. On the other side of the door Logan was waiting for me. He was carrying the metal suitcase handcuffed to his right wrist.

'We've scanned the package,' he said, 'it's all clear.'

He took out a small key. Unlocked the handcuffs. Handed me the suitcase.

'OK,' he said, 'he's waiting.'

The driver turned around and went back to his car. I followed Logan down a carpeted corridor. When we got to the end he knocked on a polished mahogany door. The door was opened from within and we walked through.

'Hello, Mr Stewart,' said Officer Jones who had opened the door for us.

'Hi,' I said.

The room was wood-paneled, with artwork on the walls, lush carpeting, a table with dining chairs and green leather loungers.

Sitting in one of the loungers was Toni Malguzzi wearing a grey silk suit complete with matching waistcoat. Sitting in another was a man in a much darker suit, crew cut hair and the look of a bodyguard. Toni Malguzzi looked relaxed and didn't bother getting up. Logan nodded to the second man who got up and left.

Toni Malguzzi smiled.

'Well I've got to say, Michael, I'm impressed,' he said.

'I just did what you asked me to do,' I said.

His smile broadened.

'Well let me see,' he said.

I took the suitcase to the table, laid it on top and clicked open the catches. Toni Malguzzi got up and came over to join me. Officers Logan and Jones hung back but observed every move.

I lifted the package from the case reverentially, as if it were an offering. The brown paper looked flat and slick, the colourfulness of the ribbon was in stark contrast.

Toni Malguzzi took the package from me, put it down in front of him and leant over to untie the bow and slip the ribbon from the parcel, winding it carefully into a roll. Lifting the roll to his nose he sniffed,

'Tied with her own fair hands,' he said, his eyes sparkling, his lips drawn back maliciously, 'Sky was always fastidious. There was even a time when I thought we should get together, the perfect succession plan. But it didn't work out.'

That could be because you're a manipulative, conniving brute who always wants to take more, much more, than you give, I thought. But now wasn't the time to express an opinion so I just nodded.

'Ah well,' he said, placing the ribbon in his pocket, 'life always throws you curved balls.'

Unwrapping the brown paper he lifted out the picture and carried it to the window, angling it to catch the light, moving it around, examining it closely before holding it out at arm's length and gazing at it for a few seconds. Then he returned to the table.

'Nice picture,' he said, 'Do you think they knew who they were dealing with?'

'Did you want them to know?' I asked.

He grinned, 'You ain't as dumb as you look,' he said.

I was flattered.

'So it was never about the picture,' I said, 'it was all about getting it.'

Toni Malguzzi looked across at Officers Logan and Jones.

'Leave us,' he said, 'you're going to hear me sing like a canary, you're going to clear up so many cold cases that the judges' heads are going to be spinning, there are gonna be so many convictions that you're gonna need to add an extra wing to more than one penitentiary. But before that I want you to get out so I can have a private word with Mr Stewart here.'

'We can't…' started Officer Jones.

Logan interrupted '10 minutes,' he said, 'and we'll be right outside the door.'

'But…' said Officer Jones as Logan took a strong hold of her arm and marched her out of the room.

When the door had closed behind them Toni Malguzzi leant in close to me and said,

'I thought that coin was real,' he said, 'I got it from a guy I thought I could trust. But I was wrong. I got it looked at. It was an expensive job. Radiography, you know anything about that?' I said that I didn't, 'well anyways it showed that the coin was contaminated at parts per million or trillion or something, I forget which and it doesn't matter, by impurities not present in the gold used for coins in 1933. I was not happy and had a word with the fella I got it from, Ray Chaucer his name was, the guy they found in an alley, the guy I used as a pretext to go in to the station and make my offer. They could never have pinned it on me. I freely admitted having met with the guy in a bar an' got into a real intense conversation with him. Any DNA or other trace evidence they found on the body could easily have been transferred from me to him then.'

'Clever,' I said, just to encourage him to keep talking.

'I was planning to grass on the Vandlas and their crew anyways, those two cops just happened to be the ones I talked to. They're lucky. They're going to be heroes.'

When he said "the Vandlas and their crew" he meant his old friends and colleagues; nice guy.

'I was really pipped when I found out I'd been duped with the coin. I thought I might have to destroy it and then I saw the Picasso on the dark web. It was like someone was smiling down on me. I knew whose picture it was, I knew what his collecting passion really was. So now it was my turn. I thought it was worth a try to swap a fake coin for a painting worth around C$2 million if it was genuine. I wasn't worried it was stolen or that it was reported as being destroyed. I knew you guys would authenticate it for me and even if it was a fake I would still take it. I wanted Lejon to have the coin. It's such a good copy it's almost impossible to tell. But I would know.'

'So you set me up,' I said.

He smiled.

'That's why I'm telling you,' he said.

'You expected me to fail?'

'There was a good chance. But hey, I'd'a grassed on the Vandlas in any case. I just wanted to see if I could get one over on him.'

'You wanted to give them a poke,' I said, 'you wanted a last win.'

'Well whatever it was I wanted I got it thanks to you, Michael.'

I couldn't help thinking that he'd thrown me to the wolves and expected me to get eaten. I should have done. I couldn't understand why Sky's experts didn't pick up the discrepancy? Had Malguzzi been duped, I wondered? Was the coin actually real?

Toni Malguzzi laid the picture back onto the brown paper wrapping, and put it back into the suitcase. He snapped it closed.

'I'll put the picture into a vault,' he said, 'then maybe in a few years, when I'm resettled all nice an' cosy and I got me a nice spot to hang it, I'll get it out. It'll be a nice memento in my old age. You got to plan ahead, Michael, that's the key thing. I don't need it now but later it'll be a real bonus.'

'It's at least stolen,' I said, 'and reportedly destroyed.'

He grinned.

'Yea,' he said, 'great ain't it.'

'Are we done?' I asked.

'Oh no,' he said, 'I owe you and I always pay my debts.'

He reached into his inside jacket pocket and pulled out a manila envelope. I could see that it had the word 'SPIKE' written on the front in capital letters.

'Just like I promised,' he said, 'inside here is enough information to take Spike off the streets for a very long time. Here, it's yours.'

The envelope wasn't sealed. I opened it and took out the folded papers. I unfolded them and quickly scanned through, making a mental note of a couple of things.

'Names, places,' said Malguzzi, 'the locations he hides his souvenirs, and his routines, he's a creature of habit is our Spike.'

I re-folded the papers and slipped them back into the envelope and then I handed the envelope back to Toni Malguzzi.

'Do me a favour,' I said, 'when Officers Logan and Jones come back in give it straight to them.'

'You're a strange fish, Michael, you should make something out of this for yourself. What's the point of giving things away for free?'

'Just humour me,' I said.

'Then I think we can call it quits,' he said and came and slapped me on the shoulder, 'Good job, Michael, good job.'

I didn't enjoy the physical contact and I wasn't sure his praise was worth having.

Like AB had once said to me "you don't have to like somebody in order to work for them". I opened the door to call Logan and Officer Jones back into the room. I didn't want any more alone time with Toni Malguzzi.

'Everything alright?' asked Logan.

'Just fine,' said Malguzzi, 'and as a mark of good faith I've got this for you.'

He handed over the manila envelope.

'What is this?' asked Logan.

'It's a taste of the treasures to come,' said Malguzzi and he explained what was inside.

'Thank you,' said Officer Jones.

I wanted to tell her that her thanks were misplaced but I kept shtum.

'I'll be going now,' I said.

Toni Malguzzi held out his hand. I didn't want to shake it but I did. No point parting on bad terms.

'Farewell, Michael,' he said, 'may you get to heaven half an hour before the devil knows you're dead.'

You'll need at least an hour, I thought.

'Thanks,' I said, and turned to walk away.

'Just one more thing, Michael.'

'Yes.'

'Just remember; this never happened, we never met…you know that, right.'

I bit my tongue, clenched my fists and dug my fingernails into the palms of my hands to control the surge of adrenalin that was encouraging me to hit him; to hit him hard.

'I got it,' I said.

'Good. Now you can go.'

Being dismissed in this way, by a thug, was hard to take. I felt like he was goading me, taunting me, inviting me to have a go. I was seeing a glimpse of Toni Malguzzi's true character and why he was so dangerous to know. He was a bully. It was only because I knew he wanted me to rise to the bait that I didn't.

'Live long and prosper,' I said.

His grin followed me, digging in between my shoulder blades. I left him in the capable hands of Officers Logan and Jones. I wished them luck, Toni Malguzzi wasn't going to be easy to deal with, he would play and tease them all the way. The dark suited guy escorted me back to the limo. The driver was there waiting. As calmly as I could I climbed into the back seat and the driver closed the door.

'Get me the hell out of here,' I said to nobody in particular.

Chapter 51

The limo took me back to the hotel. I got out without a word. The driver closed the door behind me, got back into the driver's seat and drove away.

I felt lightheaded. I walked through the hotel reception area and over to the elevators. The acceleration which followed the closing of the elevator doors made me feel woozy and I staggered out and down the corridor to my room. Once inside I went straight to the bathroom, fell on my knees and vomited into the toilet bowl.

After splashing my face with cold water and rinsing and spitting my mouth clean I forced myself to undress, get under the shower for a few regenerative minutes and then move dreamlike, naked and wet, to collapse on the bed.

Even though it was not even midday I drifted in and out of an uncomfortable sleep for an hour or so before eventually the topsy-turvy of my dreamscapes settled into a concrete focus; I could feel I was naked, I could feel the pillow beneath my head, the bed beneath my torso and legs. My eyes brought objects slowly back into focus; a headboard, a bedside light, the mirrored door of a wardrobe. And in the mirror I saw the poor wreck of a man lying prone on top of a bed. Whoever he was, I thought in my drowsiness, he'd seen better days.

I spent the afternoon recovering some of my humanity. I'd helped two criminals successfully do a deal, producing what appeared on the face of it to be a win-win outcome. You'd think I should be overjoyed at this successful outcome achieved against the odds. But I wasn't.

As a byproduct I'd helped to clear the way for members of the Canadian authorities to unlock information that they intended to use to clear up a large number of otherwise cold cases. I might even have helped some people on their way to promotion or re-election. But this wasn't the way I wanted to spend the rest of my life. No, sirree.

It was time to bid farewell to Officers Logan and Jones. I thought it only fair to Logan that we meet in a restaurant so he could enjoy his last "on expenses" meal with me as the excuse.

He definitely made the most of it; 3 courses, each one the most expensive dish on the menu and a bottle of Grand Reserve Meritage from the Jackson-Triggs Niagara Estate Winery, a mixture of Merlot, Cabernet Sauvignon and Cabernet Franc grape varieties to accompany the main course.

He let me try the wine.

It was a dry red with cedar prominent on the nose and a smooth complexity of dark berry fruits on the tongue. Logan kept the majority of it for himself. It wasn't cheap.

Officer Jones ate more frugally, sticking to salads and fish with a glass of the house white and declining a dessert.

I just went for straightforward ribeye steak, medium rare, with pepper sauce.

Over the meal the chat was mundane, where we liked to holiday, favourite foods, anything but the thing that had brought us together.

Over coffee I asked,

'Do you think it was real?'

'Was what real?' said Logan, sipping the Spanish brandy that he'd ordered to go with his coffee.

'The picture,' I said, 'the Pic…'

Logan interrupted, 'What picture?' he said, 'you're not talking about that suitcase are you? We have no idea what was inside and we don't want to know.'

He nodded across to Officer Jones. She nodded back.

'All we know is that, for good or for bad, we agreed to help Toni Malguzzi with something, and it's done now.'

'Why would you agree to help somebody like that?' I asked.

'We didn't,' said Officer Jones.

'I don't understand politics,' said Logan, 'never will, never want to, but Toni Malguzzi convinced the powers that be that he has gold dust to sprinkle but before he starts to sprinkle it in earnest he wanted to know that he could trust them, he wanted something done for him first as proof of their good faith.'

'And he chose this trade?'

'God knows why,' said Logan, 'but he dangled the bait and they bit.'

'So why were you two chosen as his nursemaids?'

'We were the ones he first opened up to…' began Logan.

Officer Jones interrupted, 'It's simpler than that,' she said, 'he asked for us.'

'We don't know why,' agreed Logan, 'maybe he thought that if things went wrong he'd like to see us take the fall,' he paused, 'but once it was clear we needed a go-between, someone from out of town, someone that nobody here in Toronto knew, someone who wouldn't immediately be suspected of being associated with the police, then our problems got much smaller.'

'To be honest we thought it was an impossible task,' said Officer Jones, 'I couldn't believe that we'd agreed to help him. I kicked back but they told me it was way above my pay grade,' she broke eye contact, 'Logan and me agreed we needed to be seen to be helping you as much as possible while never taking our eyes off of you. The last thing we needed was another problem.'

'And that's why you went way overboard with the surveillance?' I said.

'We didn't know who was going to arrive, we had no choice in the matter, you could have been a real ass hole, you could have been completely incompetent, whatever you were our job was to be nice and helpful,' said Logan.

I looked at Officer Jones, 'The first thing you said to me was that I drank too much coffee, you were looking after my health right away.'

She laughed. It relieved some of the tension.

'I couldn't help it,' she said, 'the last thing we needed was someone with hyperactivity.'

'And I thought it was because you cared,' I said smiling, 'but seriously, you expected this deal to collapse?'

'We couldn't see it panning out any other way,' said Logan, 'I'm sorry, Michael, but in a situation like this you've got to look after number one first.'

'But you couldn't have got away without being tarnished with some of the blame,' I said.

'That's true,' said Logan, 'our personal mission was damage limitation.'

'And me?'

'You chose to be in the firing line,' said Logan.

'Or was chosen,' I said.

'Whatever the case, Michael,' said Officer Jones, 'I'm sorry but you were the one who was going to take the fall. Whatever went wrong, it wasn't going to be our fault. If it was anybody's it was going to be yours.'

'If it had gone wrong there would have had to be somebody to blame,' said Logan, 'the higher-ups who had pandered to Toni Malguzzi's request would then have been desperately trying to make it up to him, trying to ensure he didn't clam up and leave them high and dry. He'd already whetted their appetite to the point that he had them drooling.'

'Is his information really worth all this?' I asked.

'I really don't know,' said Officer Jones, 'as someone once said, "you don't know what you don't know" and Malguzzi is playing on that, he keeps insinuating that he has lots of precious, never before seen information. I don't know, he's a difficult guy to trust.'

Now there was something I could heartily agree with.

'He was on the inside,' said Logan, 'he's got to know something and he's got lots of old scores he wants to settle, maybe that will play into our hands.'

'Although every act of revenge is a link in a chain that can only be finally broken by forgiveness,' said Officer Jones philosophically.

'Or not,' said Logan, 'in my experience it is forgiveness and not revenge that's always in short supply. If there was too much forgiveness a lot of us cops would be out of work.'

'On the other hand,' said Officer Jones, 'a lot of the people Toni Malguzzi's likely to finger are either dead or already or in jail, convicted on other charges. Not many of these kind of people only commit one crime.'

'But cold cases are like old wounds,' said Logan, 'they keep aching, and politics is politics, if we can clear a lot of this stuff up then there'll be positive headlines for once and people in office can declare that "every crime matters", that they're "tough on crime" and that the world is a safer place thanks to their efforts. They'll big up the Vandlas, make them seem like modern day versions of Al Capone, make it clear that they're clearing the streets of people like that.'

'But they'd retired already,' I said.

'Not a fact that would interest the newspapers,' said Logan, 'why let a little thing like that get in the way of a good story.'

'Well I'm pleased I didn't let you down,' I said, 'even though I find it difficult to understand how this has all worked out the way that it has.'

'Never look a gift horse in the mouth,' said Logan, 'and remember Toni Malguzzi has already coughed up enough on Spike to get him off the streets for a very long time. Hopefully that's a sign of the things to come.'

'Does the information hold up?' I asked.

'We're checking through it now,' said Officer Jones, 'but it's looking good so far.'

'We'll be picking Spike off the sidewalk real soon,' said Logan.

'So I guess my work is done,' I said.

'Yea,' said Logan, 'nice to meet you and thanks for the food.'

I was pretty sure that at least one of these sentiments was from the heart.

'Yea, thanks,' said Officer Jones, 'is there anything else we can do for you?'

I thought about it.

'Just one thing,' I said, 'your first name, you can tell me that.'

'My first name?'

'Yes, I'm guessing you've got one.'

She smiled.

'Felicity,' she said, 'my first name is Felicity.'

'Well Felicity Jones, thank you for all your help and I promise I'll try and cut down on the caffeine.'

'Oh yea?'

'Oh yea,' I said.

When I got back to my room I was surprised to find there was a "missed call" on my phone. I'd left it behind when I'd gone out to meet with Officers Logan and Jones to avoid distractions. I wasn't surprised there was a missed call. I was surprised that the missed call was from Sky Vandla.

I dialed into my voicemail in some trepidation. Was Sky going to pull the rug out from under my feet at this late stage? Her voice came out loud and clear.

'I guess you're surprised,' she said, 'you probably didn't expect to hear from me again but I just wanted you to know that I managed to show my father the coin. It meant a lot to me to do that. So that's all, I just wanted you to know. Goodbye, Michael.'

And that was it.

I thought it was a strange thing for Sky to do but I felt like there were some hidden messages here that I was missing. The only message that was blindingly obvious was that she knew how to contact me directly and that was no longer a good thing so I destroyed the phone and flushed the SIM card down the toilet. It seemed appropriate somehow.

As for Sky I couldn't work her out. I knew that I'd warmed to her a lot more than I'd warmed to Toni Malguzzi. I knew that, with her father, she was top of Toni Malguzzi's hit list and was therefore unlikely to be heading towards a bright future. I knew that her father's time was limited and that she cared about him. I knew that completing this trade meant something more to Sky than just completing the trade but I didn't know what and I didn't know why. I probably never would.

I decided to take a shower and began to take off my clothes.

My soul needed cleansing.

The Next Night

The man who exits the night club is tall and rangy, his head is topped with a shock of white hair, like snow atop a mountain. It is city dark, moonless but lit with the multitudinous colours of artificial light.

It has been raining. The rain has turned the tarmac and the sidewalks into mirrors that give back a rainbow of reflections.

It is not raining now.

The man reaches into a pocket and brings out a small plastic bottle of peppermint mouthwash, he takes a swig, swirls it around his mouth and then spits it out. He puts the top back on the bottle, makes sure that it's secure, and then puts it back into his pocket.

Every city has its alleyways, cloaked in shadow during the day, black slits bitten between the shop fronts at night.

The man walks on confidently.

He is not drunk, he has more nous than to let alcohol fog his senses when he's out on the streets. He could have taken a cab but he's on his way to an apartment where a woman is waiting for him, a married woman, and he's not her husband.

What a perfect way to end the night, he thinks.

As he passes yet another black slit an arm reaches out of the darkness, grabs him around the neck, knocks the breath out of him and drags him deeper into the dark. It is the work of less than a second.

His body topples. His head hits concrete.

As his eyes struggle to focus, to become dark adapted, he hears a voice in his ear.

'I don't like you,' it says, muffled by a black balaclava.

Spike regains some of his composure, he pulls against the grip of his assailant but cannot break free. Turned onto his front his nose is already smeared with the oily grime of the alley floor. The assailant's knees are lodged in the middle of his back, a forearm clamped across the back of his neck.

'Do you know who...' says Spike.

'Of course, do you think I do this for fun?' comes the answer.

There is a moment's silence, Spike is struggling to breathe.

'I'll...' he manages to spit out through gritted teeth.

'You won't do anything. You'll lie quiet that's what you'll do. When you're rotting away in jail I want you to remember this moment.'

'They won't...'

'Everybody gets caught eventually and now is your time.'

'Wha...'

'So enjoy your freedom while you can and take this little present from me.'

Expertly a single blow is delivered and Spike's consciousness disappears in a shower of sparks. The assailant removes a watch from Spike's wrist. It is a Rolex GMT Master II with a black face, a bi-coloured black/blue cerachrom bezel and a finely polished stainless steel strap. There is a single scratch on the watch-glass running directly from above the 2 on the dial down to the 5.

Outside the alley, on the street, there is the sound of a police siren. The assailant gets slowly to his feet, removes his gloves and balaclava and throws them into an open skip. Then he takes an iron bar and prods them down into the sludgy detritus.

Seconds later he emerges into the lights that colour the main street; red, yellow, white... flashing blue.

As he walks away a police car pulls up alongside the opening to the alley. A torch is switched on and sweeps into the darkness.

'There he is,' says Logan, 'he appears to have had a fall.'

Back in the hotel Mark Wilson bags his clothes for the hotel laundry, lays his watch on the bedside table, showers and gets into bed.

'Ooo you're cold,' says Teresa as she feels the touch of his skin against her back. Her arrival only a few hours ago was a welcome surprise. She couldn't stay away she'd said.

'Sorry,' says Mark, making to move away.

'Don't move away,' says Teresa, 'you'll warm up fast enough.'

Later she says, 'Are you feeling better now?'

'Much,' says Mark, who is soon breathing evenly, deep in a dreamless sleep.

One Week Later

I was back in London, in AB's office, my auburn hair colouring was starting to grow out.

We were sitting in studded green leather Chesterfield armchairs, the arms rubbed and worn with age. Between us was a low, oval, hardwood table. Each of us held a cut-glass tumbler and on the table, on a silver tray, was a half full bottle of whisky, a bucket of ice cubes and a small jug of ice cold water. The condensation on the outside of the jug coalesced into droplets that trickled downwards towards the pristine, absorbent surface of a white napkin.

'I just don't know how to feel,' I said, 'was this assignment a success or a failure? Did we help a criminal acquire a stolen painting and another acquire illegal currency?'

'You survived didn't you,' said AB, 'that's a good start.'

'But was the coin a fake?' I said, 'Was the Picasso a forgery?'

'Does it matter?' said AB.

'What do you mean?'

'Well,' said AB, 'if Toni Malguzzi believed he got one over on the Vandlas and if Lejon Vandla believed he got the coin that every serious North American numismatist covets then what does it matter if they're both mistaken?'

'As long as they each believe they've won then that's OK?'

'Can you think of a better outcome?'

I mulled it over. I couldn't. I really couldn't.

'They are both from the world of the backstabber,' said AB, 'where there is always someone plotting your downfall. They knew the ground rules.'

'You mean all that choreography on the island was all unnecessary?' I said, exasperated.

'Theatre, dear boy, only theatre,' said AB, 'when two parties want the same outcome then nothing can stand in their way.'

'But the feedback from our experts, Meredith-Taylor and Kieran Lansbury, that was real?'

'Yes,' said AB, 'thankfully. As for the Picasso it would have had to be a poor fake to conclusively prove it wrong in such a short time,' he paused, 'and "inconclusive" was more than good enough under the circumstances. I would have had a tougher job if the experts had come down heavily on the side of forgery. But let's be honest here, I would have used my right of veto and voted in favour of the picture in any case.'

'And do you think that it was the same for the other side, accepting the coin as genuine I mean?'

'Undoubtedly,' said AB, 'if Toni Malguzzi handed us a fake coin then at least it was a good one.'

I remembered what Toni Malguzzi had told me. He was clear in his own mind that the coin wasn't genuine. He was just taking a punt.

'But,' I said, 'I'm sorry, sir, but I'd like to know. Why did you give such personal attention to this assignment? It's not the most important thing in your diary.'

'Don't do yourself down,' said AB, 'every assignment is important.'

'You know what I mean,' I said.

AB considered for a moment.

'You've decided to leave us,' he said.

'Yes,' I said, 'I think my time as a go-between is done. I want to be front and centre in whatever comes next.'

'Good for you. I wish you and your bride-to-be all the best.'

So he knew about that too! I was constantly astounded by how much AB knew, the multitude of minutiae that he could retain in his mind.

'And the reason you showed such an interest?' I persisted.

'Ah,' he said, 'you probably do deserve an explanation and I can't see that it can do any harm, especially as you're leaving us.'

I didn't really care about his reasoning. I just wanted to know.

'You will remember,' said AB, 'that I did not want to accept this assignment.'

I thought back to the first briefing in his office. I could remember that very clearly.

'The reason for that is that I have rules, I have rules that I play by, that keep me sane. This assignment broke one of those cardinal rules.'

I could understand that someone with the background AB had, private school, military service, would have had the need for discipline and the adherence to clearly defined rules drilled into him from birth. So much so that it would now be a part of him and flow through his system like blood. But other than grasping the concept I had no idea what he was talking about in this specific instance.

I just kept quiet. If he wanted to tell me he would.

'I do not believe in revenge,' he said, 'I believe in the system. I accept that the system is not perfect and that there will be some who escape the justice they deserve. But I accept this and will never step outside the system and carry out my own form of justice, no matter the temptation.'

I had always thought AB was a stronger and a better man than me.

'In our line of work,' he continued. 'the temptation to turn vigilante is sometimes extreme. We walk on thin ice but I have always tried to do the job objectively and keep within the bounds of my own beliefs and training. Otherwise I do not think I could sleep at night.'

You're right, I thought, reflecting on my own disturbed slumbers.

'But on this assignment I overstepped the mark,' he said.

'How?' I asked.

He looked at me. I could see the pain in his eyes,

'I know Toni Malguzzi,' he said, 'he will not remember me but we have met before.'

'Oh,' l said.

'Yes, I spent some time in North America when I was younger.'

AB glanced at me. I was listening.

'Believe it or not I had this idea of trying to make the world a better place,' he said, 'and managed to almost get myself killed.'

He refilled his whisky glass and passed me the decanter. The straw coloured liquid rolled into my tumbler. I filled it to halfway. I wasn't planning on doing anything very much for the rest of the day.

'A colleague and I were trying to infiltrate a street gang but our cover got blown.' He took a mouthful of the fiery liquid from his glass and swallowed hard, clenching his teeth. 'My colleague, a woman, was shot dead. I barely escaped. I won't forget the face of the shootist. He was completely unemotional, just matter-of-fact in his dealing out of death. We were just a tidying up job that he needed to do.'

His head dropped, his gaze fell unfocused on the floor.

'The woman?' I asked.

He didn't answer.

That was answer enough.

'Toni Malguzzi was the shootist?'

He cupped his glass in both hands, it was almost an attitude of prayer.

'He was a younger man then,' was all that he said.

There was silence in the room. I knew that outside cars would be jostling through the streets, pedestrians would be walking purposefully, pursuing their secret journeys. Life would be passing by.

In AB's office the closed windows blocked out all external sound.

'But,' I said, 'you helped Toni Malguzzi get what he wanted. Why would you do that?'

'Why indeed,' said AB, 'Do you think Sky and Lejon Vandla could guess who was behind the leaking of information to the authorities, information that had already resulted in Lejon Vandla being incarcerated? Do you think that they might have considered who could have developed such a grudge against him so late in the game?'

'You think they knew it was Toni Malguzzi?'

AB held up a hand, 'In the world of the backstabber it's always important to know who's holding the knife. Maybe they did, or maybe they just suspected it, but in either case what do you think they might do?'

'Go fishing,' I said, 'throw out a baited line and see if anything bites.'

'Quite right,' said AB, 'that's quite the logical thing to do, and Sky is a logical woman.'

'You think Sky was behind it?'

'Her father was incarcerated on suspicion, he is dying of inoperable pancreatic cancer. By her own admission she is her father's girl, don't you think she would want to try and help him? Don't you think she would want to find the source of Lejon's pain and take it away in an effort to gain for him a little more time in the outside world?'

'And she knew about Toni Malguzzi's interest in art.'

'She is trained in art herself. Maybe Sky remembered the envy Toni Malguzzi showed when he saw the Picasso in Lejon's private collection. If they were trying to come up with suitable bait...'

'Then the Picasso was worth a go.'

'Especially with its colourful history. Toni Malguzzi would know the story, maybe it was even Lejon who originally told it to him.'

'So then they had to cast the line out and into the right pond.'

'The dark web. A pond they knew that Toni Malguzzi liked to visit.'

'It was speculative,' I said, 'a shot in the dark.'

'What better did they have? Maybe they threw out other baits but we don't know about them because Toni Malguzzi never found them.'

'But he found this one.'

'Yes, and he immediately knew who the seller was.'

'But why bother, why not just cough up all the information he had, get Lejon and maybe Sky convicted and then go disappear into the sunset?'

'Because for Toni Malguzzi this was about getting even. This wasn't about social justice or in order to salve a guilty conscience, this was about settling a grudge and in the end he wanted Lejon and Sky Vandla to know who it was that had done it to them.'

'So he dangled his own bait?'

'He knew Lejon's passion for coins. He knew he could never turn down the chance to own a 1933 Double Eagle even if they are completely illegal tender.'

And he'd got one, I thought, and had just been disappointed in its authenticity. He could offload a problem and make a win at the same time.

'So he made his offer.'

'Yes, and the Vandlas knew that such a strange offer could only come from someone who knew them well. Chances were they'd hooked their fish.'

'But why didn't Toni Malguzzi just buy the Picasso for money?'

'Because he didn't have the money. And anyway he didn't know how many other people had seen it on the dark web and shown an interest. He didn't want to get involved in a bidding war in which the Vandlas were in control. He wanted to be top of the list and so far top of the list that he was the only one the Vandlas would consider dealing with.'

'So he made an over-the-top offer?'

'He certainly did, massively over-generous, his idea being that he would pretend not to know the true value of what he was offering, he'd say he got it in settlement of some other debt and didn't know what to do with it, that he'd realised it was illegal tender and wanted to get rid of it.'

'So the Vandlas took the chance that they'd hooked the right fish,' I said.

'And were reassured when the real purchaser hid away and we, you to be more precise, were put in the middle. A completely unnecessary additional complication to completing the deal.'

I wasn't sure I liked being called "a completely unnecessary additional complication" but I let it pass.

'And the rest is history,' I said.

'As you say,' said AB.

I tried to get this all straight in my head. I was sure there was one critical point I was missing. It came to me.

'But why did you help him get what he wanted?'

'You have to be careful what you wish for,' he said, 'you may get more than you bargained for,' he paused, took a drink of whisky, 'do you like history?' he said.

This seemed to be a sudden digression but I went along with it.

'Yes,' I said.

'There's a lot to be learned from studying the past,' he said.

I agreed with him.

'Someone like Napoleon for example, he is reputed to have once said "Never interrupt an enemy when he is making a mistake".'

'Interesting,' I said, not understanding the connection.

'Not just interesting but apposite,' said AB.

'I'm lost,' I said, 'I'm afraid, you'll need to spell it out for me.'

'Well,' said AB, 'if you want to do something nasty to somebody what's the first thing you need to know?'

At least that was an easy one.

'Where they are,' I said, 'how to get to them.'

'Precisely,' said AB, 'and in this case, unless you have zero confidence in Canada's witness protection scheme and their use of safe houses, then that would be a difficult thing for the Vandlas to find out.'

'But how does all of this help them find out where Toni Malguzzi is hiding?'

'Technology,' said AB, 'I told you about it; solar cells as thin as threads, nanotechnology, tracers that can "sleep" to avoid detection and then be reactivated remotely.'

I thought about it.

'Oh shit!' I said, 'the ribbon! We scanned the package but it could have been in "sleep" mode.' I thought back, 'Toni Malguzzi put the ribbon in his pocket! We've got to tell someone!'

AB held up his hand.

'But!'

'How closely do you follow the Canadian newspapers?' he asked.

'Not at all,' I admitted.

He walked over to his desk, pulled open the top right hand drawer and took out a newspaper. He brought it over and handed it to me and then walked back to sit behind his desk. The newspaper was opened and folded to reveal a short article on page 9.

I started to read,

Ex-Gangster Found Dead

The body of Mr Antonio Malguzzi was found yesterday on a beach not far outside of Sydney, Nova Scotia. His remains were identified by a distinctive tattoo of a spider on the back of his left hand. Mr Malguzzi is known to have played a part in Toronto's criminal underworld but was never convicted of any criminal offence. He is understood to have retired to Nova Scotia quite recently.

We understand it is likely that the body had been floating in the water for some hours and was only washed up early yesterday morning. What little information we have from the Investigating Authorities informs us that the body was spotted by a local woman walking her dog.

The only other information we have is that the body was fully clothed and that the deceased was wearing a red, white and yellow striped ribbon around his neck from which hung a small silver urn that, on inspection, was found to contain some sort of ashes. Compared to the rest of his clothing such a necklace is incongruous although it is not thought to have any bearing on Mr Malguzzi's death. Indeed the Police are not anticipating the need for any further investigations as it is believed that Mr Malguzzi's death is solely the result of some kind of tragic accident.

Details of Mr Malguzzi's funeral will be released in due course.

I put the paper down. So this was why AB had said this conversation couldn't do any harm. It was because it was too late.

'It didn't take them long,' I said.

'I don't think they could afford it to,' said AB.

I got up to leave.

'Of course,' said AB, 'everything we just discussed is pure speculation.'

'But…'

'But you're leaving us and this conversation never happened.'

I thought for a moment.

'What conversation,' I said.

AB got up from his desk, came over to me and patted me on the shoulder.

'Go well, Mark,' he said, 'and thank you for your service.'

I took a final look round and then left AB's office for the last time closing the door behind me.

'How did it go?' said Samantha.

'As well as could be expected,' I said.

'So you're definitely leaving us?'

'Yes,' I said, 'the time is right I think, better to move on than to overstay your welcome.'

'You were always a pain in the ass,' she said.

Was this her way of saying she was sorry to see me go?

'Thanks,' I said, 'I always thought you were on top of everything.'

She smiled.

'Like a swan,' she said, 'gliding over the surface…'

'…while paddling like mad underneath,' I finished it off for her.

'Something like that,' she said.

'I'll miss you,' I said.

She smiled again, that was twice in one day. I was definitely one of her favourites.

'You're so full of shit,' she said, 'now go on, push off, I'm busy.'

She was good at everything else but she wasn't good with emotion. It was as I was walking out of the door that I heard her say,

'Good luck, Mark,' into my shoulder blades.

I didn't turn round. I didn't want to embarrass her.

2 Weeks Later

The man, tall and in a tailored pin stripe suit pushed open the black-painted, pealing metal gate. It gave way complainingly on its encrusted hinges. The man entered the grounds and took a clean white handkerchief, with maroon embroidered initials, from his breast pocket and wiped the specks of rust and dirt from his hands.

He wore a bespoke pale blue shirt anchored by a regimental tie with a precise windsor knot. The gloss on his shoes was be-speckled with brown dirt and he tutted as he looked down at them. Raising his bald head he looked forward with purpose and made his way along the gravel path and deeper into the graveyard.

The gardener was on his knees, pulling up weeds and tending to the flowers. His hands were work hardened and stained brown, his clothing frayed and soiled. He was too engrossed in his task to hear the approaching visitor and gave a start when he was greeted politely but unexpectedly from behind.

The visitor apologised and the gardener started to get up. It was an evident struggle for muscles, tendons and bones worn by time and the visitor reached out a strong hand to help. After a short exchange of niceties the visitor asked if the gardener knew the whereabouts of a particular grave.

The gardener nodded and asked if the visitor would like to be shown the way. The visitor gratefully accepted and the mismatched couple set off together, the gardener leading.

It was not far and soon the gardener stopped and pointed. The visitor thanked him and reached into an inside pocket, extracting a thick wadge of folded notes that were clipped together by a silver clasp. He offered the entire thing to the gardener saying that he wished to make a donation to the upkeep of the grounds. The gardener did not seem surprised but smiled and reached out his hand to touch the visitor on the shoulder saying that he did his work voluntarily, that it was his privilege to do it and that he had no need of extra funds. The church roof on the other hand... the restoration fund would hugely appreciate such a generous contribution. The donation box was inside the church if the visitor would care to enter. The visitor promised that he would do that before he left and thanked the gardener who shambled off, back to his weeding.

The pinstripe suited man turned and looked down at the headstone.

Jade Kirkbride
Aged 23
Beloved daughter...

The man's eyes misted over and tears flowed freely down his cheeks. He did not attempt to stop them or to wipe them away. One or two dropped from his chin and fell onto the green grass that now grew over the place where the coffin had been lowered into the ground. How long ago? Yesterday? 5 years ago? 10? 20? More?

The man put his hand on the top of the cold stone.

'Jade, you were much more than a colleague,' he said, 'you know that. I loved you. I should have been able to protect you. He should have shot me, not you.'

'I'm sorry, I'm so sorry,' he whispered and then he told her about Toni Malguzzi's death, that, as she had begged of him in the hospital, he had not gone hunting for revenge, that it was Toni Malguzzi himself who had brought about his own demise. If he had done anything then it was only that he had done nothing to stop it. She had to forgive him that. He had kept his promise.

He thought about the life they thought they could have. The life that was taken away from both of them.

He lowered his head and his eyes fell to the ground, his gaze passing over the final line on the engraved headstone, subconsciously absorbing the words...

NOW AT PEACE

He knew he was not at peace, would never be at peace with what he'd lost. But he'd obeyed her rules.

It was starting to rain.

'I miss you,' he said, 'every day.'

He turned and made his way towards the church. The gardener had gone. When he got inside he found the donation box. The church would have its roof repaired.

It's the least he could do.

Back in his office the next day the intercom on AB's desk buzzed. He reached forward.

Click.

'The Minister is here to see you, sir,' Samantha said.

AB thought for a moment.

'Give me a minute,' he said.

He had been looking at a framed photograph of two young people with their arms around each other, soaking wet in red plastic ponchos, Niagara's Horseshoe Falls raging behind them. They were both smiling into the camera.

AB slid open the left hand drawer of his desk and put the picture, face up, inside. He closed the drawer and locked it. Then he straightened his shoulders and reached for the intercom.

'I'm ready now, Samantha, please show him in,' he said.

'Certainly, sir.'

The heavy mahogany door swung gently open. Samantha stood aside to allow a smartly dressed individual in tailored clothing and well polished shoes to enter.

'The Prime Minister,' she said, although the familiar features and gait needed no introduction.

AB held out his hand,

'Prime Minister, do please take a seat and tell me how can I help.'

Samantha closed the door quietly on her way out.

2 Months Later

Ex-gangland Boss Dies in Prison

It has been reported that two days ago Mr Lejon Vandla an ex-Toronto gangland leader was found unconscious in his cell. Although still breathing when he was found he never regained consciousness and died 10 hours later. It is known that Mr Vandla was suffering from inoperable pancreatic cancer and it is almost certain that this was the ultimate cause of his death. Although Mr Vandla was being held in a correction centre on suspicion we believe that he was due for imminent release due to lack of evidence.

Mr Vandla is survived by one daughter to whom he is said to have been very close.

Out of the blue I got a call from "The Store" telling me that a small package had arrived for me and that they would forward it on to my London apartment. When it arrived I noted that it was addressed to "Mr M. Stewart". I opened it. Inside was a note,

Dear Michael,

I'm sure you will have heard that my father has now passed away. He died as comfortably as possible in the circumstances and without ever backing away from the fight he waged against his tumour even though, ultimately, he

lost it. Acquiring the coin that you helped to get into his hands was one of the last joys of his life. I never knew, nor want to know now whether it was real or fake and have no further use for it. I hope that you will accept it as a gift from me and that it may be of some value to you.

Yours,

Sky Vandla

I lifted the package up by one corner and the coin, still encapsulated in its protective plastic shell, fell onto the table.

Well that is somewhat unexpected, I thought.

I prized open the plastic case, took out the coin and gazed at the eagle, the date, the face value and wondered what on earth to do with it.

The sensible thing would be to turn it in but that somehow didn't seem right. After all it was a gift and Toni Malguzzi had declared it a fake.

I weighed it in my hand.

There was quite a weight of gold there and I was in need of two matching wedding rings. Why not, I thought, it would take it permanently out of circulation and Teresa need never know that she and I may be wearing two of the most expensive wedding rings in history.

I decided to melt it down myself before taking the gold to a jewelers and I knew that Kieran Lansbury's laboratory in Manchester had the right equipment.

With a melting point of over 1,000 degrees Centigrade I decided I'd better invest in some gloves.

I'd promised Kieran a get-together so this could a great way of killing two birds with one stone. I was sure he'd recognize me now that my hair was back to its normal colouring and we could invite around some of our old chums. I'd get a good bottle of whisky, maybe more, and we could talk about old times.

4 Months Later

It was a small wedding, nothing fancy, a few family and friends that's all. The chapel was cosy and ancient beams spanned the space above us. My daughter was best man.

'Have you got the rings?' I asked, not for the first time.

She answered in the affirmative.

The day itself was a bit of a blur. As far as I can remember everything went well. The matching gold wedding rings were a hit.

I remember seeing Brett rather fearfully holding Amelia, it looked like he was praying she wouldn't kick off. As far as I can recall she didn't.

I also remember that AB had snuck in at the back and stayed long enough to shake my hand and kiss the bride. That was a real surprise, I didn't think we were that close.

Teresa and I had talked about what music should be playing as we walked back up the aisle as newly-weds. My suggestion of AC/DC's "Highway to Hell" was an early casualty and Led Zeppelin's "Stairway to Heaven" came close but in the end we settled on Tom Petty and the Heartbreaker's "Learning to Fly". I have no idea whether this was actually played or not because by this time my mind was all at sea.

After the reception we had the intention of dancing late into the night. Although I wasn't really paying attention Teresa didn't seem to be drinking much, but I was. I wasn't drunk, I'm not quite that stupid, but I was what is commonly called "happy". To be fair this was one occasion when I didn't need alcohol to achieve this condition.

Early on in the evening Brett came to tell me that he, my daughter and my granddaughter had to be going, it was well past their bedtime. It was amazing that they'd traveled all the way to Scotland to be at our wedding. Teresa and I saw them off.

'Thanks for being a perfect "best man",' I said to my daughter, 'your speech was great.' Although I had already forgotten every word, but then again I'd have remembered it if anything had gone badly wrong. I'm that kind of guy.

'My pleasure,' she said.

'And Brett,' I said, 'thanks for looking after Amelia, it was a lot for her to cope with.'

Brett let out a huge sigh, 'Just glad it's over, pops,' he said. Then he realised what he'd said, the dig in the ribs from my daughter probably helped.

I laughed. I was starting to like him, 'I know what you mean,' I said, 'I was pretty on edge myself.'

Teresa said to my daughter, 'Thanks for all your help.'

'Oh that's OK, I know what a pain he can be.'

I'm still here, I thought!

'And anyway we women have to stick together, especially at these life changing moments.'

Teresa gave her a strange look. My daughter smiled.

'How did you...?'

'Like I said, we women understand each other, we need to stick together.'

I didn't understand any of this, it was as if they'd switched into speaking Klingon.

'I'll look forward to it,' said Teresa.

There followed a mutual bout of hugging and kissing and the shaking of hands. I might be warming to Brett but I didn't feel like getting too close.

Once they'd left I turned to Teresa,

'What was that all about?'

'All what?'

'That "We're all girls together" stuff.'

She took my hand,

'Come on Mr husband, let's go and dance.'

As we walked in she said.

'And I hope you're not a man that needs a lot of sleep.'

Was this a promise for later? The look on her face spoke of something deeper, but the significance didn't register at the time...

'How's it going?' asked my daughter about 5 months later, pointing at the bump.

'We've had the scan,' said Teresa.

'And?'

'And all looks good.'

'And?'

Teresa looked across at me. I nodded.

'It's a boy,' she said breaking into the largest smile that would fit onto her face.

My daughter hugged her and the next few moments were simply a incoherent gaggle of everybody congratulating everybody else, even Brett joined in.

Later, glass of red wine in hand, granddaughter in bed, the two ladies chattering away at the end of the garden, Teresa with her fruit juice, Brett, the young dad, snoozing beside me, grabbing any opportunity to catch up on missed sleep, I sat back, relaxed and thought for a moment. All being well I was going to have a son, a son who would be younger than my granddaughter. My daughter was going to have a brother who was younger than her own daughter. My granddaughter was going to have an uncle who was younger than her.

I smiled.

Families can be so complicated, I thought.

Bring it on!

New Public exhibition - Artist says 'Interpretations must not be confused with fakes.'

By Fiona Faber, British Columbia Art Critic.

The Vancouver Art Gallery today unveiled the first solo exhibition of the work of an up and coming Canadian artist who prefers to be known only as SV. This artist, as our regular readers will know, controversially splits her portfolio of work between interpretations of classical artwork and her own wholly original pieces. This exhibition explores both of these aspects.

I caught up with SV at last night's opening party and asked her first about her ability to accurately recreate the artwork of others, 'If you are to do it with respect,' she says, 'then you must pay careful attention not just to the artwork itself but to the pigments, the substrate, the brushstrokes.' Such close attention to detail has brought SV both plaudits for authenticity and criticism for walking a fine line between interpretation and fakery. 'I declare all of my artwork as my own,' she says, 'there is no attempt at subterfuge, these paintings are my attempt to pay a kind of homage to the original, to learn how they were created by recreating them and in so doing to learn how I can apply some of their techniques to my own original compositions'. When asked if she would ever consider trying to pass one of these paintings off as the work of the original artist she answers with a very emphatic 'of course not'.

When you view the works of this growingly popular artist you are immediately struck by her lively and experimental spirit. From portraiture to landscape you experience her pursuit of style, her constant flow of ideas and the vigor with which they are delivered.

If you're at all interested in the direction contemporary Canadian art is taking or want to view the controversial 'interpretations' of works by Matisse, Van Gogh and Picasso that have caused such debate then this exhibition is a must see for you.

Sometime Later

What Makes a 'Successful' Business?
Anna Lesley looks at a small business with big dreams to find out.

By Anna Lesley, Assistant Editor, 'Business is Awesome Magazine'

While there can be no foolproof method of building a business talking with up and coming company owners can bring both salutary and meaningful lessons. This month I had the pleasure of meeting Teresa and Mark Wilson the co-owners of "Teresa's Costa Rican Coffee and Consumables – From the Artisan to your door – Original and Hassle free" to talk about their success so far and their plans for the future.

I asked Teresa first what she thought was the secret of her success 'I am from Costa Rica,' she said, 'and I am proud to be from Costa Rica, my roots are there, my extended family. I know how to select the best coffee, the best spices and the best cosmetics for export to the US. In our company we want to be known for the quality of our products, the reliability of our delivery.'

'I knew there was a market,' she told me, 'Costa Rica is a great country with some great natural products that I knew would be welcomed by a lot of people in the United States.' And she was right, customers have given rave reviews to her Coffee, Cosmetics and Spices and word of mouth has grown the customer base. 'As an online business,' Teresa said, 'customer reviews are really important to us. A happy customer is not just a returning customer but also an advocate for our products.'

This model has certainly worked for the business so far with turnover increasing by a factor of five in the last three years alone.

As I looked around their office I saw what looked like the front flap of a manila folder with the word "Agaricus" written on it in large neat script that had been framed and hung on the wall. It seemed incongruous. I asked Mark about it, 'It's a reference to our famous mushroom sauce,' he said, 'a reminder of where we've come from'. For me, although I obviously missed the connection, it reminded me that all businesses have a history, are on a journey and picking up mementoes along the way can provide positive reminders of progress.

'We'll be opening more distribution hubs soon,' Teresa said in answer to my next question about their plans for the future, 'we need to make sure we can continue to give our growing number of customers an excellent service ensuring that they each get what they want, when they want it.' Teresa is obviously enthusiastic about these core principles and the importance of expansion. 'Mark will take charge of all that,' she added.

When I quiz Teresa on how the split of responsibility works between her and Mark she said, 'I do the product choice, procurement and development, liaising with my contacts in Costa Rica and I lead on the sales front, Mark does everything else.'

'I'm getting better at following instructions,' Mark quipped when I asked him what "everything else" actually meant. 'I look after the financials, our employees, the storage and distribution and I like to explore how technology can be best used to streamline what we do, technology is moving so fast there's no chance of getting bored,' he thought for a moment and then he added, 'But the dividing line is fluid,' he smiled, 'meaning that Teresa gets involved in whatever she wants to and I keep the pieces joined together.'

I asked Teresa if she has ambitions to move onto the high street or remain wholly online, 'I'm happy to remain virtual,' she said, 'that way we can treat all of our customers the same and not favor some over others depending on where our stores might be located.'

I came away believing that here is a business with its head screwed on right, it has a clear mission to sell goods manufactured in Costa Rica into the United States, two equally committed owners and a growing number of satisfied customers. 'It's all about managing relationships,' as Mark explained it to me, 'from our suppliers and developers through shipping and storage to distribution and sales. It's all geared to ensuring our customers are satisfied.' And long may it continue, I say. The most important relationship evident to me in this company was the one between the two co-owners. As long as they share a common goal, are happy working together and avoid stepping too heavily on each other's toes then I can only see "Teresa's Costa Rican Coffee and Consumables" continuing to go from strength to strength.

As I was getting ready to leave a small boy rushed in holding out his hand, 'Mummy, Daddy, look what I've found.' In his hand was what looked like a large slug, 'That's wonderful Alex,' said Teresa. Mark just smiled. I guess I'd just witnessed another good reason for these two sticking together and making a success out of their business.

This article was written by Anna Lesley, Assistant Editor and Roving Reporter and is also available online at the 'Business is Awesome Magazine'© website, blog or via our Facebook or Twitter feeds.

Next month I'll be talking to "The Mobility Research Institute" about their incredible breakthroughs in the use of exoskeleton technology to help people with mobility issues together with their branding and marketing successes. Until then I wish you good business and happy days and don't forget 'Business is Awesome'.

Agaricus

Agaricus is a type of mushroom whose genus contains some of the most commonly cultivated and consumed mushrooms in the Western world. It also includes a stinky variety that can cause stomach cramps, nausea, vomiting, sweating and diarrhoea (although for unknown reasons a minority of people can devour these particular fungi with no ill effects whatsoever) and at least one that is deadly poisonous.

They are distinguished by their chocolate-brown spores and a stem that elevates them above the substrate on which they grow and from which they take their nourishment.

Agaricus Homo: A sub-species generally kept in the dark and frequently fed with lots of well-rotted manure.

ACKNOWLEDGEMENTS

I'd like to thank all those who have given me positive support and constructive criticism during the writing of this trilogy. I would like to especially thank M. W. Craven (for reading/reviewing and pointing out my Use and Abuse of Capitals and over-use; of semicolons;), Janet Williamson for reading and editing and for sound advice, Jean Taylor for her enthusiasm about my work, Jackie Baldwin for being the big sister I never had and driving me to produce the best quality work that I could, all those at Crime & Publishment who act like an extended family of crime writers and of course to the one and only Janet Langley for everything including reading the manuscript of a genre she doesn't really like and making constructive suggestions for improvement – some of which I listened to.

Thanks to Fiverr for the artistic and creative contributions to the cover artwork. It was a collaborative process and I enjoyed it – Thank you.

My respects to Moffat Crime Writers and the 'Twisted Sisters', especially Linda, Ann, Irene, Jackie, Beth, Rose, Fiona, Christine, Andrew and Derek. It is fun talking Crime with you all and learning from each other's experiences on this journey of writing and publishing.

Thanks also to Ian Rankin for a brief but memorable chance conversation in Kendal about cruise ships, death and deep freezers.

And finally thanks to the Open University for helping me develop my writing skills and for giving me the certificates to prove it!

In writing this third book I have used some license with a few of the dates and details in service of the plot but the core facts of the real life robberies, artworks and coins referred to are, to the best of my knowledge, correct. The missing Picasso, as far as I know, has never resurfaced.

Praise for the "Agaricus" books:

"The narrative is excellent. This is a really well written book… Krai is a superb creation."
M. W. Craven, *Author of 'The Puppet Show'*

"Mark Wilson is like Bond with a conscience"

"Page turner, unexpected twists and turns… a recommended read"

"…a new approach to a traditional genre. Liked it."

"the main characters are flawed and complex, just like us all…"

"Enjoyed it, look forward to the next instalment"

"Should come with a health warning, I stayed up until 2am to finish it!"

"A crime novel with a sense of humour, what more could you want…"

"…a really good read. Recommended…"
H. Citeau, USA.

www.ingramcontent.com/pod-product-compliance
Lightning Source LLC
Chambersburg PA
CBHW061347190726
48288CB00005B/1628